MURDER
ON
EAGLE
DROP
RIDGE

MURDER ON EAGLE DROP RIDGE

AN IT'S NEVER TOO LATE MYSTERY

DONNARAE MENARD

To my godparents and Uncle Roger (Senior) Fortin, and my Aunt Estelle (Benoit) Fortin, who allowed me to run through their house, play with their children, and pat their cows. The best memories have a cow barn smell.

Praise for Murder on Eagle Drop ridge

"Murder on Eagle Drop Ridge by DonnaRae Menard is an evocative mystery that pits good against evil, nature against development, sin against saintliness, and true love against small town opinions. An easy and quick read with just the right number of twists to keep one turning the page."—Debra H. Goldstein, author of the Sarah Blair mystery series

"[DonnaRae Menard] has created a warm household full of life and love."—Katherine Fast, author of *The Drinking Gourd*

Chapter One

The vibrant oranges, reds, and golds that signal autumn in Vermont were showing off their best as Katelyn reached out, offering her hand to her new love. Their romance still as fragile as the crisp leaves beneath their feet, delicate as the lashes on the doe bounding away, and so new both Katie and Marlie blushed at each embrace.

"I thought," said Marlie, accepting Katie's hand, "you already made a plan to settle your grandmother's debts."

Katie sighed. "So did I."

Only months before, Mr. Wilkins, the lawyer, had called her in Illinois, telling her of the death of her grandmother. He told Katie she needed to come home, and she had returned after ten years gone. She had expected it all to be the same. Gram had always been like that. Instead, Katie found the family property in a sad state and on the verge of loss.

"I'm so green, grass is envious and somehow expected Stan's idea about selling gravel out of the old pit to be the answer. I found a ready buyer and everything." Katie's steps slowed. "However, that stinking accountant appears to have been right. There's a lot about owning farm property I don't know. At the end of each lesson, somebody is standing there waiting with their hand out for a check."

Her eyes drifted away toward the west. Life had been less complicated a year ago in Illinois. The seventies were upon them, yet at her house, life went on like twenty years before. Katie had a wishful daydream in which young, free, and a couch-surfing party animal who loved to laugh, she took off unencumbered, running with the wild dogs.

1

Marlie squeezed Katie's fingers, drawing her back to the deer path they followed. "But you have an idea, right? That's why we're out here?"

Katie looked down at Marlie's round face with its liquid brown eyes, dimpled cheeks, and full wine-stained colored lips. "Yes," she said. "I do." Her steps picked up. She drew a breathless Marlie along with her.

"I read in one of Gram's *The Old Vermonter* magazines," said Katie, "about this company in New York that trains rock climbers. The guy talked about all these new ideas like indoor climbing walls and yak-yak. Very cutting edge, he called it. His group sponsors clubs throughout New England. I sent him a letter asking how they find places to climb. I told him about this ridge, the shale mountain, and how its virgin territory. You know, rugged wilderness with wildlife and untouched flora and fauna, fascinating views, and all that stuff. They'd have to hike in and camp out. It would be rough and natural."

"Holy cow," said Marlie, in awe. "How did you come up with all that?"

"I must have inherited my grandmother's gift of gab," Katie laughed.

Marlie stopped walking, her grip on Katie's hand holding the other woman back. Katie turned to find Marlie peering into the brush.

"Did you see something?" Katie paused, looking around nervously. If Marlie had seen something ominous, like a snarling bobcat, they needed to get out of there. They hadn't come outfitted for such a confrontation.

"No," said Marlie. "I'm just trying to see all that stuff you've been talking about. We've been walking for a while; all we've seen is one deer and some bunnies."

"Cottontails," corrected Katie. "I've been up here with Poppa in all kinds of weather and in every season." She swung both arms wide. "It's all here. You just have to look for it. But I gotta warn you, if you started running, you'd be off the edge of the slate cliff before you knew you were falling."

Apprehension darkened Marlie's eyes. Immediately, Katie regretted her words. Her friend had come willingly, her long-sleeve shirt and pants topped by a blaze orange vest and orange knit cap. Katie wore the same fluorescent orange vest, but her faded bill cap had been old when Poppa passed away fifteen years prior, leaving it hanging on the bedpost.

"Poppa always said in Vermont you go uphill, downhill, or around a corner, and once away from the pastureland you should walk, not run," said Katie.

"You loved him dearly, didn't you?" asked Marlie softly.

"I never really knew my father," said Katie. "My mother isn't so much a visual memory as a feeling, a sense, you know, a faint smell on the breeze now and then. I'd just turned three when they died. My grandparents took me in, and my grandfather became everything to me."

Her arms cupped the empty air before her, drawing into her embrace the invisible image of the old man she had both loved and revered. Suddenly embarrassed by her emotional words, Katie laughed and took two bounding steps ahead, landing on the thick bole of a downed oak. From there she leaped off the far side and, much to Marlie's surprise, with a single yelp, disappeared.

"Katie!" gasped Marlie, rushing forward and belly-flopping down on the log, landing with her nose inches away from Katie's shins.

As quickly as Katie had vanished, Marlie's shrieking scream rose, ricocheting off the hidden rock walls and echoing over the vale.

"I'm okay. I'm okay," panted Katie, struggling up on her elbows. She tried to pull her feet toward her torso. A hard, brittle rib cage kept them trapped in one place. Immediate fear was a forgotten bear trap, but as her eyes traveled the length of her own legs, gorge rose in her throat.

The trap proved not to be man-made, or of vegetation or animal making either. It was human in all aspects. The skeletal remains tucked beneath the fallen tree, pinned in place by withered branches, encircled her feet. The bobbing skull caught between her locked shins moved with each jerking motion as Katie tried to escape. Scattered about were other bits of branches that were both without bark and of a faintly mottled shade. Katie knew they would prove human. Unable to pull free, unwilling to touch the remains, Katie fought for calm. Marlie had disappeared from sight. Katie wasn't sure if the other woman still stood behind the log or had taken off running back toward the truck. She lay still, trying to gather her own courage. Above her, Katie heard the rush of hard breath and a voice that, even though it didn't sound like Marlie, had her particular lilt.

Chapter Two

"It's okay," the voice said. "Yes, you got startled, but it's okay. Just start right here and do this the way you were trained."

After a pause, in a more normal tone, Marlie spoke again.

"Katie?" she asked, tone more deliberate. "Are you hurt?"

"I'm not really hurt, just kind of stuck, you know, grossed out maybe?" Katie spoke in a hoarse whisper that ended with a squeak. Clearing her throat, she tried again. "Are you okay, Marlie?"

"I'm fine." Marlie gave a small, embarrassed laugh. "Just startled by having my big French-Canadian nose six inches from whatever that is."

Katie heard Marlie exhale in a long, slow sigh again.

"If Sheriff Lewis saw me lose my lunch," said Marlie, "he'd fire me in a heartbeat. I'd be all done working for the sheriff's department, for sure. This might be a crime scene, Katie. Either that or at least a questionable, accidental death. We need to keep it as untainted as possible, so I'm going to stay out of it if I can."

"Okay," said Katie, sounding suddenly small. The immediate feeling of being alone with the grisly remains shook her confidence.

"Can you get back on this side of the log?" Marlie asked.

Exhaling through gritted teeth, quarter inch by quarter inch, Katie moved backwards. She focused only on her own dilemma, knowing Marlie's instincts were right. With a little pull and then a twist, Katie freed one foot. However, as she twitched back another bit, the skeleton began inching along with her. She stopped, exhaling until her lungs were empty, then refilled them slowly, nose up, drawing in from above the musty dust. Refocused, she looked again, seeing only one way out. Placing her free foot against the bones, Katie closed her eyes and shoved until a sharp crack sounded and the tension around her ankle released. The exhilarated rush of freedom disappeared at the sudden dip in her stomach's control.

"I'm coming, Marlie," she panted.

Her whispered words were more soothing to herself than to her friend. Katie rolled onto her side and, then, unable to stop herself, vomited.

"As if this weren't disgusting enough," she coughed.

"Katie?" called Marlie.

"Coming." Katie coughed again, spitting out the remnants of bile.

Once on her feet, she circled to Marlie. Nearby lay evidence the novice deputy had also thrown up her picnic lunch. Katie saw no reason to point it out as Marlie looked terribly embarrassed.

"Come on," Katie said. "Let's get out of here."

Marlie nodded. The deputy backed away from the log, trying to memorize the exact scene. To her confusion as they moved through the forest, everywhere she looked, the specter of the scattered bones amid dark branches imprinted in her mind materialized, creating a confusing collage of imagery and dread.

Both wished for a quick return along the ridge, neither now interested in the plants or trees or the clear blue sky. But Marlie's insistence on circling wide around other downed trees slowed their progress. Katie silently agreed. Her apprehension would only have been deeper if they would have gotten caught out in darkness, or the nightmare continued, and they stumbled on more remains. A deer carcass at this point would have sent them running like banshees. She tried to laugh at the thought, but the solid lump at the base of her throat brought out a harsh cough instead. As they went, Katie could pick out places she and her grandfather had camped years before. Sitting around a campfire had always been exciting, with just the tiniest tingle of fear. But she knew, without question, what they had found that day would never let her linger on the ridge again.

Katie's concern mounted as they bumped back down the farm lane in Gram's old pickup. She tried to think of something to say to lighten the mood. But her teeth remained clamped together. On the other end of the bench seat, Marlie huddled against the door, practically hanging out the window. Parentville was a small town. Marlie was a deputy sheriff who spent most of her time chained to a desk. Had the bones on the ridge traumatized her?

"You know" Katie said, through dry lips. "If I hit a bump and that door opens, you're going to fly out."

Marlie didn't reply, inching marginally away from the door. Her shock dissipated. Coming face to face with the bones and reacting as she had, un-nerved her. Sheriff Lewis demanded better. He also had the ability to ferret out what others didn't want to disclose. His disapproval created her apprehension. He wasn't easy to get along with, ever, and her story would make his temper boil. Shame stopped her from sharing her concern with Katie.

Parked in the dooryard, Katie shifted into neutral and set the emergency brake.

"I'm going to call Sheriff Lewis," said Marlie, opening the kitchen door.

"I can do it," Katie volunteered.

Marlie wanted to laugh. "No, I'm the deputy. He's, my boss. If you make the call and he finds out I stood there right beside you while you did, he'll never let me forget it." Hanging up the phone, she entered the living room, unaware her fingers twined and loosened repeatedly. A tell how truly upset she felt. "Katie, Lewis is going to ask a lot of questions. This is a small town. I'm the first female sheriff's deputy. If people, particularly Lewis, find out about us, we'll both be all done around here."

"I know," said Katie, softly.

She had been done in Parentville and left before. Locally, Katie's sexual orientation had been unknown when she'd run away the night following high school graduation ten years before. Now she had returned and considered it her business only. But to Marlie, their relationship presented a terrifying problem that, brought to the attention of her bigoted boss, would destroy her career.

* * *

The women sat on the farmhouse porch waiting for Sheriff Martin Lewis to arrive. Marlie still wore her hunter's orange. Ruth had joined them, along with several cats. Returning to Parentville after her grandmother's death, Katie had found a very confused Ruth and seventeen cats living in Gram's house. Katie had wanted none of it. Her single plan had been to sell the farm, take the money and run. But the cats were a stipulation in Gram's will. Eventually, Katie realized Ruth's problem wasn't medical, but medicinal. With the help of a doctor in a neighboring town, they had fixed the problem. From there, the older woman's mind and clarity improved daily. Over time, Katie and Ruth had become a family, solving Gram's murder, and working together tending the brood of elderly felines.

"This is bad," said the old woman, seated in the solid pine rocker, a cat high in her arms and another in her lap.

Marlie cringed.

"It's okay, Ruth," said Katie, with one eye on Marlie. "Well, not really okay, but none of our doing. The sheriff will straighten it out."

The noise of the cruiser coming up the grade on Fire Lane 61 reached them before the car came into sight. Katie stole a look at Marlie, whose lips pressed together. A sheen of sweat coated the deputy's face. Katie wanted desperately to console her love, but they had sworn to keep their relationship a secret, even from Ruth. She bit her tongue, stepping out only as far as the top step as Marlie advanced to the cruiser.

Ruth sucked in a hard breath, alerting Katie of her unease.

"You go inside." Katie turned to Ruth. "I'll be right in as soon as Marlie and I explain to Sheriff Lewis what we found. Go ahead." She shooed the cats through the door, along with her housemate.

The screen door slapped into place. Katie turned back to the conversation between Deputy Marlie Foster and her boss.

"We can't drive up there?" Lewis asked Katie over Marlie's head, ignoring his deputy. Marlie moved back a step.

"No," said Katie, reminded again of the sheriff's displeasure at having a female deputy assigned to him. "It's rough until you get to the high meadow. From there it's darn near impossible unless you don't mind scratching up your car and maybe twisting the frame. Once on top, it's a two-mile walk along the ridge. It's slow going in broad daylight. Now it's getting dark. It'll be dangerous."

"On the ridge top?" He turned to Marlie, voice gruff. "You're sure it's in Parentville, not Charlotte?"

"I don't know," Marlie murmured.

Just then Bonnie, the one-hundred-fifty-pound pig Katie had rescued as a shoat, ambled around the corner. Katie had taken over Gram's job as the animal control officer, expecting the twenty dollar per retrieval offer to include only cats and raccoons. Somebody had deserted the pig in the sheriff's parking lot, tying it to his bumper and running off months before. Lewis had shoved the squealing critter into Katie's car and ordered her to haul it off. Bonnie hadn't forgotten his abusive handling. She moved toward the sheriff. Lewis sidled away. Katie intervened, reaching out to scratch Bonnie's back. The pig leaned against the woman, satisfied to stay there as long as the scratching continued.

"There aren't any markers up there," said Katie. "And it doesn't matter because I own both sides of the ridge in both towns. The piece on the Charlotte side came as my gram's inheritance from the Roser family."

"Which town it's in matters to the police," said Lewis.

Once before, Bonnie had stepped into a fray to rescue Katie. At Lewis' tone, her ears perked up. She made a huffing noise Katie knew meant agitation. Bonnie was growing fast and getting harder to handle. Katie applied two hands, and used her foot to turn Bonnie around, trying to get the pig to leave.

"Ruth?" Katie called.

Ruth, who had been just inside the door eavesdropping, stepped outside.

"Can you see if Bonnie will go down to her stall?" asked Katie, stumbling back a step as the pig tried to get closer to Lewis.

Offering a cookie from her apron pocket, Ruth lured Bonnie around to the side yard and away.

"Did you secure the scene?" Lewis snapped at Marlie. The pig already fading from his thoughts.

Katie opened her mouth, ready to jump to Marlie's defense, but the deputy beat her to it. Lifting her head, Marlie said.

"Because Katie had already fallen into the remains, I felt our best move would be to leave the area immediately," said Marlie, an angry frown between her brows. "I hadn't taken police tape with me when we left in the morning." Then remembering she spoke to her boss, she said. "The site is way up there. If someone went looking at this time of day, securing the area wouldn't make any difference."

"Then," said Lewis, looking up into the darkening sky, "we'll head up there first thing in the morning."

* * *

First thing proved to be five-fifteen. Dawn crept over the horizon across the valley. Katie stood on the porch, a rucksack at her feet and a tall coffee cup in her hand. The night before, the cruiser had followed Marlie's car away. Now two cruisers and a black van with the Vermont Forensics logo on the side pulled in. Katie could see Marlie in the second cruiser, with Deputy Brad driving.

"That's a lot of cars. There's not much parking up there." Katie frowned.

The cat at her feet, the only one outside, looked up, listening. Without waiting for anyone to exit their vehicle, Katie started Gram's pickup and crept down the farm lane, leaving the cat and cup for Ruth to find. Deep ruts dried and hard, filled the long-deserted road. Normal traffic, tractors, and hayricks were high enough to navigate the dirt wales, muddy potholes, and stumps left from clearing the overgrowth. Katie laughed, knowing the scraping branches were nothing to her. However, the drivers of the other three vehicles were probably cringing.

When they had driven almost to the top of the shale mountain, Katie stopped in the middle of the track and climbed out.

"Not bad," said the first of the forensics guys to exit the tall van.

"Seriously?" asked Katie.

"Yeah, we've been to lots worse," he said.

There proved to be three techs, two men and a woman, in the state vehicle. Katie and the techs led the way. Marlie followed Lewis into the brush, while Brad hesitated, running sorrowful fingers along the new abrasions on his cruiser.

"We need to know if we're actually in Parentville or in Charlotte," said Lewis.

Katie stopped and looked around the heavily forested area.

"How are we going to know?" she asked.

Lewis turned away without answering. Though she tried to hide it, Marlie grinned at her superior's displeasure. Katie, Lewis, Marlie, and the forensics team were all wearing boots and pants made of jean or duck, while Brad wore his gabardine uniform. Everyone wore a heavy jacket and a bright orange vest and hat.

Once again leading the way, Katie headed into the dense underbrush filled with prickly and thorny brush. The members of the sheriff's department carried items taken from the forensic van. Katie wore only her own rucksack. Marlie followed Katie's instructions from the previous day and kept her hands and arms up and out of the worst brush. Behind her, Brad muttered curses loud enough to warn the wildlife to stay away. When they were thirty feet away from the fallen oak, Katie stopped.

"There," she said, "directly against the bole of that tree is where I fell."

Lewis and the lead tech, Edward Richardson, advanced. Then backed away in their same path.

"Did you notice if the skeleton had remained articulated when you came upon it?" asked Richardson.

Both Katie's and Marlie's jaws dropped.

"You're kidding, right?" asked Marlie.

"If I had seen it, I wouldn't have jumped into it," said Katie. Unlike Marlie, the tech's question surprised her, but she was more offended at the sheer stupidity of it.

Richardson blushed, "Yeah, sorry." He and his people set up two perimeters, one fifteen feet around ground zero, the other twenty feet beyond that.

"What do we do now?" Katie asked Lewis. They were watching Brad pick thorns out of his trousers while Marlie had stepped forward to assist the techs as needed.

"Brad," Lewis called out. "You can go back."

"How? The forensic van is blocking me," said Brad, his voice mid-range between complaining and whining.

"Move my truck, keys are in it," said Katie. "Keep on straight up and over the ridge. Down the far side is a little steep, but you can do it. You'll come out on Kitteridge Road in Charlotte." After the deputy left, Katie turned to Lewis. "If he thought this side of the ridge is bad, he's in for a nasty surprise."

Lewis ignored her. But before he turned away, Katie saw a look that might easily have been anger or maybe frustration. She didn't know if he had any experience with found remains, or perhaps just a nasty memory. Katie clamped her mouth shut, though she wanted to ask if his poor attitude had anything to do with his lack of expertise, the group of forensic techs who wanted her guidance, or maybe just his petulant male rising-star deputy.

"I believe the brow ridge over there marks the town border," Lewis said, pointing west before pulling out a small notebook and settling his amble buttocks on a stump.

Marlie joined them. After rummaging around in her rucksack, Katie handed each a small jar of water.

"I froze these last night," she said. "The center will stay a solid ice cube for a bit."

"Thank you," said Lewis, uncapping the jar. "How did you two end up out here yesterday?" Lewis looked straight at Katie. Beyond him, she could see the distress on Marlie's face as it blushed darker.

Katie stared Lewis straight in the eye, casually holding his attention on her. Marlie had complained Lewis and Brad both got training, but she received none. Katie had heard a similar complaint from both the town clerk's and the postmaster's replacement. As animal control, Katie went in and out of the town office regularly. Anyone, including Brad, could have remarked on the lack of training employees suffered because of budgetary cutbacks. She took a chance.

"There's a lot of gossip around the town hall about how the budget doesn't stretch to include training out in the field for anybody," Katie continued. "It's almost hunting season. I know a fair amount about the woods and wanted to walk the lines. I offered to take Marlie with me and maybe share some of what I know with her. You know, like about the poison ivy Brad was standing in."

Lewis looked around at the ground surrounding his own feet. Marlie stifled a giggle.

"This is a rural area," Lewis said stiffly. "My deputies grew up out here."

"Yeah," said Katie, "but there's a difference between being a village kid and a farm kid."

When Lewis' mouth pinched up, Katie changed subjects.

"We were just about to turn back because there's a slate ledge up ahead," she said. "I got up on the log showing off and fell. Like I told you, the skeleton thing got all wrapped around me. I had to fight to get free. Marlie didn't touch it. Not wanting to mess it up, you know? She stood right there and directed me until I got out. Then we headed straight back to the house. That's when she called you."

Lewis turned to Marlie.

"Yup," she said. "That pretty much covers it." The deputy had her poker face in place. Lewis accepted her word, for which both Marlie and Katie were grateful.

Richardson walked over to where the others were sitting. He had some additional questions about how Katie had moved the bones while she'd been caught in them. While they were talking, his female assistant stepped into the feathery young pines that bordered the further side to relieve herself. Suddenly she sprang out of the thick cover, and making a wide circuit around the police tape, ran toward her boss.

"You've got to come with me," she panted. "There's a cliff beyond that mess of pines."

"Yeah, there is," Katie agreed, but the woman was already dashing away. The other five followed her vanishing orange vest.

"Careful," Katie called out. "It's a long drop."

The short parade of people moved toward the cliff area she hoped would interest the climbing organization. She had offered pristine territory and didn't want clumsy feet messing it up. Biting her lip, Katie followed. The joy and beauty, the heady odors of Autumn were only a memory now. They walked barely two hundred yards beyond the bones before they were standing at the edge of the rocky precipice. The woman pointed down. Together, the group leaned forward. Below them among the reeds and wild oats, they could see the glint of metal. The assistant offered her field glasses to Richardson. He stared long and hard.

"Oh god," he said. "There's a body down there."

Chapter Three

A chill skittered down Katie's arms. She couldn't tell if the cause stemmed from the crash site far below, or the winds of disaster blowing away her aspirations of developing a steady income stream. Dead bodies strewn around the area would destroy most people's perception of pristine. The owner of the climbing company had told her they were fairly new in business. Even if they were old hands, there were probably other sites offered throughout New England which didn't come with a case of the heebie-jeebies. After a few minutes of speculation, Lewis herded everyone back to the fallen tree. Richardson tried to quicken the pace of his team.

"I tell you what," sighed Katie, returning to her sitting spot, "you guys don't need to get in an uproar to get done here and down there, because that isn't happening today."

Everyone stopped, turning to look at her.

"No one here has climbing gear, and to get there on the ground requires a long haul through the bog," she explained, crumbling a fallen oak leaf. The wind carried the tiny fragments off.

Lewis and Richardson put their heads together while the assistants went back to sifting through the debris by the log, looking for bones and clues. Lewis returned to his frozen jar of water. A few minutes later, Richardson followed, opening a discussion on the findings with Lewis. The sheriff stopped him short. His eyes were on Katie, who obviously could hear everything said. Turning away from Richardson, Lewis took a step in Katie's direction.

"You should return to your car," he told Katie.

"Can you find your way out of here alone?" she asked.

She tried to look concerned, not angry at being ordered off her own property by the man that had deemed Gram's death accidental. Katie hadn't believed it and put herself in danger to chase down the clues. She had decided to stay and defend, at least in the short term. If she was going to do so and keep any hope of salvaging her plan to develop the land, she needed to know what Richardson and his team found.

Overhearing Katie's question, two of the assistants looked at each other, then at their boss. Both were obviously nervous at the idea of being deserted in the woods.

"Sit over there," Lewis ordered. "Deputy, keep an eye on her."

Katie and Marlie moved far enough away to be out of hearing range. Katie sat on a log.

"Thank you," said Marlie, "you know, for trying to keep Lewis from believing I'm totally incapable."

"Mie logga, es su logga," smiled Katie, patting the seat beside her. "Neither one of us wants to get burned by this."

Over the next several hours the techs bagged the remains, collected, and tagged other items including dirt samples, and finally signaled they were done and ready to trek out. Katie and Marlie had enjoyed the benefit of food and drink from Katie's rucksack and set a fast pace. Getting the large, heavy van turned around to face the way they had driven in took finesse. Finally, with Katie bringing up the rear, they drove out.

The cruiser and van drove past the farmhouse. Katie offered a silent prayer of gratitude to be back in the warm house. She enjoyed a long soak in the antique claw-foot tub, emerging warm and wrinkled. Ruth waited in the kitchen ready to treat Katie to one of the older woman's world-class grilled cheese sandwiches. Ruth's friend Rick joined them for supper, bringing with him a quart jar of homemade sour pickles.

"These are really bad," said Katie, squinting her eyes and smacking her lips as pickle juice ran down her chin.

"Yeah, but really good," grinned Rick.

Besides being Ruth's sweetie, Rick had also been Katie's grandfather's best friend, and currently worked with Katie at the feed store. Katie and Ruth nodded in agreement to Rick's assessment of the wickedly sour treat.

"What did you find out there in the hinterland?" Rick asked.

"Just the left-over bits of somebody," said Katie.

"So, it's all done, right?" Ruth cringed at the cavalier attitude of her dining companions.

"Nope, we found another somebody at the bottom of Eagle Drop Ledge," said Katie.

"What?" squeaked Ruth.

"Yes, folks," said Katie, reaching into the pickle jar, "the circus continues tomorrow. It's a good thing I don't have to go to work, because I'd be missing another day."

Intent on selecting just the right pickle, Katie failed to notice the stricken look on Ruth's face. But Rick more perceptive and always concerned about the woman he often referred to as the one who got away, looked to soften the blow of the younger woman's words.

"Ah, Katie," he coughed. "You know, over on the other side of the barn driveway is a big flat space, all overgrown with sumac. There's a telephone pole there."

"Yeah," she said. "The electric wire ran over to that pole for the bunkhouse."

"That's right," he said, sitting back in his seat. The glow of sudden enlightenment on his face. "I forgot about the bunkhouse."

"Ah-huh," Katie explained to Ruth, "Poppa had a couple of Canadians who came down every year to help with the planting. They'd stay until harvest. They ate in the house, but that's where they slept." Turning her attention once more to Rick, thinking he might be hinting about a pen for Bonnie, she asked, "Why are you asking?"

"Well, ah, I've got that spot in Charlotte where the Roser house burned down all cleared. The trailer pad and everything is finished. It's ready for me to move my trailer from Saint George over to there," he said.

Currently, Rick's mobile home sat in a tiny trailer park in the village on the far side of Parentville. In the tiny space, the only thing separating one person's living room from the next person's kitchen was the driveway. The

Charlotte, or Roser site, marked the end of Lover's Lane, exactly where Deputy Brad would have reached the bottom of the shale mountain that morning. From there, he had to drive across the Roser property to access Kitteridge Road. At one point, Brad would have been within one hundred feet of the trailer pad Rick had to have poured.

"That's the plan, right?" asked Katie.

"Actually, I've been thinking, you could rent the spot," said Rick. "You know, get some return."

Katie sat still, the dripping pickle in her hand forgotten.

"You paid to put in the septic, restrung the electric, and paid for the pad." Her eyes narrowed. She honed in on the elderly man suspiciously. If he demanded a payback so he could forfeit their deal, there would be trouble.

Rick placed his elbows on the table. Rubbing his face with his hand, he reevaluated what he had been about to propose. Ruth, sitting quietly, aghast after Katie's revelation about a second body, looked toward Rick. She read the conflict on his face and distress that the conversation wasn't going as hoped. Drawing a breath, Ruth said to Katie, who had helped her so much, and then allowed the elderly woman to remain on the farm when she had nowhere else to go.

"What Rick is trying to say," Ruth said, reaching out to touch his arm, "is he would actually like to live closer to Parentville and his job. And us." With a quick peek at Rick, Ruth continued. "If you rent out the Charlotte lot to someone else, you two can split the money until he gets back what he paid out." She paused, the tip of her tongue touching her upper lip, then jumped into the rest of what Rick had explained to her about his proposal. "He wants to clear out the sumac, do the prep work, and put his trailer there. He could pay rent."

"What about water?" asked Katie, looking at Rick.

"The well for the barn is on that side," he said. "If I get started, I might get the plumbing in and a pad poured before it's too cold."

"Or Katie," said Ruth, offering her own version of Rick's idea, "you could move into your grandmother's room and Rick could park his trailer then rent your bedroom through the first winter." She nipped her lip. "You know, if it can't all get done by snowfall, that is."

"How does that work?" asked Katie. "Parking the trailer?"

"Just like closing up a house," said Rick. "You drain the pipes, winterize it, and let it sit. Instead of giving my money to the trailer park owner, I'd give it to you."

Katie leaned back in her seat; the forgotten pickle dripping juice down her wrist. This would be her first winter in the old house alone, and Gram hadn't kept it up. Rick had been a lot of help. It might be good to have somebody handy around if problems popped up. Her eyes darted to the ever-growing needed repairs list hanging on the side of the refrigerator.

LG, the youngest of the remaining fourteen cats, rubbed against Katie's leg. LG, a Houdini in training pro at escaping capture and being locked in the attached garage turned cat room while the humans ate, was ready for some attention. Katie's fingers stroked the tiger cat's ears.

"I need to think on it," said Katie. She had cultivated a different idea. Her hopes had been Rick would move his trailer to Charlotte, then he and Ruth would get married. Together, they would live in the trailer away from the farm. *They could take one or two cats with them. I could let the others sleep outdoors at night, see how that works on thinning them out,* she'd thought. Finding a place for Bonnie might actually resolve itself with a little advertising. But Rick, living in the farmhouse, meant not leaving. Her eyes drifted to the two sitting across the table, anxious looks on their faces. Katie offered a small smile. She needed time to sort this new wrench-in-the-works out.

Ruth and Rick nodded, smiling back.

* * *

That night Katie lay in her twin bed, in the room that had been her space until the day before her eighteenth birthday. That last night, just like tonight, somebody else's words kept her awake. Back then it had been Gram demanding her head-strong granddaughter toe the line. High school was done. It was time to make a plan and stick to it. In response, Katie had waited until the old woman slept and walked away, headed west to Illinois.

But her father's family in Illinois made it clear when she arrived that even though her two older brothers had grown up there, she had not been invited, and therefore not welcome.

Rising, Katie cracked open the door. She could hear Ruth snoring. She walked across the cold hall floor, listening to the silent house. Gram's room on the front of the house offered windows facing the south and west. The old wrought iron bed had been left made up, waiting for the old woman to lie down. Gram's glasses still lay on the bedside table. Katie had cleaned out the closet and dresser, leaving one drawer filled with pieces too hard to let go of. Wrapping herself in Gram's flannel shirt, Katie sat in the bentwood rocker, holding a silent council with memories that brought tears to her eyes. With no one else watching, she allowed herself to drop the tough guy, or girl, facade.

She woke at dawn, curled up on the bed with LG laying across her ankles. Outside, the sun woke the land, but Katie still had not reached a decision regarding Rick's question of the night before, or the financial fears she regretted sharing with Marlie.

Chapter Four

The sheriff's cruiser and forensic van arrived with the dawn again. This time, there were no deputies riding along. The sheriff wore tall waterproof boots for slogging through the bog. At the end of Fire Lane 61, right in front of the farmhouse, the dirt road went from being a private road to just a wide space between old trees. The Moores, Katie's paternal grandparents, had owned one side, that being to the north and west, while the Deans who lived on the other side of Fire Lane 61, owned to the south and east. Katie drove her truck, leading the other two vehicles down the farm lane the same way they had gone the day before. Just before the road started climbing up the ridge, she turned off to the left, following the edge of Dean's high meadow.

Near the far end of the meadow, in a wide place among the maples, Katie parked the truck, signaling the others to pull alongside. The ground crunched beneath their feet, crisp with frost. Grass stems and weed stalks crackled as they knocked together in the wind. Katie could smell the heavy autumn scent of trees preparing for sleep and drying grasses bursting to release their seed heads. No other season held her heart, as Autumn did. Out of the clear blue, Lewis struck up a conversation as she led them through the brush toward the bog.

"You must be busy this time of year," he said, "with the animal calls."

"You mean like with skunks and raccoons trying to invade human space for a place to hunker down and hibernate?" Katie asked. "Yeah, it is. Practically every day, I get at least one call. This is where I let them all go. Far from town and with lots of cover."

They broke through a small copse of swamp maples. Ahead of them, the bog stretched level, tall cattails already feathering out nodded in the breeze. On the far side, the slate cliff rose. Katie, already wearing waders, adjusted her rucksack. Before she could take a step, Lewis spoke again.

"This is as far as you go today."

"What?" asked Katie. She shot a look at the forensic team, who were pulling on their own waders. The woman, whose name badge said Cox, looked concerned.

"It's a straight shot from here," said Lewis, stepping around her. "I'm sure you've got a lot you should be doing."

Katie watched them clamor from hummock to hummock for a few minutes. "Ah, you're welcome," she muttered, before turning back towards home.

* * *

Katie called her boss. When Stan told her she could come to work that day, Katie yanked off her waders, dumping them by the cellar door, and headed out. This should have been her day off, but she'd missed the day before going up on the top of Eagle Drop with Lewis and the state people. She had spent years not caring if she had a dime or not, now every day's pay filled her foremost concerns. She stepped off the porch, almost to the truck, when the phone rang in the house. Katie hesitated.

"Katie," Ruth called, hanging out the front door. "It's a man from New York. Do you want to talk to him?"

Katie sprinted up the dirt walk.

"This is Katie," she said, dropping the rucksack on the kitchen floor, ignoring the sound of her metal lunchbox clunking against the thermos.

"Hi, Katie." The voice on the other end of the line sounded as though the speaker smiled. "This is Armand DeNoi, with High Ridge Climbing School. Listen, I know this is short notice, but what are the chances we could drive over this weekend and have a look at what you've got to offer? It'll give us a chance to meet, and my wife will get to see the foliage on the way. Shoot down two birds with a single stone, you know what I mean?"

They settled on Sunday, and Katie snatched up her bag and headed out again. Then suddenly, shifting from reverse to drive, she gasped, remembering the bodies. The climbers would arrive in a couple of days. Would she be able to get the New Yorkers in and out without them hearing about the bodies?

Yes, we can do this, she thought. *I'll just keep them out of town.*

She smiled all the way out to the main road. Her plan might have been flimsy, but she'd carried off escapades with less before.

"It'll be okay," she decided. "The bone folks will be gone before the climbing people get here. No one will be the wiser."

Even though her words were confident, deep in her chest, a niggling little ember of doubt burned.

Chapter Five

Taking a break to step out of the dusty confines of the feed shed, Katie slugged water from a gallon jug, spilling an ample amount on her flushed face. Rick came around the corner, making a wide turn. A pallet of fifty-pound sacks on the raised front tines of the forklift he drove. The brakes squealed as the trundling load came to a halt right in front of her.

"Did Ruth tell you I'm bringing ribs for supper?" he asked. "I've got them marinating in a cooler in the truck."

"That would be great," sighed Katie. "The reverend called. I have to stop and reset the live trap at the parish. Seems his cat likes the trap better than the raccoon does."

With a deep, chortling laugh, Rick shifted back into drive.

No wonder Poppa liked him so much, she thought, watching Rick pull away. *He's one heck of a good guy.*

Right from the first day on the job, Rick had been in her corner. Rick and Poppa had fished, hunted, and hung around together almost daily. With Katie's grandfather gone, Rick had stepped into his old friend's shoes, ready to put his sixty-year-old self between Katie and any danger. She found it hard to keep him at arm's length. His friendship and the affection Ruth showed toward her every day whittled away at Katie's determination to leave Parentville behind. Ten years ago, she had decided this wasn't her place. She wanted a big city life with street lights, parties, and something happening every minute. Now, full circle, she had come back to the tiny rural area where she'd grown up. This time she knew she didn't have to run away in the night. She could just get up and go. Yet, in the same thought, she considered she could stay too. If she wanted.

* * *

Frail Father Metevier couldn't seem to get the hang of resetting the live trap for the marauding raccoon. Nor could Katie get the elderly cleric to understand Boots, who kept getting caught in the trap, didn't need to go outdoors until the unwanted guest had been removed.

"She's a house cat," Katie explained. "Just keep her inside for a few days. She'll be fine."

The reverend looked doubtful.

At the corner of the Parentville/Charlotte Road and Fire Lane 61, three-quarters of a mile from home, Katie inhaled, sure she could smell the ribs grilling. She loaded the sandwich sign Rick made to advertise Ruth's barn sale into the bed of the pickup and headed up the grade. Grandma Irma had spent years dump picking, chasing yard sales, and collecting free items from lawns. Now Ruth and Katie were trying to find new homes for all the leftover treasures that filled the barn.

There was a strange sedan parked in Rick's space in the driveway. Katie didn't recognize the woman perched on the step. The stranger dressed like she should sit in an office, perched on the wooden stoop, and watched as Katie pull in.

"Can I help you?" Katie asked, walking up to the step.

"Don't talk to her, Katie," Ruth hollered from behind the closed door. Her next words were unclear as the woman rose, extending her hand, and said in a loud voice, "Good evening, I'm Colleen Johnston, from the Montpelier Sentinel."

Katie didn't have to hear anymore. She had fought with the press over the reports on her grandmother's death, reporters who took the instant word of the sheriff, not concerned about the truth.

"Get out," she growled. "This is private property, and I want you out of here."

"Ms. Moore, or Took, whichever," smiled Johnston, showing a full mouth of large teeth. "I just want a moment of your time."

"Get out," Katie repeated, "and don't park out on the road. It's private too. I'll have you arrested for trespassing. Read the signs, we aren't kidding."

The woman hesitated.

"Five. RUTH," Katie yelled, "Four. GET MY BASEBALL BAT. Three."

"Coming, Katie," Ruth called out. The look on her face through the screen was somewhere between a question and a giggle.

The door squeaked, sending the city woman sprinting for her car. Katie watched the sedan speed away, barely edging between Rick's truck and the ditch as the road curved.

"Here's your bat," Ruth said.

"What did I miss?" grinned Rick, climbing out of his truck with the green and white Coleman cooler in his hands. At the look on Katie's face, he paused. "What's up?"

But Katie stalked into the house. Ruth, however, followed Rick around the corner to the barbecue grill where coals were already smoldering, explaining as they went. Bonnie had come running at the sound of Katie's voice. Now, with her snout high in the air and the rounded disc at the end dancing, she followed Rick. Her love for Katie forgotten for a moment in the hope of a handout.

Her insides shaking with anger, Katie twisted the radio dial until she found the county news station. It didn't take the announcer long to get to the article about human remains being found in an area residents referred to as Eagle Drop Ledge. Crestfallen at the man's elaboration on what the state team had found, Katie's concern grew when she found the same story on the national news station.

Later Katie did dishes while Ruth and Rick closed up the barn sale and put Bonnie to bed.

"Katie," said Ruth on her return.

"I haven't had a chance to think about Rick's proposal," said Katie, cutting the older woman off. "I spent all day trying to figure out how to keep the New Yorkers from hearing about the bodies, and now all they have to do is turn on the car radio."

"Katie." Rick appeared in the doorway leading to the living room. "There's another car pulling in out front."

Scowling and sputtering, Katie pushed past him, headed toward the front door with a baseball bat in her hand. She returned, slamming the door behind her, which sent cats scurrying in all directions.

"Looks like I'm sleeping on the sofa here tonight playing guard dog," Rick said

"Nope," Katie spat out. "It'll take me a half an hour to get my stuff moved to Gram's room and you can have mine."

"O...kay," said Rick. The look on Katie's face making him unsure if his moving in had been such a good idea.

Behind him, Ruth smiled. "Oh goody," she whispered.

Chapter Six

Sunday morning found Katie up early, dressed for hiking, and filling her rucksack with sandwiches and jars of frozen water.

"I gave Armand DeNoi directions from the ferry landing to the Kitteridge Road. I'll meet them there and take them up to the ridge on that side," she told Ruth. "If I can keep them out of town, maybe they won't be asking questions. I just need the gossip about the bodies in the woods to settle down and go away."

"I made these yesterday for you to take."

Ruth handed over a Tupperware container filled with date bars. Ruth's limited expertise in the kitchen extended mostly to grilled cheese and box mixed desserts, but Katie appreciated the effort and offered a smile.

"That envelope on the sideboard is for Rick when he gets here." Katie's smile had faded. "If he doesn't agree to everything and sign it, he doesn't move anything in. Do you understand, Ruth?"

"Yes," Ruth answered. "But he doesn't think you're charging him enough rent."

"For crying out loud." Katie spun around. "He buys just about all the groceries, that's got to count."

Ruth held up her hands, surrendering. "I understand what you're saying. Right now, you better get going or you're going to be late."

Katie had cleaned out the cab of the truck, expecting the visitors to ride up the rough trail with her. To her surprise, the couple had another man with them and were riding in a four-wheel-drive Jeep that looked as though it often traveled off-road. Katie rode in the front passenger seat, directing

Armand.

"This is a good place to stop," she said when they arrived at the top of the ridge. "There aren't a lot of places up here wide enough to turn around."

They were several minutes into the hike before she remembered the yellow police tape outlining the search area of the first body.

"There are a couple of different approaches," she said, changing direction. "We can go one way and come back another." Beneath her flannel shirt, sweat heavier than the weather called for gathered.

Katie's last look back at the fallen log site as she led the forensic team out had showed the area still marked with two rows of tape. As they hiked closer, Katie worried the bog might be similarly marked with yellow tape. She led them on a roundabout route to avoid the log site, arriving eventually at the top of the ledge. Peeking over the edge, Katie could just make out a bit of fluttering yellow where the cliff base met the bog. No one mentioned it, so she didn't either. Katie sighed with relief at the sight of the one small marker.

"If you approach from the bottom," she said, "the easiest trail is on the neighbor's property, but if you hike instead of drive, you can come in through the maple forest, which I own."

They shared the lunch in her rucksack and what the DeNoi party had brought while she answered questions. Then Mrs. DeNoi said,

"I'd like to walk around the woods a little."

Katie's heart fell. She had hoped the DeNois would stay on the cliff top long enough for her to dash through the pines and pull down the marking tape. There hadn't been a chance. Now she and the men followed Mrs. DeNoi at a respectful distance. Suddenly Katie realized the fallen tree lay to her direct left and almost laughed aloud when she looked. Someone in the tech team must have taken down all the orange tape markers while she had been talking with Lewis and Richardson.

"It's a beautiful place," said Mrs. DeNoi as they climbed back in the Jeep. "Hiking in at the bottom, as opposed to driving, would add to the remote experience allure. Then, too, we wouldn't have to worry about getting legal permission to cross somebody else's property."

"And I believe," said Tom, the second man, "we could use it in all seasons. We ice climb in the winter," he explained to Katie.

"Now don't be jumping with joy," Armand grinned. "There are a lot of details that need to be worked out. We'll throw it around for a few days, then I'll send you a proposal that will detail what we'd like or think needs to be done to enhance the experience. You should compare it against your own plan and get back to us."

Katie waved as they drove away.

What plan? She thought.

* * *

Instead of driving the thirty-plus miles around to get home, Katie drove back, up, and over the ridge. The nine miles weren't much faster than the longer route, but more soul-soothing.

"I forgot to tell them we call this Lover's Lane," she laughed, thumping down on the Parentville side.

When her grandfather Moore had been courting her grandmother Roser, he had used the old fire lane regularly. After they wed, it grew back over to its woodsy self. Katie's mother had been Arlene Moore, their daughter, and only child.

Coming off Lover's Lane onto Fire Lane 61, and down her own driveway, Katie saw a sight that had her braking hard. Fifty feet away parked where the drive circled down to the barn lay a fourteen by sixty-foot mobile home still attached to the red tow truck that belonged to Philip Carwell. Katie's jaw dropped.

"How the heck did you get that thing here so fast?" She asked the men who were putting cinder blocks beneath the heavy steel towing tongue.

"Only took about an hour to get it unhooked and forty minutes to drive over," said Rick.

He stacked bricks while Philip worked the jack. A third man, who Katie had seen several times working with Philip, wandered over from the barn.

"Nice looking hog you've got," he said.

29

"It's a pig, not a hog," Katie said more tersely than she had intended.

"So, you're not going to eat it?"

"It's a pet," she snapped. Turning back to Rick, she said. "You guys did all this alone?"

"Yeah, well," he blushed slightly. "We probably should have had an electrician. Maybe a plumber."

"Oh yes," laughed Philip, "and a permit."

Once again, Katie felt her mouth opening. "I don't want to know," she said, turning toward the house. All she needed now was Lewis to have a reason she should do some jail time. Her original idea to sell the farm and split resurfaced.

"Yup, you don't," said the hired man. "And you don't want to know how fast we were traveling."

Preparing for the day, Katie had left chicken stew simmering in the crock-pot. The aroma made her mouth water and stomach rumble, taking the edge off her anger.

"I made biscuits," said Ruth. "We've got leftover date bars and ice cream for after. Should I ask Philip and his guy to join us? We've got enough."

"I'm surprised you have to ask," said Katie, once again sharper than she met. Silence behind her stopped her headlong move toward the bathroom and a wash-up. She turned to see Ruth biting her upper lip. "What?" she demanded.

"It's just that, well, it's your house now, Katie," said Ruth, standing with both arms wrapped around her middle.

Katie went back to give the old woman a hug.

"You're not putting on a roof, you crazy old lady," Katie laughed. "Just feeding a couple of hungry guys."

* * *

"These are good date bars," said the hired man as they finished up their meal.

"Yes," Katie agreed, "and biscuits. Ruth has only had a couple of lessons and she's already way past grilled cheese."

30

"Yup, mighty good." The man took another bite and smiled at Ruth, who blushed all the way to her salt and pepper curls.

Rick scowled at them both.

Then the hired man commented on the number of cats he'd seen around the property.

"Not so many," said Katie. "We're down to what? Fourteen, Ruth?"

Ruth nodded. "Yes, now that all the kittens have been adopted." She turned to their guest. "People drop them off all the time, all hours. Are you looking for one?"

The man blanched. "Ah, no."

"Well, keep us in mind if you are," said Ruth, in her most businesslike voice.

The other three people at the table grinned into their hands.

After supper, Katie found an envelope on the windowsill over the sink. The signed agreement she had written up for Rick folded inside. She had spent the better part of the last ten years squatting in one place or another. Her first-hand knowledge of how easily forgetting the rules of residence became prompted the agreement. Generous to a fault, Rick seemed to be constantly giving, donating, or maybe simply helping out her household more than need be. The single piece of paper might remind him of barriers. He had signed the handwritten document and left the first payment inside. Rick also left a note that read, *You don't have to tell the government about every little dime you have.*

She tucked the envelope away. With everyone else seated in the living room having coffee, she took a moment to telephone Marlie's apartment.

"Hi," she breathed into the mouthpiece. "I thought I'd have heard from you before this."

Marlie came back sounding stiff.

"We've been really busy," she said.

"Would you like me to bring over coffee or dessert?" Katie blushed.

"No," said Marlie. "But thank you for calling." The line went dead.

Katie fought the urge to call back or drive over to Charlotte to ask what was wrong. Marlie never came across as short or bad-tempered. Maybe someone else had been in Marlie's apartment. Katie's heart whimpered at the snub.

Leaving the others to visit, Katie went up to Gram's bedroom. She still had trouble thinking of this room as hers. In July, she'd arrived on the doorstep with a change of clothes and a box of books. Six months later her personal effects were still meager even though it felt like her world had tripled. She sat in the bentwood rocker, book in hand, with only LG for company. Across the room, the door firmly closed would keep the other cats out. Once in, they covered the double bed, leaving her to wonder where to sleep.

Beyond the window, the top edge of Eagle Drop Ledge had disappeared in the dark. The cliff edge may have been out of sight, but its presence and issues were still on Katie's mind. LG, paws tucked under, laid on the window ledge. Her rasping purr barely discernible to Katie, who reached out a finger to stroke the feline. Two soft pats and LG's ears laid back. LG had a well-deserved reputation as a biter. Katie had learned to watch the cat's ears for a warning to back away.

"Well," sighed Katie, "at least I can touch you now without ending up with a bloody slash."

She wondered about Marlie. Had she been alone? Katie had assumed their relationship was monogamous. Perhaps Marlie hadn't made the same commitment. Katie sighed, afraid to think on it further.

Chapter Seven

Just as Katie and Ruth put supper on the table, Armand DeNoi and his party were discussing their day on Eagle Drop Ridge. The all-terrain Jeep idled in place, parked in the loading lane for the ferry crossing from Vermont to New York. Cory dozed in the back seat; an open wine cooler tucked between her thighs. Armand and Tom, however, were joyously discussing the fresh territory. It didn't matter, the heat of the Indian Summer afternoon had been more suitable for napping than a long hike. Or that other motorists hemmed them in, all waiting for the ferry to unload before taking them on for the return to New York. Every car or truck had its windows down. People laughed, talked, and if anyone noticed the two men taking sips from their long-necked beer bottles, they didn't say anything. A local news station ran an update on the two bodies found in Charlotte, but nobody listened. The afternoon was too glorious for anyone to care.

"It's raw up there on the top," said Armand.

"True," Tom agreed, "but did you notice the ground slopes enough, so the face probably gets a radical ice cover?"

Armand nodded, Adam's apple jumping up and falling down with another sip.

"Also," said Tom, "I don't think the woman is such a tree hugger that she'd have an issue with clearing an adequate space on top for tents and a campsite."

"Yeah, that's true," said Armand. "But I think we should sell it as a park and leave your vehicle at the bottom, hike in, camp, climb, hike out."

"We should absolutely climb it, you know. I mean, we gotta know what we're selling." Tom winked at a teenage girl seated in the rear of the car parked beside them. She blushed and turned away, but soon returned to ogling the handsome man with his flippant attitude to the no alcohol law.

"Oh yeah, a couple of times anyway," Armand agreed. "What do you think, Cory?"

"Shut up," she grumbled, settling further into the tweed and vinyl seat.

The two men roared with laughter. Up ahead, the last of the cars were inching off the ferry, including a pale blue Chevy Vega with New York license plates. In a short time, the ferry bucked the waves out on the broad lake. Cory slept while the two men sat on the hood, exhilarated by the find capable of catapulting their fledgling company upward.

* * *

The Vega traveled directly to Kitteridge Road, the driver not interested in letting anyone know he had entered the village, or even in the state. Once on the Roser property, he drove past the sandpit, wincing when he realized it was now a working enterprise complete with a small guard shack. The heavy metal bar blocked the entrance, a shining padlock in place for the night. But the mere possibility other people could appear there at any time caused already taut nerves to ripple. The man's stomach clutched. He drove slightly up the ridge road until he found a space between two tall pines wide enough to back in the car, their overhanging branches concealing the vehicle from sight. Daylight had faded, it was too late to go further, but the man had come prepared. Resting on the backseat beside a cooler with food and drink, leaned over a neat stack of hiking gear. He had no interest in climbing or the views, or even the gruesome sight Katie had fallen into. His concern had him rubbing his hands across his face as he contemplated the drive over the ridge and what he would find at the bottom of the cliff. Coming from this side, would take longer, but he didn't want to chance being noticed by anyone living on the farms.

Long before dawn broke, he started the Vega and crossed over the ridge.

Chapter Eight

"I'm going to leave a few minutes early for lunch," Katie told Rick, who loaded grain bags into the company delivery truck, "and slide over to the town office. I think I'd better find out if I need a permit for the climbers." Stan had assigned her the boring task of scooping bulk beans into five-pound bags to restock inside the store. She folded the hemp sack, adding it to the stack ready to ship back to the cooperative. Walking past Rick, she averted her face in the event he could see through her pupils and read her mind. She swore sometimes he could pull that trick off and right then didn't want him questioning what she was up to.

Katie made it to the town office minutes before Janice, the town clerk, a friend of both her mother and Gram, closed the door.

"What can I do for you?" Janice smiled.

Katie explained about the climbing company. "Do I need a permit to let them hike and climb there?" she asked.

"Are you opening a business? Or is this going to be a regular, like a weekly event?" Janice asked.

"No and no," said Katie. *At least not yet.*

"Then it's just between you and your insurance guy," said Janice, reaching for the sliding door panel. "Oh, by the way, the people from the historical society were asking about you. Have they been in touch?"

Katie, already headed toward the connecting door to the sheriff's office, turned. The top of the Dutch door had already closed with the out-to-lunch sign in place.

Sheriff Lewis had been clear when she first arrived that the inner door should be used by town employees only. Katie reasoned if the town paid her to answer animal calls, she qualified as an employee. Once through the door, she could hear loud male voices within the sheriff's office. Marlie sat at the front desk, head bent over a stack of forms.

"Hey, Marlie," said Katie, friendly but not softly sensual in the event someone should overhear. From experience, she knew Janice could stand on her desk and listen through the air vent.

Marlie's head didn't rise, but her shoulders went rigid.

"Can I help you?" Marlie asked all business.

"I, ah, had to come over to see Janice." Katie wet her lips. "So, I thought I'd just stop in, say hello, see how you were doing."

Marlie raised her head. She looked so sorrowful, Katie wanted to race around the desk and hug her.

"I told you before, Katie," Marlie said in a low voice. "This is my job. I like it. But my boss is a small-minded bigot. I need to be careful, here and everywhere."

The door to the sheriff's office opened. A pinched look gathered on Marlie's normally smooth brow.

Katie took a step backwards, staying focused on Marlie. "I need to find out about permits for the rock climbers."

"I don't know about that type of permit. Perhaps the town clerk has them," said Marlie. She stared straight ahead, not acknowledging the tall man exiting the sheriff's office.

"That office is closed for lunch," said Katie. A casual glance verified she didn't recognize the man.

"Well, I can check into it," said Marlie. "If I come up with anything, I'll let you know."

Katie nodded her thanks and left. *Maybe he's some kind of inspector* she thought before her mind jumped onto a different track. Janice had mentioned insurance. That could be an issue.

* * *

"You got a call right after you left." Stan Baldwin, the owner of the feed and hardware store and Katie's boss, stepped out of his office as she punched the time clock. "Seems the reverend caught himself a big, old raccoon. He wants to know if he can let his cat out."

Katie laughed. "Yes. I'll pick the 'coon up on my way home."

In the back of the feed shed, Rick had left a newspaper spread across the stacked bales of straw where he spent his lunch break. A black-and-white photograph stopped Katie in her tracks. The man she had seen fifteen minutes earlier in the sheriff's office looked back from the picture, his arm wrapped around a thin woman weeping into a handkerchief. The caption above the photograph read REMAINS OF MISSING SON FOUND. Before Katie could read further, the PA sounded, announcing a customer coming around to pick up an order. Without hesitation, Katie ripped the page out of the paper and crammed it into the back pocket of her jeans.

All the feed store employees had Sunday off, after that their second days off were rotated. Willy, who usually made local deliveries on Monday, Katie on Tuesday, and Rick on Wednesday. With Willy gone for the day, Rick picked up the slack and made deliveries. That left Katie alone in the shed, and today, busy. Rick pulled in about half an hour before closing.

"Hey," he called out, "did Stan tell you about the raccoon? I'm taking a load of trash down to the dump. Want me to pick it up and let it out there?"

"That would be awesome," said Katie, wiping her sweaty face against her shoulder.

"See you at home," said Rick, waving as he drove off.

Katie wished she could be in Rick's place at that moment. On his own, driving away from work with the window down and an Autumn breeze cooling her cheeks.

* * *

Pulling up to the farmhouse, Katie tooted the horn, signaling Ruth she had arrived home, and the elderly lady should lock up the barn sale for the night. With the first sandwich sign lying in the bed of her truck, Katie drove past the second one, which stood at the end of the barn drive, pointing the way to the actual sale. Taller and of more substantial weight, they let it stay out all the time. Just as she'd crested the rise, Katie had seen the gleam of a vehicle in front of the barn. Ruth had a customer and a little hint it was closing time might shorten Ruth's gab session with the poor person corralled and listening.

"Maybe," Katie told LG, and the other assembled felines as she entered the front door, "she'll have made a whole dollar this time."

The kitchen door slammed open, banging against the counter edge.

"Katie," called Ruth, "I need your help. There's some people down at the barn that won't leave."

"Because you won't drop your price?" Katie asked with a grin, dropping her lunch bucket and thermos on the table.

"They're not buying." Ruth shook her gray curls. "They're just asking questions."

Katie didn't ask what questions; she already had a fair idea and followed Ruth back outside.

"Can I help you folks?" asked Katie. She stood, feet apart, and unsmiling at the top of the small slope that led from the house down to the barn. Above her, thunderheads gathered, and a rumble rolled down from the ridge. The few cats following the women turned tail and scuttled back toward the house.

"Mrs. Moore?" said one of the three men. "We'd like to talk to you about the human remains discovered on your property."

Katie looked at the vehicles lined up in the drive. The first one had probably knocked at the front door. Getting no response, he'd followed the arrows on the sandwich signs. The rest had tagged along.

"No Mrs. here," she said, looking back directly at the speaker. "You're going to have to back out." An old cleat track tractor Rick tinkered with blocked the exit sweep of the drive.

"We're news reporters," explained the second man, whose suit jacket blew open in the wind, exposing large sweat circles under his arms and around his neck. He did not smile as the first man had. Instead, his words made it sound like they were official and had no choice but to do as he suggested. "Perhaps you would like to come down here?"

"No," said Katie, "I'm not interested in talking to you at all."

Two of the men opened their mouths, but Katie cut them off.

"I heard about the remains. We didn't find them here. I heard they were discovered in Charlotte on a farm that burned out years ago. You're in the wrong place." She motioned for Ruth to move back.

"Well," said the third man, whose paunch hung well over his belt. "Mr. Ash, the father of the dead boy, said differently."

Katie remembered the paper in her pocket.

"I don't know Ash," she said, "but I know Rick. He's got a bust-your-headlights-out attitude when he's crossed." She turned to where a plume of dust rose from the road coming up the hill. "And if I'm not mistaken, that's him now. Good luck, gentleman. You'll need it." Heavy rain droplets fell around the feet of the men, raising their own dust plumes. Taking Ruth by the arm, Katie moved quickly back to the house where LG and two of her counterparts cowered against the door as lightning flickered and another clap of thunder roared right on its heels.

"That one was close," Ruth said, shushing the cats off the sill as she pulled the window closed.

Rick got inside while the men were still jockeying their cars around in the barn drive.

"Who's that?" Rick asked.

"More reporters," said Katie, pulling ground beef out of the refrigerator. Suddenly, she spun around, pointing out the kitchen window. "Did you see that? I think one of them just hit your trailer."

Rick bolted out the kitchen door and with long strides crossed the side yard, uncaring of the rain and sending their four hens squawking.

Ruth leaned over the sink, peering out the window.

"Shame, Katie," she said. "You told a lie."

"Three, maybe four by my count," said Katie. Leaving the meal preparations, she went into the bathroom. Once behind the closed door, she pulled the ripped piece of newspaper out of her pocket.

Mr. Ash received several inches in two columns of paper space. Katie read how Scott Ash; the son of the prominent Charlotte businessman had disappeared two days before Christmas over a year before. Remains found at the bottom of Eagle Drop Ridge had been tentatively identified as Scott using evidence found at the accident site.

He went out on his snow-machine, said Mr. Ash. I thought to meet with friends and didn't worry when it got late. I got up the next morning and realized he had never come home. My wife and I started calling around. No one had seen him the previous evening, and as far as we could deduce, he hadn't gone out to meet anyone we knew.

One short line remarked on the other remains. *...those of a female hiker from a previous accident have also been discovered.*

Katie knew that hiking on the ridge could be dangerous, even in broad daylight. The shale shifted, often unstable, and years of overgrowth hid dangers that made the way treacherous.

"Only a fool would go up there on a snow-machine at night," she said to herself.

Just as they sat down at the dinner table, a knock rattled the front door. Moments later Rick, who had insisted on answering and confronting the caller, came in from the living room, ushering Marlie before him.

"Look what I found on the doorstep," he said. "Ruth, get another plate. Sit here, Marlie."

"No, no," stammered Marlie. "I just stopped by with some information for Katie."

"Later," said Rick, "after we eat."

Marlie knew from experience she was no match for the bossy old man.

While they ate, she told them the same thing Janice had regarding permits. Ruth had risen to fetch cookies and coffee when the subject of Scott Ash came up.

"How did you people come to identify that bit of leftovers as Scott?" asked Rick.

Ruth put her cup in the saucer and pressed her eyes closed at Rick's question.

"Honestly?" asked Marlie. "By the registration number on the snow-machine."

She stared downward, busy picking up crumbs with her finger and dropping them on her plate. Only Katie noticed Marlie's lack of enthusiasm on the subject. Sitting back, she waited for the meal to be over.

Leaving Ruth and Rick to pick up, the two younger women migrated to the front porch. After the sudden rain shower ended, Katie had shut the chickens in their coop for the night and locked Bonnie safely in the barn stall that had been her home since being rescued. Neither man nor beast appeared to interrupt them.

Taking a chance there were no peekers and Marlie, who had seemed so cold earlier in the day, would be receptive, Katie reached out to stroke her lover's cheek.

"I've missed you," she said.

Katie rarely spoke of the time she had been gone. So Marlie, knew nothing of the last ten rough years, could not know how much it took for Katie to say those words.

"Oh Katie," said Marlie, stepping closer and laying her forehead on Katie's arm. "It's such a mess down at the sheriff's office."

"You're in a mess?" asked Katie, concern growing as her arms encircled Marlie.

"No," whispered Marlie. "I mean in general. No one has really figured out what happened to either the woman or to Scott Ash. His dad is a big shot over in Charlotte and the head of the town council, a big property owner, practically the mayor. Geoffrey Ash comes slamming in whenever he wants to, demanding this and that. He even got information from the official forensic report before Sheriff Lewis did. And Ash threatens everybody, says he's bringing in the federal marshals. For crying out loud, Katie, he's even got the governor calling."

Katie frowned. Before this she had never even heard of Geoffrey Ash.

"Then there's his wife," continued Marlie. "Hysterical on the phone, equally irrational in person. We should have had her take the alcohol breath test when she came in. Barely ten in the morning and she's so lit she's stumbling

41

around, and I could barely understand what she said. We don't have any answers. The state hasn't released the remains yet. It just goes on and on." Marlie shivered. Katie put her arms around her. "It's scary. I tried to be calm and empathize with Ash, and he jumped right down my throat. He even scares Brad. And Sheriff Lewis can't let go about the other body. Every time Ash goes on about *his* son, Lewis has to bring up the unknown woman. I don't know why, but that sends Ash off the deep end."

"That makes everything worse, I'm sure," murmured Katie.

Marlie pulled away, swiping at her eyes. "I have to go. Tomorrow I give my statement to the State Police Major Crimes Unit again. If they haven't been out here yet, get ready. I'm sure you're on their list. They are not friendly people."

Katie watched Marlie drive off. In retrospect, it did seem odd no one from law enforcement other than Sheriff Lewis had approached her. She had written out a report for Lewis and had not talked to him since.

Standing in the full dark, Katie could smell the damp left from the cloudburst and feel its chill seeping through her shirt. The autumn night smelled like more rain coming in. Snow would follow soon. Katie rose from the porch swing, ready to call it a night. The sudden glimmer of headlights coming up the road caught her attention. With one hand on the screen door, she considered fetching her bat as she waited. The car pulled into the drive. Sheriff Lewis stepped out.

"Good evening, Katie," he said, walking to the bottom step.

"Hey, Martin," she replied, relaxing.

He held something out, and she reached for the folded paper.

"Katelyn Moore-Took, consider yourself served," he said. "You are hereby summoned to appear tomorrow morning at eight o'clock at the Attorney General's office in Burlington. There you will meet with the Attorney General and the Major Crimes Unit."

Chapter Nine

Katie sat in the dusty hall outside the attorney general's office, cooling her heels. Her night had been long and sleepless, and so far, her morning had been equally lousy. When she came downstairs, she had found Rick sitting at the kitchen table, dressed and ready to go. He wanted to drive her into Burlington. A heated discussion had followed when she declined his offer.

"It'll be easier than giving you directions," he frowned.

"And we'll both lose our jobs," Katie retorted.

Then, when Ruth had come downstairs and found Katie dressed in her work clothes, the old woman sent her back upstairs to change into the one skirt and blouse she owned. Somehow the gauzy fabric, bought for an August fete, seemed more inappropriate than her jeans and flannel shirt.

Finding the courthouse at the corner of Church Street and Champlain Avenue had been easy. An open parking spot had been more difficult to come across. Katie raced into the building at eight-fifteen. The first person she talked to, a court clerk, stopped Katie in her tracks, asking what time her lawyer would arrive.

"I don't have a lawyer," Katie said, gaping at the clerk. "All I did was take a walk in the woods."

The clerk didn't seem impressed. Now, two hours later, and Katie still waited. Others had gone in and out when the heavy oak doors had opened. So far, no one called her name. She recognized the forensic tech and walked toward him, a smile on her face.

Holding up his hand, he said. "We're not supposed to talk to each other."

So Katie returned to her seat.

"Katelyn Moore-Took?" The caller, a stern-faced elderly man in a light gray suit, held the door open for her to enter.

Katie had been in court a few times during the ten years she had squatted in one place or another around Illinois and South Dakota. This time it worked the same way right up until the man behind the bench scared the bejeezus out of her. Then it became an inquisition.

"We're looking at a possible homicide here," said the Attorney General.

Katie's mouth fell open. Her blood ran cold.

"Therefore," continued the Attorney General, "we are also looking for a motive and a killer."

"What?" squeaked Katie.

She told her story twice and then answered random questions until finally, as the neighboring church bells chimed twelve, the Attorney General called lunch recess. Katie sat on the toilet in the lady's room with a wastebasket in front of her, sure at any moment, she would puke her guts up. The attorney general had told Katie she could leave for the day with a warning they could call her back. Her original plan to return home and start winterizing the house disappeared from memory. Now she wanted to get in her car and drive out of the state of Vermont and never look back. To hell with the farm and all the problems it had brought with it.

Katie drove back to Parentville without noticing how beautiful the day had become. Once out of the car in her own driveway, she inhaled deeply, surrounded by sunlight that shone both crisp and bright. She felt recovered. The tension in the attorney general's office had faded slightly from memory. *I'm okay*, she thought. *This is the perfect day to get things done.* However, an hour later, she still sat on the edge of Gram's bed staring at the ridge. She tried to force herself to stand up, zip her pants, and go. It wasn't happening.

Get up, she mentally scolded herself. *Get with it. That big roll of plastic sheeting won't put itself up.*

Knuckles rapped lightly on the bedroom door.

"Katie," said Ruth, "did you forget the furnace man said he would come today? As long as you're here, do you want to talk to him?"

Irma and Ruth hadn't used the furnace in years. Instead of paying for oil, they closed most of the big house, which had been a stagecoach stop and a hotel. Between the huge cook stove and the wide living room fireplace, they had made do living in only those two rooms. Stan had suggested if Katie were going to use the antiquated furnace, a cleaning would be in order for safety reasons. Katie led the man into the basement.

"Holy cow," he gawked, stepping off the bottom-most stair. "I haven't seen one of these monsters in, I'll bet, fifteen years."

They stood inside the tin hood bigger than most ice fishing shanties, flashlights lit and showing the actual burner unit, rusted beyond recognition.

"The original furnace burned coal," Katie said to Ruth as they sat at the kitchen table after the furnace man had left. "At one point, someone converted the burner unit to oil, probably before I came here as a child. Now it's garbage." The estimate for a new unit lay on the table between them. "The only thing salvageable is the big vent grate under the rug."

"We'll figure it out." Ruth patted Katie's hand.

A car pulled into the drive just as the phone rang. Leaving Ruth to deal with the jangling instrument, Katie grabbed her bat and headed outside.

"Going to hit a few balls out to the pig?" Marlie smiled, more relaxed than the last few times Katie had seen her.

"Thinking about it," grinned Katie. "I made coffee, c'mon in."

"I've only got a few minutes," said Marlie, spooning sugar into her mug. "I wanted to let you know Ash is pushing his investigation ahead."

"You said he came across as pretty intense about it," said Katie.

She wanted to talk to Marlie about her meeting with the attorney general, maybe compare notes. However, Ruth sat right beside her.

"Yeah, well, the female remains are possibly a college girl who went missing in Syracuse, New York. Major Crimes called Lewis; they said the state thought they could use dental records to make an identification."

"How would she have gotten here?" asked Ruth.

"I don't know, but Lewis left the forensic report on his desk, and it might have accidentally fallen into the Xerox machine." Marlie pulled three folded pages out of her shirt and laid them on the table. Her radio squawked. "Gotta go," she said, gulping coffee before running for the door.

Katie reached, fingertips drawing the pages back to her. Both she and Ruth knew Marlie had a specific reason for bringing the illegally copied papers. Her eyes scanned the page, not quite focused on the words. Then, like lightning in a summer sky, Katie jumped to her feet.

"Later," she said, dropping the xeroxed copies. "Daylight won't last forever. We need to get that plastic up first."

With scissors and hammer in hand, they rolled out the long sheet of folded plastic weather protector. Earlier, Rick had cut boards scavenged from the collapsing barn into long strips. Ruth held the sheeting in place while Katie tacked up the strips. They worked steadily, accompanied by the radio music wafting through an open window muffled by two fuzzy cats dozing nose to nose. As the afternoon waned, the wind chilled. They were nearing the end of the last side of the house and the end of the sheeting when Raymond Dean from the farm across the road rolled into the drive. The mud-spattered tractor pulled a hayrick half full of rectangular hay bales.

"These were left from last year," he said. "They're too rotted and moldy to use for feed. If you space them out on the plastic, they'll hold it down against the wind until the snow comes in." He unhooked the hayrick. "Let me know if you need more."

Katie eyed the bales, reluctant to begin handling them when Ruth said, "I think we've got maybe a foot or so extra on the plastic. Ha. We cut that one close!"

The older woman sounded winded; but, came to stand beside Katie. Tugging a bale to the edge of the hayrick, Katie let it fall into her arms and staggered backward before dropping it to the ground.

"Holy cat crap," she swore. "I forgot how heavy hay bales are."

"Especially old ones that sat out in the rain for months," said Ruth. "Whoa, I need to sit for a minute." She plopped down on the bale Katie had dropped.

Katie spun around, taking in the older woman's flushed, sweaty face. Ruth puffed for breath, mopping her brow with her sleeve.

"That's it," she said, "you're done."

"Are you saying I'm too old to keep up?" growled Ruth.

"That's exactly what I'm saying." Taking Ruth's arm, Katie walked them into the kitchen where she poured lemonade. "Rick can help after supper," she said.

While Ruth fussed with the cats, Katie turned her attention to the forensic report. Most of the writing held a lot of technical jargon she didn't understand. The other information seemed irrelevant until she got to the end. Under OTHER NOTES, Richardson had entered. *Though initial inspections of the remains and their respective sites show a time discrepancy of several weeks to a few months. It is my opinion both incidents occurred within only two to seven days of each other. The partial remains of the female were exposed to both the weather and animal predation, while the snow-machine laying on top of the remains of the male protected them. The male most likely pressed deep into the snow and virtually froze solid. We have not yet discerned cause of death for the female, but the male died of severe trauma. That being the fall from the cliff top and the crushing of the machine.*

"A week or less?" Katie said to herself, incredulous at Richardson's obvious need to voice what she believed to be perfectly clear. "How could anyone in their right mind not realize there's a connection?"

Katie reached for the phone. She needed to talk to Marlie, then remembered the ringing from earlier.

"Ruth," she called out. "Who phoned right after lunch?"

"Oh," said Ruth, "I forgot." She came around the corner. "The man from New York called. He wants to come over and, I think he said, test the climb?"

Katie leaned her forehead against the wall.

"If it doesn't rain, it pours," she groaned.

*　*　*

By the glow from their headlights, Katie and Rick placed the bales around the foundation. She'd pull a bale into the wheelbarrow, but Rick grabbed each bale by its twine and muscled it into place. As they went along, Katie told Rick about her day, the tense interview by the team in the attorney general's office, the furnace man's disappointing evaluation, and finally about the climbers who would arrive the following Sunday for a series of test climbs.

"You going to meet them up there?" asked Rick.

"Yes." Katie nodded. "Nothing is probably going to come of all this until next summer, but it's a start."

"Yup," Rick agreed, dropping the last bale into place. "Looks like we're short by about ten or twelve bales. I'll walk down and tell Raymond he can pick up the hay rick. Maybe he'll drop a few more bales tomorrow if he has time."

"Okay," said Katie, twisting the kink out of her neck. "I'm going to just sit for a few minutes."

"I'm planning on driving over to Hardwick tomorrow," said Rick, rubbing the edge of his right hand over his mouth. "There's a big auto salvage yard there. If you don't need Ruth here, I'd like to ask her if she wants to ride along."

"Go for it," said Katie. *They're so cute.* She grinned as he disappeared in the twilight.

On the backside of the house, behind the tractor shed, were the remains of the stagecoach garage. The structure had at one time been a tall, wide tunnel where the stagecoach could be pulled in during bad weather, allowing riders to dismount and enter the hotel out of the storm. On the side attached to the house, a wide concrete platform with stairs on the off-coach side were all that remained. The wooden platform long gone. Katie stared off towards the west while she sat alone on the highest step in the darkness. LG mewled from the other side of a screened-in window, begging to come out. In the early moon glow, Katie could see the sharp jut of the cliff. Then, a tall, fluffy cloud slid in, and with the blink of an eye, the cliff disappeared.

I wish my problems moved on so fast, thought Katie.

She turned her mind to the oncoming winter, considering how they could make it work with the three of them in the house. The bathroom door opened off the kitchen beyond the wood burning cook stove, and only during the severest weather had the pipes frozen. With Rick there, they were going to have to use the empty parlor as well. Normally, they left the wooden pocket doors closed because there wasn't any furniture in the room.

The cats wandering in and out would have made it just another place to clean.

It'll be chilly, she thought, *but Ruth and I could sleep in there. If we keep the cat room closed, that will help.*

Besides the original two floors, each with four lofty rooms under the gabled roof, and the kitchen and pantry added later, there had been an attached tractor shed or garage. The space had been a depository for junk throughout Katie's youth. Eventually, Irma had converted it to a kennel room. She'd borrowed money for major repairs and equipment, which added debt to Katie's list of financial woes. Katie's imagination took over her exhausted brain and took her to a sandy beach under a tropical sun when headlights caught her eye and announced Raymond's Ford pickup. Rick sat in the cab and Raymond's two boys sat on the tailgate. The missing bales filled the body.

"Go on inside," Rick waved her away, "we got this."

For the first time that evening, Katie noticed the frosty plume of his breath. Trick or Treat, for villagers, not here so far out of town, loomed weeks away, and the nights were steadily growing colder. She rose, back creaking and knees protesting.

So tired, all I want is a hot bath and an early night.

Inside, she found Ruth feeding the cook stove fire. The sweet and salty smell of hot popcorn and melted butter filled the air, creating a change of plans. When he came in, Rick found her sitting at the table with a bowl of popcorn and a cup of tea, reading the paper.

"Hey, that's my paper," he said.

"I know," said Katie, sweetly. "And you're first right after me."

Chapter Ten

T hat night it snowed. Not the work-stopping cover of deep snow, but a light sprinkle that crisped up the lawn. The thin covering of white came as a warning of what could be expected. Katie dragged Irma's old barn coat with its tattered cuffs and stained pockets out of the closet.

"It'll do," she said, at Rick's raised eyebrows. Grabbing her lunch pail, she left Rick and Ruth behind as she dashed out the door.

Stan met her at the time clock. It seemed, he told her, one clerk, heavily pregnant, had gone into early labor.

"Allergic to snow, I guess. Anyway, I need you to work in the store," said Stan. "At least for a while."

"I'm alone in the feed shed today," she said. "And Rick can't come in, he's already gone off for the day."

"I'll shuffle the guys around out back," Stan replied, pointing toward the front of the store. "Cindy will show you the ropes."

Another surprise! Cindy, Stan's wife, normally came in two afternoons a week to do the books, and always with her three small children in tow. Now she darted around, busy setting up registers. Katie looked, but Cindy had no babies circling her feet.

"Look at what's on the racks," Cindy directed. "Then go check the inventory out back. Keep it stocked up. And Katie, take a fresh flannel shirt off the shelf, we'll call it a promotional advance."

Katie looked down at her outfit. She sighed, agreeing with Cindy. What she wore did well in the feed shed but made her look a little scruffy behind the counter in the store. New shirt in hand, she told Cindy to add a note on her account.

"I'm never going to get that balance paid off," she muttered, coming out of the communal restroom with her old shirt in hand. Stopping short, she gaped. People rushed in as soon as the doors were unlocked. A piece of paper would have a problem squeezing between them. The cheery, red-cheeked crowd let it be known the first pretty sprinkle of snow blew through people like an electric current, zapping them into action. Every department in the store bustled with rushing customers seeking bird food, shovels, salt, and other winter paraphernalia. Beyond the regular inventory, Baldwin Feed and Hardware carried a full line of insulated gloves, hats, work boots, and jackets. Notebook and pencil in hand, she rushed off to follow Cindy's directions.

As she returned from lunch, Cindy caught Katie by the arm.

"Take a dolly," Cindy said. "Way out back is a pallet that has boxes of snow brushes and windshield scrappers. Get one of each and fill the racks at both doors, okay?"

Katie nodded, and using the dolly as a wedge, made her way through the crowd. She finished the first rack only to watch hands grabbing the fresh stock. Someone behind her said her name.

"Miss Took?"

"Yes," said Katie, "what can I help you with?"

She turned to find Mr. Ash behind her.

"My name is Geoffrey Ash," he said. "My...son, you found his remains on your property. I'd like to speak with you."

Katie felt herself pale. Marlie had warned her the man was bad news. Now he showed up where she worked. She wanted to get as far from him as possible.

"I'm sorry, Mr. Ash." She tilted the dolly, ready to move away. "I didn't find your son. Sheriff Lewis wouldn't let me within half a mile of the accident site, and this is where I work. If you'll excuse me, sir." Without waiting for an answer, Katie forged into the crowded aisle and away. For the rest of the afternoon, she jumped every time a tall man crossed her path. None of them were Ash. Her relief lasted until she left the store at five.

On the windshield of her old Subaru, pressed into service because using the headlights the night before had drained the truck's battery, lay a business card. The glossy bit of paper fluttered under the wiper with the message handwritten on the back, asking Katie to call Ash's office.

"Huh," she said, dropping the card to the ground, "must be he doesn't know the lock on the driver's door is broken."

* * *

Tired out down to the very bone, Katie's heart sank when she crested the hill to find half a dozen unknown vehicles in the drive.

"What's going on?" she asked Ruth as she came into the kitchen through the front room.

Leaning around the other woman, Katie blinked in surprise. Ruth's cooking abilities ended with grilled cheese and biscuits, but both the wood cook-stove and the gas range were covered with fry pans, and a large peach cobbler cooled on the washboard.

"Rick's friends are helping out," said Ruth. Something sizzled and spat. She spun back to the stove.

The arrival of the tractor gifted to Rick by, Katie guessed, a friend desperate to get the eyesore off his property, had created a social hot spot. Most Sunday afternoons, Rick and a couple buddies took their shade tree mechanic knowledge and invested it into the tractor's innards. Sometimes the men came alone, other times a wife or granddaughter might sit and visit with Ruth while they waited. For that, Katie felt grateful.

"It's going to run," Rick declared regularly. "We can use it around here, wait and see."

But Wednesday fell in the middle of the week, and darkness had set in. Suddenly, right below Katie's feet, something crashed, and someone yelped. Ruth rushed to the cellar door.

"Supper," she called down the stairs.

Katie squeezed past and rushed downward, stopping short when she encountered the first bearded farmer.

"What the heck is going on?" she demanded. Because the structure built to house stagecoach travelers leaned closer in design to a hotel than a residence, and sat on a hill, it had a cellar eight feet deep. At this moment, the stone and dirt floor space seemed filled with sweat-stinking men in overalls.

"Hey, Katie." Philip Carwell, auto mechanic and Grace Dean's brother, grinned. "We got it out."

She pushed past to find a large space where the tin hood had stood. Even the decomposing firebox had been removed, exposing the brick chimney she had missed seeing before.

Behind her, the men filed upstairs. Still confused, Katie followed.

"Where's Rick?" she asked.

One man exited the bathroom, wiping wet hands on his overalls, and another entered.

"Coming around," said Philip. "He went up to shut the bulkhead. You're probably going to need to replace the doors. They're rotting right through."

"A good place to pick up scrap lumber is the heap at the dump," said a man Katie didn't know as he walked by.

She nodded.

"Can you help me, Katie?" Ruth called.

In a daze, Katie filled plates with fried ham and green beans, mashed potatoes, and Hubbard squash. Each man took a plate, silver, and a cup of coffee, then wandered into the living room to find a place to sit. Most parked their butts on the floor, leaning against the walls, leaving the single chair and sofa for the ladies. As they filled miss-matched plates with hot food, Ruth explained the planned foray to the salvage yard had been shelved for the day.

"Where are the cats?" asked Rick, reaching for a plate.

"Are you kidding?" laughed Ruth. "I put them to bed a long time ago."

Katie held one edge of the plate tight while Rick tried to tug it free.

"You want to tell me what's going on?" she demanded, eyes dark beneath scowling brows.

"That dinosaur relic of a furnace had to go. These guys wanted to help."

Rick frowned. "The whole thing had to be disassembled. Too heavy for you and me to do alone. It's all on the trailer, ready for the salvage yard. I thought you'd be happy."

Laughter broke out in the living room. The three in the kitchen edged to the door to see what caused the hearty male guffawing. One plump gentleman sat on the floor with LG, who had escaped capture, lying wrapped around the back of his neck. Every time the man raised his fork, the cat reached out, trying to snatch a bite.

"LG!" gasped Katie.

Even the plump guy laughed. "No matter," he said. "I don't mind. Me and the Mrs. lost our old puss a few weeks back. Yup, miss her, we do."

Ruth went over and sat down on the floor next to him, plate on her knee. "What color did you say your kitty was?" she asked.

"It's a good thing," said Rick, from behind his coffee mug, "we've got one of every color."

The men spent the next hour exchanging stories while they emptied plates and devoured the cobbler. When they finally rose to leave, Katie stood at the door thanking each one, especially the plump fellow hugging the cat carrier.

"I'll make sure you get the carrier right back," he gushed, cheeks pink with excitement. They both laughed when a despondent meow came from inside the carrier.

Ruth rushed away, already elbow-deep in the dishpan, so Rick and Katie picked up dishtowels.

"Tell me," Katie said.

A headache sparked behind her brow. She caught herself squinting to focus.

"I bought a ham," Rick explained, "and we used the vegetables Grace and Ruth canned last summer."

"That's not what I mean," said Katie, stepping right in front of him.

His sigh said he had been hoping to distract her.

"I talked to the guy down at the scrap yard in Monkton where we took the old barn stanchions. He's going to take the hood," said Rick. "He'll meet me there Sunday."

Even though Katie had him hedged between herself and the kitchen table, Rick didn't make eye contact. Katie knew he held something else back. She waited, but he didn't share. Eventually, she moved aside. Katie and Ruth sat in the front room listening to the radio, while Rick spent the evening at the kitchen table with the newspaper. The clock chimed eleven before Katie tumbled into bed. Exhausted, she slept without her usual nightmares until Ruth shook her shoulder.

"You slept through the alarm, Katie. You're going to be late."

She barely clocked in on time. Stan told her it looked like the pregnant woman who still hadn't given birth would be out for a couple of months.

"Braxton Hicks contractions," he said. "she could be out for a while. You'll be working inside."

Katie selected two more shirts off the shelf.

Chapter Eleven

S tan came out of his office and handed Katie a slip of paper. Geoffrey Ash wanted her to call him back. Around ten, Sheriff Lewis came in asking if she'd talked to anyone else other than the Attorney General. Katie worked at the register when Lewis entered. He motioned the other customers in her line over to the second register. The clerk looked at Katie in panic. Katie focused on Lewis. She barely knew the other employees. Now internal gossip would spread about her, maybe bad stuff. She saw speculation in the eyes of the customers, some of whom were edging closer, hoping to catch Lewis' words.

"You're going to get me fired," Katie hissed. "This is unethical behavior."

"What do you think Stan's going to say when I tell him to pull you off the floor?" asked Lewis.

"It can't be any worse than all the people standing around trying to eavesdrop," she whispered. Suddenly she smiled brightly and raising her voice said, "Why, Sheriff Lewis, that is excellent news. I can't believe you would take time from your busy day to stop in and tell me. I'm, I'm flattered."

She looked away, shy, with fluttering lashes. Someone behind Lewis laughed. After all, unmarried, with a good job, and only of middle age, Lewis would be a fine catch. His neck reddened. Without looking at the people behind him, he hurried out of the store. Even though Katie wanted to slam the register drawer shut and shriek in anger, she smiled at the waiting customers, still bemused and coy.

"Can I help someone?" she asked. People rushed to her register.

Amid the customers calling out 'Hi Katie' and 'Nice to see you again,' stood a woman in a city-style outfit. She shouldered locals away to be next in Katie's line.

"I gather," said Colleen Johnston, "you prefer Took to Moore." Her smile offered the same oversized teeth Katie remembered. "I stopped in at your house, but didn't find anyone at home. The lovely woman down the road told me you work here."

The same anger Katie had felt toward Lewis rose again, filling her throat with bile.

"That's what I'm doing here, working," Katie said through gritted teeth. "Go away. Don't bother me anymore."

"Oh," said Johnston, "I'm shopping. I need some help with garden tools. And I prefer a woman's perspective to that of some clod hopping man."

Katie wasn't sure if Johnston's words were merely that, or if the reporter hinted, she knew something else. This time, the register closed with a resounding bang that caused the coins to clink.

"I tell you what," Katie smiled back at Johnston, "I'm going to get my boss's wife to help you out. While you're shopping, I'm going to take a break, walk around the parking lot. I certainly hope I don't fall down against somebody's tires with a sharp object in my hand."

"I don't take well to being threatened," said Johnston, an icy smile not meeting her eyes.

"Hm," said Katie, "seems I saw the north side of you headed south once at the threat of a bat. But just so I'm making myself clear, a promise is not a threat." She left her register and walked into Stan's empty office. From the window, Katie watched Johnston stroll out to her car.

"Need something, Katie?" asked Stan behind her.

"A roll of nickels," Katie said.

"Cash bag under your register," said Stan.

"Oh, yeah, I forgot."

Katie left the office without telling Stan about the reporter. Unfortunately, another employee previously made him aware people were visiting Katie on issues other than feed and hardware. Stan watched her walk away. Both he and Cindy considered Katie a friend. But the feed store, a place of business, should not be an open forum where she or any other employee working beside her should have to watch their backs.

For the rest of the day, Katie considered any person who approached her and was not wearing over-all's, to be suspect. Even then, periodically, someone slid in a question. She grew tired of telling people she didn't know any more than they did. Her curt remarks, aimed at one person at a time, were not stemming the flow. The bodies found on and beneath the ridge were big local news. The who, what, and why were on everybody's mind. She decided she needed a professional perspective. And she knew just the professional.

Chapter Twelve

Marlie locked the door of the sheriff's office. Both Lewis and Brad had gone home an hour earlier, but Marlie had been told to clean up the stack of reports waiting to be filed. Her shoulders sagged, showing the frustration and degradation weighing her down. Even though Sheriff Lewis hadn't said the words, his tone implied he considered clerical duties to be a woman's work. As a deputy in Champlain County, Marlie held a salaried position. It didn't matter how many hours she worked; she got paid for forty, and expected to be called anytime, 24/7. Also, as the newest employee, she got the worst days off and her schedule was subject to change on short notice. Marlie did not consider herself a fool. She knew a woman in this job walked on uncharted ground. She often laughingly referred to herself as not only the new cucumber, but also the one closest to the compost.

Exhaling in relief, she tugged at the heavy tactical belt deputies were required to wear and took the first step down. Then froze. With the onset of winter and the shortened days, the only light left on in the parking lot stood near the bottom of the steps. Across the graveled lot where she had left her car parked, she saw a movement in the shadows. Her hand eased up to her holster, middle finger releasing the strap securing her weapon. Her choices were to step down or return to the office. Either way, she would have to challenge the shadow.

Which? she thought, trying to calculate the risk. A movement across the lot took the decision out of her hands.

"Hey, Marlie," said Katie, stepping into the outer vestiges of the light halo.

"I didn't think you'd ever come out of there."

Marlie broke out in a cold sweat. As discretely as possible, she snapped the guard back in place.

"Are you insane?" Her voice shrill. "I could have shot you." Immediately, she regretted the words. Casting her eyes around, seeking anyone else who might have heard, she stepped onto the ground.

Katie blinked. Never in her wildest dreams would she have considered herself in danger, never mind being shot. Her jaw dropped.

"Why?" she asked.

Marlie strode towards her. "Deputy Sheriff," Marlie said, pointing to herself. "Night," arms reaching for the sky. "Deserted parking lot with you in the shadows," lowering her arms, she encompassed the world around them.

Katie cringed, releasing an audible gulp. "Sorry."

"What do you want?" asked Marlie. She stopped walking well within the ring of light.

"We need to talk," said Katie, jolting back and remembering why she had driven over to wait through the damp evening. Her meek tone had disappeared.

"Not here," said Marlie. "If we're going to be together, we have to go somewhere there are other people."

A new icy edge rimmed Marlie's tone. Katie didn't like it. There weren't a lot of options in the tiny village during the daylight hours, and none once the sidewalks were rolled up at supper time.

"We can go to my house, have some dinner," Katie began. When a frown appeared on Marlie's face, Katie hastened to add. "Ruth is there. Rick and some of his buddies are working on collecting all the parts of the tractor and getting them under cover."

"Okay," said Marlie. Without another word, she climbed into her car. Katie scrambled to catch up as Marlie pulled out of the lot.

At the farm, they found supper finished and the crew headed back to the barn.

"This won't work," said Marlie as the door closed behind Rick, his two buddies, and Ruth.

"Why not?" Katie demanded.

"If you need me to explain, you're not paying attention," Marlie snarled.

"Fine," snapped Kate. "Take off that lousy gun and get rid of it. I'll make us each a plate and we can eat in the damn barn." The China plates rattled dangerously together.

After locking the tactical belt with its holster and gun in the trunk of her car, Marlie walked around the house to the kitchen door. "Thank you," she said when Katie thrust an over-full plate at her.

"Just what we need," grunted Rick when the two women entered the barn through the milking parlor, "an audience."

"Hey, it's dinner and a show," said Katie, her tone backing him off. She tipped over an apple crate and sat down. A couple of bites later, she gave up trying to eat. Putting the plate on a nearby stack of boxes, she said. "Okay, so what's the deal?"

Marlie hadn't gotten far on emptying the plate balanced on her knees. She laid her fork across the top.

"You and I both know being gay isn't something people out here understand." Keeping her voice low, Marlie watched the people working twenty feet away. "I could lose my job, you could too. Well, maybe not you. Stan is pretty cool, but Sheriff Lewis isn't. He's an enormous bigot. He's down on anybody who isn't a straight, white, catholic male who votes republican."

Katie laughed, knowing Marlie's words to be true. Anyone who spent longer than ten minutes with Lewis learned about his beliefs.

Marlie dimpled shyly, then sobered. "But amazingly, he's not the biggest problem."

Katie sat quietly, watching as Marlie reclaimed the fork to push food around on her plate.

With a sigh, Marlie said. "A while ago, before you moved back here, I went out for the evening to a place in Burlington on lower Church Street. It's a kind of dive bar called The Red Dog. I mean, a real dive; greasy floors, bars made of old house doors laying across sawhorses, and a tough crowd."

"It's also," she said, "the type of place you go if you don't want to be seen. I went with some friends who are real flamers. I mean, these people exploded out of the closet. Discrete is not in their vocabulary."

Katie cocked an eyebrow. Marlie held up her hand.

"They are my friends," said Marlie. "Anyway, these people are only a small cross-section of the type of people you find at The Red Dog. The entire building, three floors, had been gutted and opened up to just one big room on each level. People moving around, dancing, drinking, the air filled with smoke. And a lot of weed. This woman walked by our table. I can't describe how incredibly sleazy she looked. The outfit she wore had less material than a good size belt, and her make-up must have been applied with a spatula she held in her left hand."

"And you think Lewis sounds like a bigot?" asked Katie, raising her eyebrows in question.

"No, Katie, listen to me," said Marlie. "If it were for me to guess, I'd say she rose from the bottom of the barrel with nothing to lose. She strutted by laughing, had one of those gigantic martini glasses in her hand, and towed this guy behind her who appeared even more out of place."

"How so?" asked Katie, once again nibbling at her supper.

"Creased trousers, golf shirt, fresh haircut, pompous attitude." Marlie waited. When Katie didn't respond, she said. "Geoffrey Ash."

"What?" Katie fumbled, almost dropping her fork. "Are you sure?"

"He looked me right in the eye," said Marlie. "Neither one of us had a chance to duck out of sight."

"Then what happened?" Katie asked.

"I didn't see him again that evening. To be honest, I left twenty minutes later. But Katie, he recognized me. I mean, maybe he couldn't remember from where, but I could tell he recognized that he'd seen me in the past. A couple of weeks later, the call came in Scott Ash had gone missing. I rode with Sheriff Lewis when he drove out to Ash's house. As soon as I walked in, Ash remembered having seen me. It was all over his face. He knows I'm gay. And if he's not sure, I bet he can find out."

"Wait, a minute." Katie's head jerked up. "You were a deputy when Scott Ash disappeared?"

"Yes, I've been on the force for almost two years."

"Awesome," Katie smiled. "Because I've got some questions."

Marlie held up a hand, quieting her. The deputy watched Ruth bear down on them.

"Are you two about through?" Ruth demanded. "We could use a little help and maybe get done out here. It's freezing."

Both women put their plates aside and jumped up to help.

With Ruth directing the men, Katie and Marlie moved stacks of boxes, bags filled with kitchen appliances, figurines, and boxes of old toys out of the way. There were heavy grain sacks filled with clothing and an impressive number of broken kitchen chairs. When they were through, they had created a space large enough for the tractor itself.

"Maybe," said Marlie, lugging the remnants of a broken bicycle to one side, "we should have been sorting as we went."

"That's Ruth's job," Katie huffed. Before shutting down the lights, she scrapped the rest of their dinner into Bonnie's dish. "Be a good girl," she told the pig and closed the stall door. To Marlie, she said, "Pick up your silverware. If we leave the dishes down here, we'll never find them again."

"After what I've seen tonight, I understand your eclectic dinnerware," grinned Marlie.

"It's not a bad thing," Katie smiled back.

She followed Marlie, who obviously still wanted to be where there were other people, and after hearing about Ash, Katie understood. A roomful of witnesses meant no person could make an assumption and from there, an accusation. Even though she would have liked to take Marlie's hand, Katie merely motioned her along the path up to the house. Once everyone had a slice of cake and a cup of coffee, most went into the living room. Katie sat at the table.

Marlie bit her lip, gazing at the living room door.

"As Poppa used to say," said Katie, "have a sit. We're in plain view, but as long as you keep your voice down, nobody else can hear you."

"Katie," Marlie began.

Katie cut her off. "You said you went with Sheriff Lewis to the Ash home when they reported Scott missing. Can you talk about it?"

"I don't see why not," said Marlie. "Most of the information is common knowledge now."

"Okay," said Katie, leaning back in her chair, cup in hand. "Start at the beginning."

Sasha, an older female long-haired tri-color, or money cat, with a friendly nature, rubbed against Marlie's knee. Scooping her up and rolling her over to scratch the soft white belly, Marlie began. "The call came in around ten in the morning the day before Christmas. No one else had come into work; Sheriff Lewis stayed home. I patched the call through to him there. It sounded like the type of thing he would want to be in on at ground level, you know. Not only that, but Ash specifically asked for Lewis. Ash wouldn't even tell me why, only that he had an emergency. The Sheriff picked me up as he drove through town, and we got to the Ash property about an hour later. Have you ever seen that place? Holy cow."

"Did you have a problem finding it?" asked Katie. "You know, get lost?"

"No, the sheriff seemed to know exactly where to go. I think he might have been there before. He didn't gape around like I did." said Marlie.

"Okay, then what?"

"We got there right about the same time as a state trooper, a corporal, but I don't remember his name. Anyway. Mr. Ash told us his son had been in the house when he and his wife had gone out the night before. When they got home, Scott's car hadn't moved, so his parents thought he had already gone to bed. The next morning, his mother went to wake him, but he wasn't in bed. Somewhere around that time Ash realized that one of his snow-machines had been taken. They decided Scott had gone out in the evening for a ride."

"They were expecting a crowd for brunch," said Marlie. "From what Ash said, his wife got pissy about it, so Ash started calling around looking for Scott."

"You were sure he'd gone out in the evening?" asked Katie. A niggling little thought took root, but as quickly as it sprouted, it died. It seemed she had heard a slightly different version of these events somewhere else.

"The night before had been freezing. Fish and Game responded to the emergency call. The forest ranger had a snow-machine on the back of his truck. We used that and Ash's second snow-machine to follow the tracks for a distance. The ranger pointed out the tracks were frozen solid. The crushed snow, in and along the sides of the tracks wasn't malleable. The trail led in a northerly direction. Then Scott got onto a busy trail, and we lost him."

"When the ranger and I got back to the house, Lewis and the corporal had just finished going over Scott's bedroom. All the bedrooms are at the front of the building, at the top of the stairs. Mrs. Ash is at the end of the hall with Mr. Ash's room on one side as you come back. On the other side, Scott's is right across from Mr. Ash, and then Robby's, then the stairs, and after that, there are a couple of guest rooms. According to Lewis, the room appeared neat, orderly. It didn't look like Scott had been in the bed. Lewis didn't find any drug paraphernalia, or any hint Scott hadn't been of sound mind."

"You mean like suicidal?" Katie asked.

"Exactly," said Marlie. "Ash also verified the gun cabinet lock hadn't been tampered with. And all his firearms were accounted for. He gave us a list of Scott's friends. When we called, every single one of them said Ash had called hours earlier. No one had seen Scott. Most of them thought he would be tied up spending time with his brother."

"Scott has a brother?" Katie straightened up.

"Well, yes, and no. Robby is a cousin. Their mothers were sisters. Robby's parents had been killed in a car accident. He might have been, I don't know, ten. Ash and his wife took Robby in and raised him. I don't believe they legally adopted him, like a son. I think the right word is ward. But the boys considered themselves brothers. Robby is older by a year or two, and there's a strong family resemblance. All the information I heard said they were close."

"What did Robby have to say?" asked Katie.

"He had been home from college for the holidays but left the same time Ash and his wife went out the previous evening."

"Two days before Christmas?" asked Katie. Considering what Marlie had just said about Mrs. Ash wanting Scott at the brunch, that sounded off.

"His girlfriend lived in Michigan. They were going to fly out there so he could meet the parents. You know how it is with love, new sweetie, bye-bye siblings." Marlie cuddled Sasha. The purr volume rose. "Sheriff Lewis talked with him on the telephone and said he was devastated. He wanted to come right back, but Ash said no, he should wait until they knew more. I heard the sheriff tell Brad that Robby had said when he left, Scott had just made himself a sandwich and as far as he knew, had no plans to go out anywhere."

"Okay," said Katie. "What about Mrs. Ash?"

Marlie laughed. "Remember, I told you she's out of control? Well, by the time we got there, she was limp as two-day-old fish. Ash said she flipped out, beyond hysterical. He had given her a sedative." Marlie paused. "I don't know what Ash gave her, but when we arrived maybe an hour and a half later at the max, he couldn't wake her up, like totally zonked. The sheriff didn't get to talk to her for a couple of days, and even then, he said she could barely string three words together."

"So, you didn't get any information from her?" asked Katie.

"Never a word." Marlie stood up, brushing off cat hair. "She did finally submit a written report, which said exactly what both her husband and nephew had already told us." Marlie gave the despondent Sasha one last pat. "Good night, Katie," she said.

Katie's face screwed up, wondering how Mrs. Ash could have been so out of touch at the time of the loss of her only child. The woman had done nothing but produce one report, which from the sound of it might have actually come from her husband. Then she had shown up at the sheriff's office totally over-wrought. The picture in the paper showed a weeping woman, but no article offered her words. Katie wondered what type of hidden issues the family swept under the rug.

After making her good nights to those in the living room, the deputy left, followed by Rick's friends. Ruth went up to bed, but Rick found Katie still sitting at the tiny dinette table.

"What'cha doing?" he asked.

"Scott Ash has a sort of brother, an orphan cousin," said Katie.

"So?" said Rick.

"How come we haven't heard anything from or about him on the news, or from Lewis?"

"Good question." Rick yawned hugely. "Good night."

"Not for everybody," whispered Katie after he left the room. "Not for two poor souls out in the woods."

Chapter Thirteen

"Y ou were up late last night," Rick said, pouring coffee as eggs sizzled on the stove.

He had taken over making breakfast in self-defense after suffering through several servings of Ruth's burned oatmeal. Katie looked down at her plate. Two sunny-side up eggs eyeballed her over a bacon smile. On either side, flamboyant toast ears with little jelly earrings stretched out to the edge of the plate.

"Take a look at this." He put the Burlington Free Press dated the previous day and opened to page five, down beside her. A small article encircled in pencil lay above the fold. The strictly factual report stated that the remains of Scott Ash discovered by hikers were being released to the family. There were no words regarding the other remains.

Ignoring the food, Katie flipped to the second section of the paper and the obits. She expected to see something about Scott. She didn't find anything. No photo, no story about his prowess in sports or his potential, or all the attributes his father had been touting to every Tom, Dick, or Harry reporter who crossed his path.

"I'm thinking," said Rick, spreading jam on his own toast, "it'll appear in a couple of days. A modest article about private services complete with a request for privacy for the family."

"Why is that?" Ruth asked.

"Because," said Rick, never taking his eyes off Katie, "*Geoffrey* Ash has the stink of really rotten fish."

Katie got up to pack their lunch for work.

68

"It's easier for me to do two," she explained, brushing off his offer to help, "than for us to be under each other's feet."

Rick studied his toes, sipping his coffee. Finally, he said. "I think I'll run over to the dump at noon instead of after work. Maybe I'll be a little late getting back. If Stan asks, tell him I'll be right along."

Katie watched him leave. Rick had an agreement with Chet, who ran the dump which involved a big plate of leftovers in exchange for bits they could use around the farm. The elderly veteran lived in an old Silver Bullet camper, which served as his office. Rick would stop on the way home, dropping off a foil-wrapped meal Chet could heat or not, his choice. For his good deed, Rick always returned with all manner of boards and planks. This time, Katie had the definite impression Rick wasn't searching for the exact piece of lumber he needed.

She stepped outside, still trying to decide if her grandfather's old friend hinted at more than odd jobs. Eyeing Rick's scrap collection, which never grew because he always had a project, she considered his abilities, or rather, how far he would go to get what he wanted, and what he would willingly do for the same.

The far back corner of the barn had collapsed years before. Without anybody asking, Rick shored up where Irma cannibalized for fuel. Using coffee cans filled with bent nails found in the barn, he repaired Bonnie's box stall. Barely twenty-four hours earlier, Rick related he had sized up what he needed to replace the bulkhead Katie had forgotten hid among the enormous bank of hollyhocks.

"We're going to need to get in and out of there," he'd told her.

Katie hadn't listened, and therefore not asked why. Now she wondered what else he had going on that maybe didn't involve a hammer and some rusty nails.

Ruth hustled by her, returning with an armful of wood chunks.

"Brr," she said. "Cold out here and cold within."

Katie forgot about Rick. Her thoughts returned to worrying about heat, plowing, frozen pipes, and all the other things she heard people at work grousing about. They now had a television as Rick appropriated the unit from his mobile home. She considered the Channel 3 weatherman an enemy, raising the alarm on consequences that never entered her mind. Day by day, Katie learned, to be a property owner wasn't all about sitting on the porch with hot dogs on the charcoal grill and a cocktail in her hand. Pride kept her from asking for help, but her closed mouth didn't stop Rick from providing it.

Business slowed down after lunch at the feed store, and Katie listened to Don, another employee, re-hash the grueling last two days he spent covering all the windows in his house with plastic sheeting. Not long after Don finished the heavy chore, the chimney cleaner created a big dusty mess.

"We couldn't air anything out without taking down all the plastic," he said. "Can you believe it?"

Katie shook her head. Her house had two chimneys. *Did I need to clean them? Or at least the one attached to the wood stove? How? Do I need to get another roll of plastic?* Rick had returned and spoke up as Don walked away.

"So, that's what I heard," Rick said, taking a hard look at her. "Are you alright? Did you hear what I said? You look kind of glazed over."

He waved his hand in front of her face, snapping his fingers. Katie jerked away giving the old man a hard look.

"I'm good." Katie shook her head to dispel the big multicolored dollar signs puffing out of tall chimneys and whipping around in the air like giant flags. "Say it again."

Rick repeated that Chet's Silver Bullet housed a regular meeting place for old-timers, a point Katie would never have been able to guess.

"A lot of male-style gossip goes through there," he said. "If you want to know what's going on, you either go to the library on knitting club day or the dump."

Katie quirked an eyebrow. "I don't knit," she said.

"But Ruth does. Maybe she should rejoin," said Rick. "Anyway, there's a lot of talk about the dead folk on the ridge. Who the girl might be, how young Ash always acted like a wild one, and his father is a world-class sleaze." Rick paused. "There's also some chat about Geoffrey Ash's reputation for being a bully. You need to be careful if you're going to go poking around in that mess."

She gave him a look. Rick just shrugged his shoulders and walked away. "You know, you're going to," he threw back as he walked away.

* * *

Katie got up with the chickens the next morning. Daybreak found her standing at the edge of the bog. She would not have a lot of time, but she needed to see for herself to understand. Barely able to make out the hummocks that would keep her from falling on her face, she moved across the wetland. A thin layer of ice covered the puddles, and reeds crackled and broke as she pushed them aside. She arrived at the cliff face panting but relieved. Then realized finding the accident spot might not be so easy. Sheriff Lewis and the techs had spent two days carrying every chip of bone, scrap of metal, any and everything that might be a clue away. Katie did not know if she stood in the right spot. Turning left, then right. Nothing. Then, twenty feet away, a tiny finger-sized bit of yellow police tape waved in her direction. Like Gram coaxing her to a special treat, the waver as thin as a sunflower petal beckoned.

Slivered rock rising above the bog made up the cliff bank. Icy shards of slate slipped beneath her feet, threatening to tumble her to her knees, slicing open both trousers and skin. Where her left hand rested on the rock face, as she tried to hold her balance, the cold stone stayed solid beneath her palm. Reaching out to the band of yellow just as the reed split in the wind, a sob caught in Katie's throat as she threw out her hand, fingers splayed, trying to catch hold before it floated away. Katie knelt on the ground, looking up the cliff towards the top, then back across the expanse of the bog behind her. Gratefully, she hugged the small bit of remnant clutched in her fist. Thin sun, bright but offering no warmth, broke over the tips of the naked maples. Now that she had finally found the site of the crash, she had no time to stay. Quickly, she gathered rock pieces until she had stacked a cairn three feet high and just as wide against the cliff. Whether it would serve as a map or a reminder of someone lost didn't matter. X marked the spot, and not trusting what Lewis or the state agents were telling her, Katie would return searching for a clue to who, and hopefully why.

"I'll be back," she promised, jumping onto the nearest dry hummock. She felt a tug on her jacket, as though the stone held her back, reluctant to let her leave, afraid her promise would not be kept.

Chapter Fourteen

"There you go," Katie said, handing the customer his receipt. The next person in line, Janice from the town clerk's office, stepped up. "Hi, Janice," Katie smiled.

The woman, Katie's mother's age, spoke often of going to school with her, smiled back.

"I thought earlier about giving you a call," she whispered, leaning over the counter. "But I didn't want to get you in trouble with your boss."

"Okay," Katie whispered back, eyes flickering around, looking for Stan.

"I talked to Charlene, she said she hadn't gotten hold of you and the meeting for the historical society grant is tonight."

"Tonight?" frowned Katie, remembering she had yet to contact the Historical Society coordinator. "This is Friday. No one holds meetings Friday evening. Why would I want to go, anyway?"

"Your grandmother had an interest in this grant. Charlene can explain it to you." Janice hefted a bag of birdseed onto the counter. "Is this good for cardinals? The committee moved the meeting up because one member has a family hooy happening this weekend. And I guess the paperwork needs to go out by Monday. What do you think? Should I buy this one?"

Katie got Janice the correct bird seed and sent her on her way. Later, when Rick wandered by, she stopped him and asked if he knew what the clerk had been talking about.

"Not a clue," said Rick. "But the word grant means money. You should check it out. Take Ruth. I'll be late tonight anyway. I've got a meeting with Philip."

"I didn't realize you guys were such buddies," said Katie, cocking an eyebrow. Rick had been doing a lot of his need to know only business lately, and often named Philip as a conspirator.

Rick shrugged and headed back outside.

So, at six-twenty, the two women entered the town hall. As they paused to get their bearings, a woman rushed up to them.

"Oh, I'm glad you got here early. This way. Let me tell you about Irma's application." She thrust a manila folder into Katie's hand before coaxing them into a side room.

Charlene Garland reminded Katie of a Chick-a-Dee. Petite, wearing her dark hair in a short bob, and with bright eyes, she didn't stop moving for a second. Even as she hip-hopped around, she appeared to have an eye on everything happening.

"So," Charlene began, "we started listing historical property sites around the village about five years ago. Irma came forward because of the stagecoach house and the old school. She did the initial paperwork but didn't come to any of the meetings. While I was driving into town, I noticed you're cleaning out around the school. This might be good for you. The stagecoach house, of course, is out."

Before Katie could ask a single question or explain they had not gotten any further than cutting the wild growth back from the building, a gavel banged in the council room and Charlene dashed off. Most of the seats were already filled, but Katie found two in the middle near the back. People she didn't know nodded to her as though she had never been anywhere else, and Ruth greeted many others.

Geoffrey Ash stood up, banging the gavel again. He called the meeting to order and apologized for the short notice. Katie rolled her eyes. Everyone there knew about Ash's family hooy.

"The state notified us that, though they gave us an end date for our application this year, the process has changed. It's more first come, first serve. Let me make it clear, we will not be discussing payments going out for the last grant. If we selected your property in the last round, you'll receive a check within the next ten days. We just need to decide how to split what we received. If you don't get one, we're trying again. I'll call your name, we'll verify your application, and move on to the next person. Again, there will be no discussion."

Katie heard disgruntled murmurs from all around. Ignoring them, Ash called the first name. While the board clarified items on the landowner's application, Katie pulled the file out of the manila envelope.

An application for $1000 filled out in Irma's neat block script, dated two years ago, lay on top of several other pages. Flipping past it, Katie found another copy of the same form dated May first of the current year. This one had several cross-outs and corrections. Beneath those two were several pages of notes, some with attached photocopies of old photographs, none in Irma's handwriting. Stapled to the back page, Katie found a neat, typed application that had been dated but not signed. She did not have time to read any of the notes.

"Katelyn Moore-Took," called Mr. Ash.

Ruth's elbow dug into Katelyn, popping her out of her seat with a yelp. She rushed to the front of the room, fighting the urge to rub her side.

"Katelyn Moore-Took," she repeated to Charlene, who appeared to be taking meeting notes.

"Miss Moore-Took," said Ash. "The committee is denying your application for funds to repair the stagecoach house."

"Why?" asked Katie. Even though she hadn't known about the application, she didn't like Ash's dismissive tone. This might be a better place to take him on than in the middle of the feed store. She knew the history of the property. Both of her grandparents had extolled its virtues to her.

"Historical grant monies are provided for the continued upkeep of buildings of historical significance." Ash sounded snide. The glint in his eye hinted he reveled in dashing her hopes. "Even if the building is being used as a residence or for a business, the basic structure has to remain unchanged. The tour of the coach house showed far too many alterations."

He had her there. She had no idea what changes had been made to the original structure. But she made a mental note to find out.

"Thank you for your consideration," Katie said.

"However," interrupted Charlene, "I believe your application for the schoolhouse is valid. I just need you to sign it and give it back to me." She looked pointedly at the folder. "Isn't that right, Geoffrey?"

Charlene didn't look at Ash, but Katie had him right in her sights and did not miss the way his lips disappeared as his mouth tightened, or the lowering of his brows. Katie pulled the application free, signed it, and waited while Charlene notarized it.

"Can I get a copy?" Katie asked, her throat inexplicably dry. After Charlene promised to mail one to her, Katie headed up the aisle, collecting Ruth as she passed by.

When they were well outside Ruth said, "Well, I'm glad I'm not the next person in line."

Katie burst into laughter. "All they can say is no, they can't take away somebody's birthday."

"Or their right to drive," giggled Ruth.

Once home, Ruth put on the inevitable pot for tea, while Katie flipped through the mail. Among the store flyers and bills, she uncovered a letter postmarked from New York. Inside a brief note from Armand DeNoi and his partner, Thomas Hefflin, said they would arrive Saturday evening to hike into and climb Eagle Drop Ledge on Sunday. If they were happy with the climb, they would consider an agreement to climb there.

"It says here," Katie read aloud, "they want to go down from the top this time. On their next trip, they'll hike in from the bottom."

"That means they're going to be here the day after tomorrow." Ruth pointed out.

"I know," said Katie. She pulled her mug closer. "Somehow I didn't realize this idea would be so involved."

Chapter Fifteen

The next day, Katie left work early.

"I have to go over to the Charlotte town office and they close at noon on Saturday," she explained to Stan. "Sorry."

"Not a problem," he said. "I'm keeping track of the hours. When it gets to be time for inventory, I own you." Laughing with false hysteria, he walked away.

Katie and Lenny, the other clerk, watched him go.

"Is that normal?" she asked over her shoulder. "For someone to cackle like the Wicked Witch of the West?"

"It is if you're some kind of lunatic," said Lenny.

* * *

Katie rushed into the town hall and directly to the office of the zoning clerk. Parentville might not require a permit for the hiking company, but Rick had reminded her Charlotte might.

"I'm sorry," said the town clerk, "Mrs. Deyak isn't in today. Is there something I can do to help?"

The words almost fell off the of Katie's tongue asking about permits when the door to the selectman's door opened and Mr. Ash entered the main room. His eyes met Katie's. He didn't look away but walked toward the two women. Out of the corner of her eye, Katie saw the town clerk step back.

She's afraid of him, Katie thought. She steeled her face, not wanting to frown or appear agitated.

"Good afternoon, Miss. Took," smiled Mr. Ash. At least Katie thought it might be a smile. The straight line of Ash's mouth barely curled up at the edges. "What brings you all the way over here this afternoon?"

"Farm business," said Katie.

"Oh yes, on Kitteridge Road. Your mother is Arlene Moore, right? Her mother a Roser?" asked Mr. Ash. His question wasn't *quite* a sneer.

Katie hesitated. She resented his tone, and Ash seemed to know a lot about her. What game did he put on the table now?

Ash eyed Katie up and down, taking in the tattered jeans and flannel work shirt.

She could see his petty little mind working, and it disgusted her. Normally, she didn't feel the need to explain herself or her origins. But Ash could easily jump to a conclusion regarding Katie's grit. Arlene Moore had been a beautiful, gracious woman of about Ash's age. He couldn't have known Arlene, she had died before he came to the area. But regardless, Katie's mother had always been a lady. If someone acted rude to her, she turned the cheek and never put herself in that position again. Gram always said her daughter had been a kind girl, unable to say crap if she had a mouthful. Perhaps Ash assumed Arlene and Katie were two peas from the same pod. If so, she had a surprise for him. Her grandparents raised her. Gram, a tough old woman, and Poppa, who respected all that surrounded him. Neither were shy about demanding fair treatment from everyone else.

Katie gave a deep sigh and, in as respectful a voice as she could muster, said, "Yes, I don't remember a lot about her, but my grandparents brought me up. Both the Moore and the Roser families have lived here for generations. It honors me to be one of them." *And protect what they had.*

Mr. Ash nodded slightly. Though still rigidly erect, he allowed his shoulders to relax, perhaps thinking she was a gentle soul, "But you're not quite like them, are you?" The glint in his eye hinted he knew something she would not want shared. He made Katie's skin crawl.

I could reach you and rip the smug, self-abasing smile off your face before you knew I moved, she thought, then reigned in her temper. *Easy girl let's not hurt him until you get what you need.*

Unable to look Mr. Ash in the face any longer, Katie turned back to the town clerk.

"Is there a form I need to fill out to rent my land? Should I schedule an appointment?"

"You need to speak with Mrs. Deyak," said the clerk. "I can have her call you." She hesitated. Mr. Ash still stood beside her. The woman licked her lips. Katie took it as a sign of unease. Sure, the cause stemmed from the self-righteous bigot hovering over them.

"That would be fine." Katie smiled. She wrote her number on a slip of paper and left. Walking down the cool hallway into the sun, she muttered to herself.

"He's watching. I can feel his eyeballs severing my spine. Relax, don't stamp your feet. This is just a normal day in a regular workplace. Don't let him get under your skin."

Katie made it all the way to her car and out to the main road before her mouth snapped open and while she pounded her fist on the steering wheel, roared one long-winded cuss after another.

"Aaargh, of all the conceited bastards. Mr. I'm-so-good. I bet he gives out bow-wrapped lumps of coal to everyone he knows at Christmas."

She wanted a cup of coffee, but didn't feel like turning around to go back to the Miss Charlotte Diner.

Don't worry, Ruth will have tea. You can wait until you get home.

Katie rolled down the window, letting in the warm, musty autumn smell, and cranked up Arlo Guthrie on the radio. Then inspiration stomped down on the brake pedal. At the town line, Katie turned back and drove straight to the Charlotte High School. The Subaru rolled down Spear Street and came to rest in the middle of the street.

"What the heck?" said Katie, leaning out of the driver's side window.

The old building had been closed up tight; the lawn covered with blown leaves. A piece of plywood covered a broken window. A large sign nailed to the door said trespassers would be charged. Katie exhaled a long breath, then another light went on inside her head.

"Next stop," she said, cranking the window closed, "the public library."

Like most towns, the Charlotte Library had a local section. Katie found three shelves devoted to high school yearbooks. Right up to 1966, the books were The Tarpon. Then the title changed.

"Because," Katie mused, "the school closed, and the town shipped all the kids over to Champlain Valley Union."

She guessed Scott Ash to have been about twenty years old when he disappeared, and selected the 1973 Tarpon, and the first two books from CVU after the merge. Opening to the individual student pictures of the senior class, she read names. The Tarpon had nothing, but the first CVU Janus yearbook provided exactly what she wanted.

She made a list of all the clubs and activities listed beneath Scott's name. Then leafed through the book, looking for any related photographs. On the same notebook page as the list of names, she placed an additional star every time she found a person included in a photograph with Scott. An asterisk meant they were hugging or hamming. The list kept growing.

"So, Scott seems to have been a popular guy," said Katie.

She rose from her seat with her arms filled with the stack of yearbooks. Then she remembered Robby. Sitting back down, she looked for Robby in the yearbooks.

"Robby Ash. Robby Ash." She ran her finger down the columns of seniors and found nothing.

"Wait a minute," she mused. "No one said he went by Ash." She flipped to the next page. "And is Robby a nickname for, maybe, Robert?"

In the book from two years before, she found a Robert (aka Robby) Daudlin. Marlie had said the two boys shared a strong family resemblance. Looking from one photograph to the other, Katie considered the pictures.

"Whoa," she muttered, "this could have been two pictures of the same guy."

However, by placing them side by side, Katie could see the subtle nuances that made them individual.

"That's downright creepy," she said, making a new list of Robby's contacts, which were even longer than Scott's.

Katie would have liked to take her list to the town clerk's office. But by this time, everyone would have gone home, and Mrs. Deyak, the zoning director, hadn't been there, anyway. She had been helpful when Katie had been searching for Gram's murderer at the time, she returned to Parentville earlier in the summer. Katie trusted the other woman not to gossip about her doings. Being a lifelong local, Mrs. Deyak might tell Katie if some students listed in the notebook still lived in the area. They couldn't have all left town. Katie stood on the steps of the library, looking over the roof of her car and around the village. Just going from place to place asking questions wouldn't work. Eventually, other people would ask her questions too.

"On another day," sighed Katie.

She had been right. Ruth had tea. While they were sipping and Katie explained her notes to Ruth, the telephone rang. Both women jumped. Katie kept the momentum going and grabbed the receiver.

"Is this Katie Took?" asked a strange voice, that of a younger man.

"It is," Katie answered, warily.

"Great!" The man's voice went from nervous to smiling. "I'm Allan Gavin, the guy from the sheriff's office gave me your number. He told me you're the animal officer and you do extractions. My wife and I bought the Anderson farm on Backberry Road. We need your help. Could you come over?"

Behind Mr. Gavin, Katie could hear a woman speaking and two or three young children squealing with excitement. They were all quite loud.

"Yes," said Katie, "I can help you ––,"

"Great! See you soon!" Mr. Gavin answered enthusiastically. He didn't seem to realize he had cut Katie off and even as the line died on his end, Katie heard him tell his family not to worry. She would be there soon.

"Wonderful," she sighed. Turning to Ruth, she said, "I have to go over to Backberry Road for a pick up. It shouldn't take long." While she pulled on her knee-high boots and collected her gear, Ruth gave directions.

* * *

"And second left," Katie said to herself.

Two and a half miles later, she turned into the driveway to a big yellow colonial house. With a snare pole in one hand and a large heavy-duty fishing net in the other, Katie walked up onto the porch. The door flew open and three children

between the ages of eight to twelve boiled out.

"Miss Took?" asked the gangling man who followed them.

"Touque," said Katie, with a smile, "like a knit winter hat."

"Okay," he said, looking towards the driveway and frowning.

His wife came out right behind him. When she opened her mouth Mr. Gavin held his hand up to quiet her.

"Are those your tools?" he asked.

Katie didn't like the little furrow between his eyebrows. At her nod, he ordered the children back in the house, telling them to stay inside.

"Why don't you leave those here," he said, "while we have a little look-see." He sounded cheerful, in a strained sort of way.

Katie went back to the pickup. After dropping her gear into the back, she took a moment to look over the man in his brand-new farmer overalls and the woman. Her outfit shone more like brand new city slicker smart than down home cow patty conservative. She had tinted Lucy-red hair in a teased-up page boy hairdo, two-inch pumps, and a cantaloupe-colored dress with a two-inch black patent leather belt and at least a couple of crinolines.

If that belt were any tighter, thought Katie, *both her eyeballs and her toes would bulge out.*

Mr. Gavin led the way, with his wife following Katie, whose skin tingled a warning as they got closer to the barn. They entered through the milk house mid-way up the length, and once inside, Mr. Gavin turned right. Twenty-five feet away, three heavy metal bars blocked their approach to the end of the barn. Mr. Gavin ducked between the lowest two. Katie hesitated.

"We had these installed," explained Mrs. Gavin, "so the children wouldn't go any further." Though she now stood right beside Katie, she made no move to squeeze between the bars. Katie looked back and shrugged. Mrs. Gavin's crinolines would never have fit through the narrow slat. Mr. Gavin hesitated, waiting for Katie to follow, which she did with serious trepidation.

When Katie stepped up to Mr. Gavin, she realized the back end of the barn contained free stalls, as opposed to stanchions. Initially, Katie didn't see anything, but even as she turned her head to the left, she heard a heavy, heated snort followed by a rasping noise similar to a claw hammer dragging on stone.

"He's right there," whispered Mr. Gavin. "No fast moves. His name is Jack."

The hair stood up on Katie's arms and waved a warning. Her first step didn't bring an errant critter into view, but the next two brought her to a double-thick wall that ended just above her eyes. Coming out of the top were steel uprights used to re-enforce the timbers. Standing on tip-toe, she saw the central wall between the two free stalls had been removed. A pair of tiny and angry black eyes ringed with an impressive rack of horns lowered in her direction, and stared back. Jack had to be the biggest and most gorgeous coal black bull Katie had ever seen. The thick brass ring hanging from his nose would have fit over her wrist, and all the time she admired him, one or the other of his foot hooves pawed up the filth beneath him.

A smile brought on by his beauty and raw power lifted her lips. Then, suddenly, with a loud and powerful snort, Jack jumped forward two steps. Katie scrambled backwards and found that Mr. Gavin and his wife had already exited the barn.

"Oh, my god!" Katie exclaimed when she got outside. Her heart pounded in her chest, and she bent over, resting her hands on her knees to quell their trembling. "Where did you get him?" She coughed to clear the shrill and give herself a moment to calm down.

Mr. Gavin stood with his hands in his pockets, his wife already halfway back to the house.

"He came with the farm."

"Who takes care of him?" Katie asked, still feeling shaky.

"I just throw feed over the wall," said Mr. Gavin. "What do you think?"

"What I think," said Katie, once more under control, "is that whatever is in there you want out, Jack can take care of."

Mr. Gavin looked at Katie as though she had sprouted balloons from her ears.

"It's Jack, I want out," he said.

Later, Katie would swear her jaw actually bounced in the dust.

"Are you out of your mind?" She demanded. "How would I get him out of there? For crying out loud, just open the gate."

Gavin handed Katie a piece of paper from his pocket. It appeared to be a note from the previous owner explaining about Jack's pedigree, and that under no circumstances should he be allowed freedom as he presented a death threat to anyone and any animal he could get to. *Neither barbed wire nor electric fence will stop him,* said the note. Katie handed the paper back.

"I can't help you." She circled Gavin.

"It's your job," he retorted.

She spun around. "*My* job is raccoons, skunks, and deserted cats. Not farm animals with a killer attitude." Katie stalked towards her truck.

Gavin didn't back down. He called out to her rigid back, "The sheriff told me to call you."

"Yeah, well, the sheriff should have known better." Then she stopped before spinning back on her same track. "Wait! Did you tell him you wanted me to remove a twenty-four-hundred-pound bull with rabies? Because if he sent me out here to be killed, you're going to be my witness for getting him fired."

Gavin held up his hands. "No, I just told him I had a problem with a nuisance animal, and he gave me your number."

Nuisance, my fat hinny, Katie slammed the truck into reverse. *Somebody ought to put up a sign at the town line telling all the trust fund babies who want to play Old MacDonald, this ain't the place.*

Before she got the truck into drive, Allan Gavin hung from the window frame.

"What should I do?" he asked. "We have kids. We've been here six weeks and my wife is afraid to let them outside."

"Do you own a 30.06?" asked Katie. "Hollow points would be better than full metal jackets."

"Be serious," he said.

Even though the truck inched along, he still hung on. Katie stamped down hard on the brake, jostling both the truck and the man.

"Mr. Gavin," she sighed, "my best advice is to get the vet out here with an over-loaded tranquilizer dart. And make sure the guy from the butcher shop is standing by with a truck and a wench."

Just before the first corner, Katie looked back. Mr. Gavin, still standing where she had left him, gazed down toward the pretty red barn.

Chapter Sixteen

Shortly after Katie arrived home, the telephone rang. Rick entering through the kitchen door swooped up the receiver. Hanging the handset off the side of the harvest gold wall unit, he called to Katie as he proceeded upstairs.

"New York," he said. "I think it's your guy."

"Huh," said Katie, thinking immediately about her appointment with the climbers for the next day. "Must be a change of plans." Retrieving the receiver, she asked, "Armand?"

"Is this Mrs. Took or Mrs. Moore?" asked an unknown woman.

"There's no Mrs. at all," Katie said, instantly suspicious. "Who is this?" She turned back to the wall unit, ready to slam the receiver back onto the hook, when a hurried voice answered.

"This is Tessa Adams," said the woman, speaking fast, seemingly aware she was about to get cut off. "I'd like to speak to someone about the remains of Daphne Carter."

Katie paused. "Who?" she asked, glaring at the phone, daring it to send the look across the line to the caller.

The woman took a sharp breath, then blurted. "Daphne Carter, a Syracuse University sophomore who disappeared last year at Christmas time. She went to Vermont to go skiing instead of going home to Michigan. No one has seen her since."

Katie pressed the phone closer to her ear. "My name is Katelyn Took. This is my farm. How is it you know the identity of the remains the police haven't yet identified?"

Tessa Adams' next sentence came back low and sad.

"I've been looking for Daphne," she said. "My gut tells me this is her."

"Who are you, exactly?" Katie asked.

Tessa explained she worked as a reporter with the Syracuse Daily News. She had covered the disappearance of the sorority sister from Putter, Michigan.

"The college responded to the parents' demand for action," said Tessa. "The parents hadn't heard from Daphne since before Christmas. Daphne worked, so she planned on staying in Syracuse over the holiday. The family had been expecting a call on Christmas day. Nothing. By the end of the week, they still had heard nothing. At that point, the parents called the sorority and spoke to the housemother. She told them Daphne hadn't returned from a ski trip to Vermont. No one there had heard from her either."

"So, they called the college?" asked Katie.

"Exactly."

"And you got involved because, what, the story leaked out to the press?" Katie's brows knitted together.

She had been right when her first instinct had said to slam the receiver back into its cradle. Another damn reporter looking for dirt. But then, maybe because Tessa Adams sounded so sad, Katie listened for another minute.

"Well, initially, I got involved because Daphne's mother and I went to school together. She called me. When the paper got wind of the story, I asked for the assignment. I might curb the pain my friend is going to suffer."

"Ah, huh," said Katie.

Tension crackled across the phone line while each woman paused, waiting for the other. Finally, Tessa stepped up.

"What can you tell me, Ms. Took?" she asked.

"What can you tell me?" asked Katie.

"I can tell you what we put in print," said Tessa. "I can even send you a copy of the tear sheet."

"Okay."

"Daphne paid for a seat on an activity bus going to Jay Peak for a three-day trip," said Tessa. "She signed up for a bed in the ski dorm, too. You know, a party bus sort of deal. No one remembered seeing her after they got off the bus. One girl described it as Daphne walked out of the parking lot into nowhere."

"Could she have been meeting someone at Jay?" Katie asked. "Like a boyfriend?"

"Her parents knew nothing about a boyfriend. I spoke with the other women at the sorority," said Tessa. "Only one had a vague recollection of another student Daphne had been seeing regularly. According to her, Daphne called her relationship with the other student minimal."

"What does that mean?" Katie said.

"The young woman I spoke with said Daphne's male friend had a messy breakup, and Daphne didn't want to be involved in the remnants of it. Until the young man got freed up, Daphne said she didn't want anything too intense, her words."

"What else?" asked Katie.

"That's all I've got."

"No one could find this guy?" Katie asked, incredulous.

"It's a big campus," said Tessa. "Also, the sorority sister couldn't swear the guy had been a student. He could have just been a local."

Katie considered Tessa's claim.

"What can you tell me, Ms. Took?" Tessa asked again.

"I can tell you we found the remains of a woman on the ridge above my house. The coroner said probably in her early twenties. The remains have been there from nine months to two years. She had light-colored hair, Caucasian. As far as I know, cause of death hasn't yet been determined. But that could be information the police are withholding. We're also about an hour and a half out of Jay Peak."

"Thank you," sighed Tessa.

"Can you tell me, before you hang up, how you knew about this?" Katie asked.

Tessa laughed. "In this business, we're super snoopers. You get to know people. Everyone is looking. If you're not afraid to tell somebody what it is you want, there's a good chance someone is going to call you with a tip that pays off. Then you get to pay it back. It's like tag. If you're lucky, you're it. I spread the word among colleagues, hoping someone would hear a whisper."

Katie hung up the phone. Behind her, Ruth worked around in the kitchen wrapping food in wax paper.

"I made you some sandwiches, Katie," the older woman said, oblivious to what Katie had just been talking about. "But I don't think you need to freeze your jars of water for tomorrow. It'll be cold enough as it is."

"Yeah," Katie agreed, "I'll take coffee in both of my thermoses." She watched Ruth, who was always happy to be puttering around. Katie considered her own life. If she'd leave other people's problems to them, everything could be much easier. She could be like Ruth, going with the flow, warm, fed, and happy. A smile raised the corners of her mouth. Ruth looked up and smiled in return.

"Maybe you should ask Rick if you can use his thermos too," she suggested.

"Holy cow, woman," Katie laughed aloud. "How much do you think I can lug?"

Chapter Seventeen

Saturday night, Armand and Tom arrived on the late ferry. They set their tents up in the small area beyond the sandpit, never noticing where a car had previously crushed the grass and parked beneath the trees. Two climbing friends from southern Vermont met them there. They planned to hike up to the top of the ridge using the fire lane in the morning and meet Katie on top.

Katie arrived first. In her rucksack, along with food and a thermos, she carried extra rope, a small first-aid kit, and a list of questions for Armand.

"There's the possibility of snow flurries later on," Armand pointed out when they arrived. "Let's get right out to the top of the ledge."

Gulping a last swallow of coffee, Katie led them on the most direct route. They walked right past the fallen oak. Katie knew once the hikers were in, she'd have time to go back and inspect where she had fallen into the remains. Her actions would be screened by the small pine tree cover. Without so much as taking a peek, she led the group to the edge of Eagle Drop Ridge. Each man carried a large pack. Katie watched, fascinated, as they pulled their gear out, testing each piece.

Armand explained one man would stay on top while the other three repelled down, after which they would scale back up.

"We need to teach it all," he explained to Katie. "Different rock requires different techniques. This is going to be cool." Everyone grinned as the men started going over the edge. Katie stepped forward to watch. Suddenly, her stomach fluttered, and her vision narrowed.

"Nope," she said, stepping back, "can't do it. Can't take the height thing."

Tom laughed; he'd be the top man. "Not everyone can."

Katie wandered back into the trees toward the site. She stopped walking where she thought the outer ribbon of tape had been. Pulling out her camera, she snapped a picture from each side, standing far enough away to get a wide view. There was a light overcast, making the day less bright than when she and Marlie had hiked in. Looking skyward toward the fast-moving clouds, Katie hoped the photographs would still be clear. Moving to the side where she had actually fallen, she moved ahead a half step at a time. The leaf litter had settled back into place, even covering the places where soil had been dug out and taken for analysis. If she hadn't known the forensic techs had burrowed around, she wouldn't have been able to discern anything. Squatting next to the tunneled area where the trunk of the tree had rested against the stump, she peered into the dark brown gloom.

According to the forensic report, Marlie had spirited away, the woman had most likely died because the tree fell on her. Katie eyed the fallen log, trying to decide why someone would stand in place and wait while the forest giant toppled.

"So," she muttered, "they had to dig out the bones because the woman got pinned a couple feet from the stump, pelvis, and left thigh crushed."

Katie got closer to the ground. She still couldn't see anything. With a sigh, she laid on her back and wriggled into the trench the techs had dug. Using her flashlight, she examined the tree itself. Right above her head, it looked normal, but closer to the broken edge, the bark appeared paler. Probing with her fingers, she could feel the inner sheath of the tree, slivered and scarred.

What's this? She wondered. Moments later, she wiggled back into the open. Her interest had changed from what she might find on the ground to the tree itself.

Right at the stump, at ground level on the back side, a carved place dug into the base. Years ago, some rot or animal had excavated right into the wood. The part of the tree left untouched had grown up on three sides, eventually growing back together feet from the ground, creating a deep cavern. An animal had filled the open area with acorns, leaves, and tufts of fur. Where the tree had broken, about nine inches up, all that remained had been the

91

narrow three-sided band. Katie snapped a few more pictures, then dragged her notebook out to sketch what she saw. Squatting in front, she could look right into the hole.

"Some mama used this for a home," Katie said. She pushed at the log, which didn't budge. Standing, she sighed, "Dumb idea."

She wanted to see underneath. Hands on hips, she searched the forest, looking for a way. Behind her, Tom called down to the men on the cliff face. Katie hurried back toward him.

"Their down on the bottom already?" Katie ventured a peek.

"Going down is the easy part," Tom said. "Coming back up will take longer. They'll take a break, have lunch, and then get started." He coiled the repelling ropes as he pulled them up.

"Listen," said Katie, "in your stuff you had some ratchet thing-a-ma-bobs. Can I use one? Maybe some of that strong rope you've got there?"

"What are you doing?" Tom asked, curiosity edging his words.

"To be honest, I want to roll a log over so I can see what happened to the tree," said Katie, offering as close to the whole truth as she felt safe to tell him.

"Oh, botany," Tom said.

"Sure," Katie agreed, rolling her eyes when he bent over one pack.

When Tom stood up, he had a couple of metal contraptions in his hands. He handed her three coils of multicolored climbing rope.

"Let's have a look," he said.

"No, actually...," Katie began, but Tom disappeared into the feathery branches of the young pines.

"This is the log you want to roll over?" He looked skeptical.

Katie licked her lips. "Yeah. See how the base got all hollowed out? I want to access, ah, see what other damage there might have been." A single drop of sweat trickled down the side of her face.

"Not a problem," Tom grinned. "I'm always up for a challenge."

He showed her how to use the climbing ratchets, stringing them from two trees on the far side of the one they wanted to roll. Together they worked the grip handles, tightening the lines and eventually moving the log.

Unfortunately, instead of rolling over, it slid toward them.

"OK, whoa," said Tom. He walked back to the log, looking over the situation.

"We need a pry bar, a long steel one," said Katie. She had seen just such an instrument in the barn.

"Well, one thing you learn to do climbing up and down different rocky mountains," said Tom, "is how to improvise." He walked around the area, returning with a rock whose weight bowed the man's legs. Dropping it near the heaviest part of the log, he said, wiping his brow. "We'll bury this one far enough under the trunk so it's going to have to come up over it. I'm going for another rock."

They tried again, this time with Katie going from ratchet to ratchet and Tom shoving smaller rocks under the trunk. With fairly little effort, the log came up and then rolled over and down.

"I gotta go check on the guys," Tom said. "Figure out what you want, then we'll unhitch."

The unhitching could not have been easier. Katie got everything ready in the event Tom came right back. She didn't want his help with her investigation.

What she found raised more questions. It appeared the base of the tree had received a long, deep slash, causing it to crack on the good side. An ax did not make the splintering cuts. Breaks were random and there weren't grooves showing a blade. The splinters were new enough, so the wood hadn't become discolored even though the edges had dried out.

"If that poor girl had been a foot closer to the stump," muttered Katie. "She would have been under the open scar area when the log got hung up and maybe stood a chance. Then," Katie ran her hand along the tree trunk, "the weight of the oak wouldn't have crushed her."

Katie took photos until she ran out of film, then packed her camera away before kneeling where the tree had originally fallen. Among the wood debris, she found a few more splinters she believed were bone. While sifting through the leaves looking for more, a quick shiny light caught her eye. Inching over another foot, Katie moved a chunk of semi-frozen dirt and twigs aside, digging further down into the mixture of soil and rotting leaves. Finally, she held a delicate silver bracelet complete with five charms: a graduation cap, a diploma, a convertible, a flower blossom, and a mustard seed sealed in amber-colored glass.

Katie curled her fingers around the bracelet, feeling the metal heat up in her palm. She spent several minutes staring at her fist, unable to continue. Then she heard the faint call from Tom to the other men. Sliding the bracelet into her pocket, Katie used the wax paper from her lunch to wrap the bone shards in and threw her discarded jacket over the exposed splintering on the stump.

Now she faced the problem of how to keep the men from noticing her jacket. A flutter of orange surveyor's tape caught her attention. A few yards further, she saw another flutter, and then one beyond that. One of the new guys had wrapped surveyor's tape around the trees as they hiked in. This way, their path out would be easier to follow when they got ready to leave. Ripping three of the tags off the trees and repositioning them slightly away, then sprinkling leaves over the coat made it less visible. By the time Katie got back to the ledge with Tom's gear, she sweated profusely. The men, flushed and smiling, were back on top.

"Awesome," said Armand. "Perfect for intermediates." He smiled at Katie. "I think we might have a deal."

She smiled in return, but a foreboding chill ran up the center of her damp back.

Chapter Eighteen

"Yeah, so it looks like it's going to happen," Katie explained to Rick and Ruth when they sat down for supper. "I don't know how quick, and Armand is going to send me the particulars for a contract."

"Lawyer," directed Rick, buttering a roll.

"Absolutely," Katie agreed, trying not to think of the cost.

"Where will they stay?" Ruth asked.

"I gather they like to keep it rough," said Katie. "There's a choice of three campsites. One behind the sandpit, the second one at the top of the ridge, and the third one will be on this side near the bog. For that one, they'll have to come in through Lover's Lane."

Beef stew had been simmering on the back of the wood stove since morning. Keeping the stove burning kept the kitchen and front room warm. She speared a carrot.

"Did you tell them anything else?" Rick asked.

"Seemed to be no reason to," said Katie. To change the subject, she turned to Ruth. "I noticed all the barn sale stuff outside has disappeared."

Ruth's barn sale had made use of the milk house on the front of the barn with the outside concrete apron covered with items the weather wouldn't harm.

"Closed for the season," Ruth sighed. "I packed it all into the milk house."

"Speaking of which," said Rick. "You're sure it's okay to move the tractor inside the barn?"

"Yeah, of course. If there's room with all of Gram's junk still out there, I don't think there's any issue," said Katie.

"Tell her your news," Ruth bubbled, watching Rick. She looked like a little girl waiting for the birthday cake, all curled in on herself, fists in knots, and shiny-eyed.

Rick couldn't help grinning. "You know, we took the tractor engine out and down to Philip's garage, right? He puttered on it, played around. I've been chasing around for parts. Today we brought it back and got it hooked up."

"And?" Katie asked when Rick paused for breath.

"It runs." He held up his hand as her mouth opened. "There's other stuff that still needs to be done, gear shift so we have reverse, and there's a hitch in the transmission. The weather's going to turn and we won't be able to work outside much longer, so using the barn will be great."

"Haul it in then," Katie said. While Rick and Ruth chatted about their day, Katie's thoughts jumped from one thought to another.

"Rick," she said, "I see you got rid of all that scrap metal from the furnace hood."

Rick almost choked. "Yeah, we loaded it on Philip's trailer and got it out of here first thing. The, ah, parts came to more than I expected. There isn't much money left."

Ruth stared at her plate, hands knotted in her lap, but Katie didn't notice.

"No problem," said Katie, whose thoughts were back on the ridge. "Put it towards gas. I mean, you guys did all the work."

Rick nodded; mouth filled with stew.

"Car out front," he choked out.

Katie got to the porch just as the taillights disappeared. On the ground lay a banana box firmly closed with masking tape. Squawking and hooting, it jittered around near the bottom step before rolling onto its side. The noise stopped abruptly, then restarted with renewed vigor.

"What the heck is that?" Rick asked, coming through the screen door, Ruth right behind him.

"No idea," said Katie. She watched the box suspiciously, waiting for the critter inside to quiet down. Suddenly, a webbed foot thrust through the waxed cardboard side.

"It's a duck," said Ruth.

"No," said Rick, "a foot that big has to be a goose. Get back inside and I'll let it out."

He pulled a jackknife out of the holster on his belt. Katie pushed Ruth back inside. They waited behind the safety of the screen door while Rick slashed the masking tape. He made one cut, before he got in another one, a full-grown brown and white goose surged out of the box. A second goose emerged on the tail feathers of the first. Rick jumped backward. His heel caught on the bottom step, sending him sprawling. The honking geese turned in his direction. Rick raised his arm to protect his face. Deliverance, however, came in the form of the long-haired tom cat who had inadvertently been left outside at supper time. Terrified by the squawking noise of the geese, he came rushing out from under the porch. With no fear of the man sprawled on the steps, the cat leaped over Rick, and straight for the door Ruth thrust open.

The startled geese waddled away, honking in unison. Rick scrambled to his feet and into the house.

"What now?" Katie asked.

"We'll just leave them out there for tonight," said Rick, brushing dirt from his jeans. "Maybe a coyote will get them. OW!"

He jumped back, grabbing his shin.

"Shame on you," scowled Ruth, ready to give him another kick.

First a pig, then geese. What's next? wondered Katie. Twenty minutes later, they could still hear an occasional honk.

Chapter Nineteen

The next morning, the leftover banana box remained as the only evidence regarding the arrival of the geese. Katie fed Bonnie and let her out in the yard, all the while keeping an eye open. Katie had learned as a child, geese were notorious pinchers and watched for them until safely inside the truck. She drove to work through an early morning shower of cold sleet with hail mixed in, but by noon the storm had passed. Mother Nature continued sending out winter warnings. Working inside proved to be a gift. A co-worker suggested they all dress up like scarecrows for Halloween, or maybe assorted vegetables. Katie laughed and avoided committing.

When two men in dark suits walked in, she gave them barely a notice. True, the usual garb for customers included heavy work pants and boots, but these two went directly towards Stan's office as would any salesman. Katie chatted with a man looking for straw bales, unaware the roving eyes of one man searched the sales floor, stopping when they found her. He turned slightly, never taking his eyes off her to give a barely perceptible nod to his partner. Both men zeroed in on Katie's location and the second man continued watching her and monitoring her movements. One man entered Stan's office. The other, who kept an eye on Katie's progress, remained against the door.

Stan came up behind Katie and touched her elbow. "Lock your drawer, Katie," he said. "Come with me."

They walked into the office past one man in his dark suit. This time, Katie looked. The man glowered at the happenings on the work floor and the hair on the back of her neck rose. The suit followed Katie and Stan into the small room where the second man waited. They introduced themselves as detectives from the Major Crimes Unit based in Middlesex at the state police barracks.

"We're here to clear up some issues regarding the remains found on your property," said Detective Riffle, the tall one.

"Oh-kay," said Katie, "but I already told the attorney general all I knew." Her eyes flicked from Riffle, who had seated himself in Stan's chair, thereby separating himself from her with the desk, to the man blocking the window glass of the door.

"You can leave, Mr. Baldwin." Detective Riffle nodded toward Stan, standing five feet from Katie.

"Actually," said Stan, taking two steps closer, "I think I'll stay." He sat in one of the visitor's chairs, motioning Katie into the other.

Detective Riffle didn't bother to answer. Instead, he turned his attention to Katie, only then removing his hat, exposing a short, buzzed frizz of coal-black hair.

"You told the attorney general you had been on the ridge twice," the detective said. "Once when you discovered the remains, and another time when you guided the sheriff up."

"Yes," said Katie, throat suddenly dry, "I went up both times."

"This morning, a team of forensics officers guided by Edward Richardson was on the ridge. Richardson traveled with you before."

"Mr. Richardson is the forensics guy. I met him the day I went up with Sheriff Lewis," said Katie, her armpits dampened.

"Yes," acknowledged Riffle. "What they found is something different from what he remembered having left behind." Riffle paused.

"My coat," said Katie.

A flicker of surprise crossed the detective's face.

He didn't expect me to own up to it: she thought. The ground rules had changed. Katie relaxed against the back of her seat. Stan's head twisting from one to the other. Katie could read both concern and surprise on his face.

"Mr. Richardson believes there is evidence of several visits to the area. Didn't the attorney general explain to you to stay away from the active crime scene?" asked Riffle. "The site is closed to all non-authorized personnel."

"No," said Katie. "What he said is I could not discuss any of the particulars of the case while the investigation is ongoing. And I haven't. Every time some slithering reporter shows up at my house or here, where I work, I tell them the attorney general shut me down and to get out."

"Using the baseball bat?" asked Riffle.

This time, Katie blinked in surprise. She ignored his question.

"I don't remember him telling me to stay away from the site," said Katie. "Maybe he thought being a woman my stomach would be too delicate to revisit the area. Must be he's never had a baby."

"Katie," Stan whispered a warning.

"He also told me I could go back to work," Katie continued. "That's what I'm doing, practically my entire waking hours. I'm either working here or on the farm." Her best hope to get ahead of Riffle would be to state her case up front. "Mr. Richardson probably told you it looked like several had been there. I guided a group of investors to keep them away from the site. However, I went back to the log. I couldn't believe that anyone would be stupid enough to stand still while a tree fell on them. To be honest, I believed Richardson and his cronies had finished there. They hauled a lot of stuff out."

"It appears you did more than forget your coat," said Riffle.

Stan moved nervously in his chair. The detective by the door didn't make a sound, but Katie could feel his attention aimed at the back of her head.

"I didn't forget it," said Katie. "I found evidence the tree had been damaged a while ago, some kind of a structural issue which might have caused it to be weak enough to fall. I got to looking at it and thinking maybe something under the tree Richardson didn't see needed to be exposed. I wasn't just being nosy. If I'd found anything worth mentioning *immediately*, I would have called Richardson. Sheriff Lewis berated the deputy for not protecting the site when we found it. That's what I did, protect what I found and thought Sheriff Lewis was going to need to know about. And I took some pictures to, ah, send Richardson." The last had not been her original plan, but it sounded good at that moment.

"Where's the film?" Detective Riffle asked.

"Mm, I sent it out to be developed. There's no place here in town," said Katie. *But there's a drugstore at Taft's Five Corners.* Rick had dropped the film off. The receipt hung behind a cat magnet on the refrigerator.

"We're going to want those pictures," said the detective.

"Absolutely," said Katie.

Detective Riffle sat for a few moments, his eyes on Katie. Hers were on his. Even Stan sat still.

"You did more than wrap the tree, didn't you?" Riffle asked quietly. "You moved it."

"I had to," said Katie. "That's how I found the damage." Once more, her mouth went dry.

"So, you, are what a hundred-and thirty-pound woman, found a way to roll a forty-foot log over to look at the bottom? Alone?" Riffle's fingers tapped the desk edge.

"First of all," said Katie. "I don't believe the log is forty feet long. Then there is the fact the whole tree suffered from rot. If you took a look at it once it was rolled over, you'd see the base had been almost eaten through. Further up on the trunk some infestation caused the whole upper half to die. If you're asking me what I found, that's it. I'm not a city kid and I have eyes." She leaned forward slightly. "Moving it wasn't all that difficult. I may be only a woman, *Sheriff,* but I'm not stupid. I used a couple of come-a-longs, rope, and some well-placed rocks."

"You hauled all that in?" Riffle's eyes snapped.

Even though she knew it might come back to bite her in the butt, Katie said, "You don't think I could carry that? If I'd thought about it, I'd have brought my four-foot steel pry bar. Besides, the rocks were already there." She stood up. "Is there anything else, *Sheriff?*"

"When you leave here, you are to return home and stay there until further notice," said Riffle.

"Am I under arrest?" Katie asked.

"No," said Riffle.

"Then we'll see," said Katie.

As Katie turned, he added. "And it's Detective."

She shrugged, not bothering to turn back. "Same small-minded attitude."

All four left the office. Stan followed Katie into the employee break room, where she pulled her jacket out of her locker.

"I don't want people coming in here tainting your business," she said to Stan. "I guess, I'm all done."

"No," he said, sadly. "You're on a leave of absence. Cindy can come in." He grinned. "My mother-in-law is going to be busy with the kids."

Katie gave a faint smile in return. Outside, the detectives were waiting. They followed her to the turnoff for Fire Lane 61. Exiting her car; she stood beneath the NO TRESPASSING sign for a full minute before returning to her vehicle. They did not follow her up the road. But that didn't mean the episode had ended.

Chapter Twenty

J ust as a few days earlier, vehicles filled the driveway. The long line of steel and chrome all facing down toward the barn. Katie could hear a heavy truck engine revving. Without bothering to go inside, she cut across the driveway, headed towards the corner of the house as she followed the noise. Then, suddenly, she stopped short as the two geese who had been lying under the porch jumped out. With both necks and wings extended, the large birds rushed in her direction.

"Whoa," she yelled. "Stop!"

Miraculously they did, turning on the spot and rushing back to their hidey-hole. They had not retreated at her order, however. Squealing loudly, Bonnie had come rushing around the corner. The geese were running from the pig!

"I'll be darned," Katie said, scratching the black and white back presented to her. "Look at you, tough girl."

Ruth came around, right behind Bonnie. "Oh, whew. Those two. They're after everybody."

"They're going to have to go," said Katie.

Ruth nervously wrung her hands, casting glances back over her shoulder. The older woman's movements weren't wasted on Katie.

"What's going on around here?" Katie's brow dipped.

"Okay," said Ruth, motioning Katie to stay put. "Couple of things. You're home earlier than you normally are. We were planning a surprise."

"I bet it's not cake," said Katie.

She went to brush past Ruth when a large dark green pickup truck with a boxed-in body exited Lover's Lane. Seconds later, another followed. This one pulled a trailer loaded with two off-road vehicles. Both trucks had the State of Vermont emblem on the door. Neither driver looked in Katie's direction. As she moved toward the road, Ruth's hand on her arm stopped her. From her sweater pocket, Ruth pulled a folded blue paper.

"It's a warrant," said Ruth. "They went out to the accident site in the bog. Raymond got one too. I wanted to call you, but he said not to bother. Just let them go. He also told me not to talk to them, not one word."

Katie watched the trucks leave. "Yeah, well, that is a surprise." She thought about Detective Riffle and felt slightly ill.

"That's not the surprise," said Ruth, tugging on Katie's arm.

They went down to the barn. Philip worked at backing his tow truck through the wide doors at the western end. The tractor attached to the tow bar, and with the help of the hired man directing the operation, edging under cover. Katie and Ruth slipped inside.

"Holy cow," said Katie. "Where did all this space come from?" Even with their work alongside Rick's friends, they hadn't created such a wide area.

Ruth giggled. "You said to get rid of anything cloth or paper. A bunch of us worked yesterday while you were on the ridge. We threw it all on the burn heap. Afterwards, we hauled all the old stanchions outside for the next trip to Monkton Metal Salvage."

Outside, an air horn sounded. Katie rushed out to find a long three-ton truck raising its hydraulic body to dump split sixteen-inch hunks of wood on the back lawn.

"STOP!" Katie ran towards the truck. "You're in the wrong place."

"It's okay, Katie," called Rick, rushing down the embankment.

"Where did you come from?" she turned, red-faced and confused.

"Stan told me about the Major Crimes guys." Rick stopped short. "I thought I'd better get back here."

"Did you tell her about the furnace," asked Philip, walking over while wiping grease from his hands on a soiled red bandanna.

"BE QUIET," Rick ordered.

Katie had turned toward Philip, but now whipped back around to Rick, face inches from his, and her forefinger burying itself in his chest.

"WHAT?" she demanded. "Is going on here?"

Just then, a voice from above shouted. "Look out below." A long piece of heavy chain slithered off the roof, falling with a solid thump to the ground.

Katie looked up to see Charlie, the diminutive bow-legged friend of Rick's, on the roof.

"Hi'ya." He waved, grinning from ear to ear.

Katie staggered backward. "What is Charlie doing up there?" Her voice as weak as her knees.

"I'm going to go put coffee on," said Ruth, running up the slope.

Men were coming up through the half-finished bulkhead. Rick motioned them away. Philip stayed put. While men formed a line behind Rick and tossed wood from one to the other, then through the bulkhead down into the basement, the truck shifted into drive and drove off. Rick stepped closer, lowering his voice as he tried to explain.

"Here's the deal, Katie," he said. "We're worried about you. All of us. You're losing weight. You look like the cat dragged you through a knothole backwards. We...I wanted to make it easier for you. Philip had a lead on a wood-burning stove. A Tarn that would vent heat up into the house through the grate system. It's maybe not a permanent fix, but it'll work. I ordered four cords of seasoned wood. It's too late this year to cut our own. These guys know what they're doing. They got the furnace hooked up today. Charlie is cleaning the chimneys. As long as he's not sober, he'll be fine."

Katie didn't laugh. Her eyes followed Charlie's progress down the long extension ladder.

That's all I need. A drunk to fall off the roof. "Anything else?" she asked, hoarsely.

"Ah, I placed a newspaper ad offering to rent the trailer pad in Charlotte and rented Raymond's bush-hog and tiller for cleaning out the bunkhouse lot and around the schoolhouse next weekend if it doesn't rain."

Surprise and shock gave over to anger. Katie gaped like a fish. Words sat on the edge of her tongue, ready to tell him to mind his own business. Then she remembered she basically did not even have a job.

"Just how am I paying for all this?" She asked in a voice brittle and cold as ice. Her throat was closing up fast. She could feel the sides constricted as she sucked in air.

"Well, there's the money from the metal salvage, ain't much, but it'll help," Rick said calmly, then his voice went flat. "And I sold the trailer."

Philip watched, waiting for Katie to explode. Her mouth snapped shut and turned on her heel, stalking toward the kitchen door. Once inside, she ignored Ruth, hurrying past to her room. The door slammed. Ruth cringed.

From where she sat in the rocker, Katie could see the open space where the house trailer had been. Try as she might, she couldn't remember if it had still been parked in the drive the day before. She fluctuated between anger and humiliation. She had taken care of herself for ten years, albeit barely.

This is all I need, she thought, *all these ratty old hicks thinking I can't take care of myself. For crying out loud, they don't even know me.*

She tried to reason out why people who had been strangers to her ten months earlier would get their panties in a twist to help her now. Unable to stop the tears, she let the tears fall. Once she started crying, she couldn't stop. There were tears for Gram, Marlie, all Katie's fears, the belief she had lost herself, and finally for two unknowns out in the woods. She woke in darkness and crept down to the bathroom.

A note hung on the mirror telling of sandwiches left in the refrigerator. Her finger traced the neatly printed words. Another tear fell.

* * *

The next time Katie woke the sun shone thin and bright, cheerfully lighting up dust motes. She had a stuffy head and eyelids stuck together like kissing cousins. Returning to her room the previous night she had not shut the door tight, and several cats slept on her bed, weighing down the coverlet. She stepped up to the window while buttoning her worn flannel shirt. She had no reason to wear a new one today. Outside, Ruth stood in brittle sunshine scattering corn on one side to four pecking hens. On the other side were the two geese, their necks extending, retracting, and coiling like serpents.

"Oh, crap," exclaimed Katie, sure Ruth did not know the geese were advancing and would bite.

Grabbing the window frame, Katie tried to yank it up, but years of paint kept the glass locked in place. She rapped on the pane. Ruth turned, waved, and headed back towards the kitchen door. The geese followed at a respectful distance. Hustling down the stairs, Katie almost collided with the closed door at the bottom of the staircase and swore under her breath. All summer the door had stayed open, they closed it now to keep the heat downstairs. The small porcelain knob slipped in her hand, slowing her further.

"Ruth," she called, bursting into the kitchen, causing the large collection of feline heads sitting around the stove to snap up. "Are you okay? Did they get you?"

Ruth looked up from the dishpan. "Who?" she asked.

"Those darn nasty geese," Katie peeked out the window. The geese had returned to the feeding area. "They get a good pinch in every time they get near."

"Not me." Ruth shook her head. "I feed them. They know better."

Katie gave Ruth a questioning look.

"Like the cats," Ruth explained. "I feed them, pat them, kind of mother them. You take them to the vet and yell at them. I'm their friend. You're a bad person." She laughed. "Well, maybe not a bad person, just not the really good one."

"Yeah," Katie laughed. "You're probably right. I never thought of it that way." She poured coffee, still chuckling. "They're afraid of Bonnie though, they run from her."

"Because," said Ruth, pushing the old tom away from the wood stove with her foot, "LG got her nosy nose near them and when they chased her, Bonnie took offense. They know the pig is dangerous." Getting her cup from the counter, she sat down with Katie. "What are you going to do with her, them, all of them? It's going to get colder."

Katie shrugged. It was on her list. Bringing home again the idea she should pack up and get out herself. *Especially after all that bull yesterday*, she thought, chewing on her upper lip.

"Katie," said Ruth, reaching out soft fingers to touch the younger woman's arm. "Rick is only trying to help. He, we…you aren't talking to us. I know you've got a lot on your plate. If you don't want us just jumping in, anywhere we think we ought to, you need to tell us what to do."

Katie sighed, pushing away the plate of toast. "I don't need to owe him more."

"Time is short, Katie. Not just for today, but all the days," said Ruth. "We are each all the family we have. Together we need to work together, like a family." She pushed the plate back to Katie before jumping up to dash into the living room. She came back carrying a parcel wrapped in brown paper. "I found this package on the front step yesterday when I came back in after the state trucks went through."

The medium-sized box had only her name written on it, with no return address. Katie eyed it suspiciously. It wasn't overly heavy and didn't rattle when she shook it. Taking a chance, she cut through the twine. Inside lay Irma's barn jacket and a note from Edward Richardson.

"Is that your old coat?" asked Ruth. "Did you leave it somewhere?'

"Sort of," laughed Katie. "There's a note from the forensic guy. They found the coat at the site yesterday morning. The police discarded it as not important, but he thought I might want it back. Huh."

"Isn't that nice?" said Ruth, neatly winding the twine.

"Yeah," Katie agreed. But her thoughts weren't really on the coat, but on the bracelet, she hadn't mentioned to the detectives. She went upstairs to check and found it still hidden in one of her socks. The silver sparkled. Winking at her in the light. Katie thought, *it's telling me it knows a secret.*

She considered driving up the ridge when Ruth asked if the police would check to see if she had stayed home. Bouncing the truck keys in her hand while Ruth waited, Katie decided she should stay close to the house for a few days.

"Maybe," she said. "I guess I'll check my list, see what I've got to do."

After Ruth headed into the cat room with a broom and dustpan, Katie opened the cellar door. From the bottom step, she looked over the area she had previously ignored. A large steel blue box sat in front of the chimney. It appeared to be hooked to the brickwork and heaven only knew what all the rest of the alien-looking gauges, pipes, and wires were for. This had to be the used but good furnace. It did not look too old. The metal shone in the overhead light. If it hadn't been for the dents around the fill door, Katie would have thought twice about Rick's definition of 'used'. Rick said he'd fire it up on Wednesday when he would be home to watch it.

"Good enough," Katie mumbled.

A neat stack of wood chunks lined one wall courtesy of the work-for-a-hot-meal guys. Once again, Rick had seen to their needs. The realization did nothing to improve Katie's mood.

"Well," she said to herself, "I could roast a goose."

Leaving the step, she pulled the chain, turning on the light over the bulkhead. Rick had constructed the stairs of weathered board. She could see the new, freshly cut edges. Then using the same lumber, he had completed a section of the bulkhead door. Canvas covered the opening left where he had run out of planks. Once outside, Katie replaced the canvas before heading down the hill to the Dean farm. Bonnie needed a warmer winter place.

"Sure," said Raymond when she caught up to him mucking out the barn, "like I told you. I've got two pens, but I only separate the sows when they have piglets. My two can stay in one, Bonnie in the other. Maybe she'll teach them some manners."

Katie laughed, promising to get Bonnie down to the farm soon.

Walking past Ruth, busy dusting the living room, Katie said, "I think we should invite Rick's friends for Thanksgiving. You know, the ones who would be alone."

"That would be fine," said Ruth, never missing a beat. "But roasting a goose is out."

"You read my mind." Katie laughed aloud, reaching for the phone. "Directory assistance for Montpelier, Vermont," she told the operator. "Office of the coroner."

After reciting the number, the operator asked if Katie needed another number.

"Yes," Katie said without hesitation. "A resident listing for Corinne Cox."

"What are you doing?" asked Ruth. With her hands on her hips, blocking the living room door. She looked as formidable as either of the geese.

"Relax," said Katie. "I just want to thank Edward for sending my coat. I'm not doing anything the cops won't like." Then she kept herself occupied, avoiding dialing the phone until she was sure Ruth could not hear.

The coroner had to forward Katie's call, but once she was in the right place, she asked for Corinne.

"I'm sorry," said the receptionist. "She's not working today."

"How about Edward Richardson?"

"He's a little tied up. Is this an emergency?" the woman asked.

"No, we were recently at a crime scene together. I have some questions about the information that came out in his report," said Katie.

"If you got a copy of the report, then you basically have everything he can give you," said the receptionist. "For any item you need clarification on, you can submit a written request through the department head."

"Alright, can you take a more personal message for Edward? Tell him Katelyn Took called and said thank you for finding my jacket." The connection ended, but Katie smiled, smug that she had done just what she had told Ruth. "And now for a little deviation."

Katie dialed the other telephone number she had gotten from directory assistance. The phone on the other end of the line rang.

"This is Corinne, may I help you?" asked the female forensic tech.

"This is Katie Took. I accompanied your team to the top of Eagle Drop Ridge after my friend and I found a skeleton up there," said Katie.

"Yes," said Corinne. "I know who you are."

"I'd like to talk to you," said Katie.

Corinne hesitated for a moment before asking, "How did you find me?"

"Your name is on the forensic report. The phone company gave me the number," said Katie. Corinne started to speak, but Katie cut her off. "Look, Corinne, I don't want to get you in any trouble, but things are pretty bad for me around here right now. I don't know if you watch the papers, but I can't go outside because of the reporters. They're also showing up at my job. Now I'm on leave without pay. And the boy's father, Mr. Ash, is in the middle of this every minute. The man has money and power. I don't. I'm a woman who he thinks is beneath him and, well, to be honest, I didn't know who else to call."

They set up a meeting for later in the afternoon at the Monkton Diner. Katie didn't realize her palms were sweating until the call had ended. Grinding her hands against her jeans, she said to herself. "I didn't lie, I really didn't."

Katie spent the rest of the morning setting up a chicken wire fence inside the hen house to keep the geese on one side and the hens on the other. Rick had rigged up heat lamps for the frosty nights and the oncoming colder days.

"You guys are just going to have to learn to be roomies." She explained to the nesting hen, who sent up a warning squawk every time the hammer struck.

"How are you going to catch the geese?" asked Ruth, when Katie came out of the hen house.

"Good question," Katie answered. She swiped across her face, wiping away the sweat, whether from the hauling and hammering or from the upcoming meeting with Corinne, she couldn't tell for sure.

"I have to go," she told Ruth. "Yeah, I know I told the cops I'd be right here, but I have a meeting in, ah…town."

After a white-knuckled drive to the Monkton Diner, Katie sat near the window in a booth whose vinyl seat had been duct taped multiple times. Like water droplets in a hot frying pan, her mind jumped around trying to figure out if she was on the right track. Corinne arrived and ordered coffee. While they waited for the waitress to return, one woman studied her hands, while the other one stared out the window.

"Corinne," Katie began.

Corinne's head snapped up. "This is unethical," she said. "I could be putting my career in danger." While she spoke, Corinne kept her head down close to the tabletop and her eyes on the door. "How did you get a copy of the forensic report?"

"It came to me through the sheriff's office," sighed Katie. She wanted to be honest with Corinne. "Let's just say some of what I know might fall under the danger umbrella, you know, if I share it."

Corinne nodded. Moistening her lips, she asked, "I don't know what I can tell you."

"Okay," said Katie. "How about…what can you ethically tell me about the happenings when you people went up there the second time?"

"There were seven of us," Corinne said after a brief pause. "Thanks for putting up the ribbons so we wouldn't get lost, by the way."

Katie didn't explain the ribbons had been left by the hiking team she had escorted to the cliff edge.

"We laid out a grid, then went from sector to sector. I think everyone was quite surprised to find the log rolled over. And, also the jacket covering it. Ed recognized the jacket as being yours, by the way." Corinne looked up. "We couldn't do that when we were there the first time. I don't know if we even thought about doing that. Yet, I heard through the grapevine you did it alone."

"I had equipment you didn't have," said Katie. "And because I'm such a tomboy, maybe some of the knowledge my grandfather shared helped too."

Corinne watched Katie closely. In defense, Katie explained how it had all worked, alluding to having hauled equipment in and leaving Tom out of the picture.

Corinne smiled for the first time.

"What?" asked Katie, immediately suspicious.

"Are you kidding?" Corinne laughed aloud. "Do you have any idea how much my status would go up if I had figured out we should roll the log and then been able to execute it? I'm at the bottom of the food chain."

"So," grinned Katie, "go to the hardware store, buy a come-a-long and a stout piece of rope. Mix that up with a nice, heavy crowbar and you should be good."

"With a little practice," said Corinne.

"It doesn't take much," Katie shrugged. "Find a place to mess around in the woods after deer season. Just make sure you have a tight hitch because if that sucker comes off, you'll literally lose your head."

Both women relaxed. "How about a piece of pie?" asked Corinne, waving at the waitress. "We didn't find much more than we did the first time. There were some bone shards a short distance away. Animal degradation. We cut out the last three feet of the log and all the remaining stump above the ground."

Katie remembered the wax paper wrapped pieces in her pocket. Pulling them out, she handed them across the table.

"I found these," she said. Corinne's eyes narrowed. Katie changed tactics. "It took me a little scuffing around to move the log. These were under the leaves. I didn't know for sure if they were bone or wood chips. Then I forgot about them until this morning."

Corinne unwrapped the splinters, then pulled a magnifying glass out of her pocket. "I think bone, yeah, definitely bone." She dunked her finger in the water glass and pressed down on one shard. When she lifted her hand, for a moment, the shard held on. "Where exactly were these? Under the log? How am I going to explain where I got these?" she asked.

Once again, Katie hid in a near truth. "I don't really know. I knelt pushing, you know, scraping around in the dirt trying to bury the rocks." *You figure out how you're going to tell your boss*, she thought.

Corinne re-wrapped the pieces. "Like I said," she sighed, "other than the tree evidence, there wasn't much. We hauled out a few more buckets of dirt. Oh, and I know what you mean about the dad."

"Mr. Ash?" Katie's ears pricked up.

"Yeah," Corinne nodded. "When we came out, he met us at the trailhead. You should have seen him jump all over the Major Crimes Unit guys demanding to know what they'd found. He kept pushing to get them to go to the other site. He didn't back off until one of those guys said they were ready to arrest him. That sheriff, Lewis? He looked really pissed. No one should have known we were up there. Yet Ash did. Lewis demanded to know how Ash found out. The man totally ignored the sheriff. Ash looked right through Lewis like he wasn't there."

"What happened?" Katie's mouth went dry.

"Our guys loaded up around them and we sat in the van. When Ash walked in our direction, Edward made me roll up the window and lock the door. We don't answer to him. He *screamed* at Ed. I thought he'd stroke out."

If the information hadn't been so serious, Katie would have laughed. They were silent for a few minutes.

"You didn't go to the other site?" Katie asked finally.

"Nope, not at all." Corinne pulled out her wallet. "I personally got some pleasure out of the day. The first time we were there that poor girl only got our attention for one day, yet we had to spend two days slogging around that swamp because of who the guy lying under the snow-machine had for a father. Well, check it out, we went back, and the girl got her second day, and Ash got nothing."

"I've got this," grinned Katie, snatching the check from the waitress. "It's my pleasure."

Chapter Twenty-One

Katie left Monkton on a fast track for Taft's Five Corners. In her pocket, she had the receipt for the pictures.

"Please," she prayed, "please let them be there."

The counter clerk explained the delivery truck had just pulled in out back. Katie could either come back later or hang around until they unloaded the merchandise. Katie opted to wait and sat out on the curb. Cold seeped in from the concrete under her butt, but the sun warmed her. *This feels like Illinois*, she thought. *All I need is a cold cup of mission coffee and a stale peanut butter and jelly sandwich.* A flock of honking Canada geese flew overhead. She looked up, watching their flight across the sky. *I could go back anytime.* But to what? She asked herself.

"Ma'am," said the clerk, holding the door open, "what's the name on the pictures?"

At the counter, Katie took the inner envelope of pictures out.

"I need another copy of these," she said to the clerk, handing the outer envelope and negatives back. She bought a small box of envelopes and a packet of stamps from a dispenser machine. The only address she could think of for the Major Crimes Unit would be care of the State Police office, state house station.

"Here's hoping you get them," she said, cringing as she folded the pictures in half and stuffed them in the envelope. She knew she'd been gone longer than Ruth would be happy about. However, there was no helping it. If she couldn't go to work, and every law enforcement officer in the county except Marlie looked at her suspiciously, she'd have to find a way to protect herself and save her own bacon.

Back in the car, she sped up, trying to make time. Daylight was fading. She thought she saw Marlie standing on the side of the road, eyes looking directly into hers. Immediately, she slowed down. She'd suffered from hallucinations before, back in Chicago when she'd gotten high to get through the day. Katie knew the vivid waking dreams could be dangerous. She'd almost drowned chasing a canoe that didn't exist: a man and a woman, two little boys, and a baby girl who weren't really there, yet who she could see drifting away. Two fishermen had pulled her out of the lake, fighting and screaming, demanding to find her parents, who had blissfully paddled down to picnic on the lake bottom. She'd spent three months in dry-out.

"Once you're addicted," her counselor said, "you are forever an addict."

She hadn't believed it until the day she'd walked into a grocery store and palmed a pint of Johnny Walker Red. Back in her room at the YMCA, she'd started sipping. She only remembered those first couple of sips. Later, when the cops showed up and hauled her away, they told her about the screaming radio, the boozers boogie down the dorm hallway. The Y blackballed her, she spent a couple of nights in jail, got to go to court, and started sobriety again. Now she refused to even smoke a cigarette.

Behind her, a blaring car horn snapped her back from the past. A station wagon she had roared past a half-a-mile back, pulled up behind her at the stop sign at the junction of Route 7. The driver's angry face shone pale in the dashboard glow. So embarrassed she wanted to get out and apologize to the woman she'd cut off, Katie turned right, waited until the left bound station wagon got far ahead, then followed it into Parentville.

"Where have you been?" demanded Ruth. Rick touched her arm, but she yanked it away. "You scared me to death. If I were your mother, I'd send you to your room with no supper." Ruth trembled with rage.

"Or," said Rick, "I could fry pork chops, and we sit down and eat, maybe talk about it."

Katie pushed past to the bathroom. Burying her face in a cold washcloth helped calm her. Tears were rising again, but she forced them down. She came out to stony silence. Circling the table, she knelt beside Ruth's chair.

"I'm sorry," she said. "You were right when you said everything would mount up and I couldn't do it all alone. Please, Ruth, I'm, I don't know, drowning."

Sobbing, Ruth threw her arms around Katie.

"You're a headstrong girl," sniffed Ruth. "You're going to do what you think you have to, just like Irma. But you have to trust me. Please know, I would never undermine you unless you were on the brink of death. Don't shut us out, Katie. We know you're thinking it would be easier to just go. Tell us what you're doing, or what we can do to help." She ran her hands over Katie's hair.

Rick cleared his throat. His was voice husky. "We, I might have overstepped my bounds. Hell, I'm sure I did. All I could think is what would your granddad have done to make sure you had everything you needed. Maybe I tried to fill his shoes."

Unable to speak, Katie slid into her chair. Moments before, she had felt stuck in the mud, unable to breathe or escape. That same feeling of being encircled held on, but now it felt more like a warm quilt on a cold winter night, making her grateful. Slicing into her chop, she told her friends where she had been during the afternoon.

"Do you think those detectives will get the envelope?" Ruth asked.

Katie shrugged. "No return address, and probably not enough postage. I'm going to say the post office will get it delivered so they can collect their missing five cents."

Rick laughed. "Yeah, they'll probably send out a bill."

Then she told Rick and Ruth about seeing the ghostly apparition in the dark. Once she got started, she couldn't stop. As they sat silently watching her, she talked about Illinois and the lake.

"Oh, Katie," sniffed Ruth.

"You know, Rick," Katie cleared her throat, embarrassed at having revealed so sordid an event from her past, "a coating of breadcrumbs would have kept this overdone shoe leather edible."

"What?" he sputtered.

"Ah-huh, but the applesauce we canned last summer is awesome." She grinned at him, willing herself not to cry.

"So, what's next?" Rick asked, wiping dishes as Katie washed.

"We catch the geese."

"Seriously," he said.

"I need to know more about Scott Ash," she said.

"How come his family is so high and mighty about him," asked Ruth, sponging the table, "he didn't go to college and it doesn't sound like he amounted to anything so great."

Katie turned. "That's a good question, Ruth. Why not indeed? And if he's been hanging around for two years, what's he been doing?"

Chapter Twenty-Two

While Katie folded laundry and Ruth chased cats, the telephone rang. Brad, another full-time deputy stationed in Parentville, had a job for the cat lady.

"Animal control call," he said. Katie had not talked with him since the day on the ridge with Sheriff Lewis, and Brad sounded as though his nose was still out of joint. "Call the woman, Theresa Higgins, 482-5505. Female cat hit by a car, kittens in distress."

"Thanks, Brad," said Katie, wondering at his stiff and formal statement, but the line had already gone dead. She blinked at the buzzing receiver in her hand, belatedly realizing she should have asked who gave her name to Allan Gavin.

"Humph," she muttered to Ruth. "What crawled up his butt and died? I'd have to call him back to find out about Gavin and I bet he still would have hung up on me before I knew."

After calling Mrs. Higgins, Katie pulled on her boots and grabbed her coat and keys. At the door, she turned to find Ruth right behind her, buttoned into her camel-colored wool jacket.

"Where are you going?" Katie asked.

"It's dark," said Ruth, pulling on her gloves. "You might need someone to hold the flashlight." Tucked under her elbow were the emergency household flashlight and a large piece of an old blanket. Ruth carried a smaller net. Before Katie could say another word, Ruth squeezed past and hurried down the steps. Rick stood at the kitchen door, waving goodbye, a grin on his face.

They drove into the village and south on Silver Street, toward Monkton.

119

At the Higgins' house, they found a tearful Mrs. Higgins shooing her children toward the television.

"My husband put the cat in a box," Mrs. Higgins sniffed. "It's on the porch."

"Is it your cat?" Katie asked.

Mrs. Higgins shook her head. Katie went outside. With Ruth holding the flashlight, she examined the remains.

"Well, it is a nursing female," sighed Katie. "I'd say from the number of swollen teats, four or five kittens."

Mr. Higgins came outside. "She's been holed up under our shed. I'll show you." Mr. Higgins had on a worn bomber's jacket and uniform trousers. Behind the house, a ten-foot by ten-foot garden shed sat in the corner of the yard. An overhead wire ran from the house, which meant the shed had electricity. When he threw the switch, fluorescent lights illuminated the entire space.

"Wait," said Katie, "don't walk on the floor."

Taking the flashlight, she walked around the shed, pushing the bushes out of the way, looking for a crawl space. She found several openings, but she couldn't make out anything underneath when she shone her light in. Back at the wide door over the lawn tractor ramp, she laid on the floor, ear pressed to the flooring.

"The floor is kind of dirty to be crawling around on it," Mr. Higgins said.

Katie held her hand up for silence. Moving sideways, she listened again. A faint scrabbling came through the plywood beneath her ear.

"I think the nest is right here," she said, with her hand pressed to a spot three feet from the outer edge. Looking at Mr. Higgins, she asked. "How old are these kittens? Are they going to come out for food?"

"I don't think they're much more than three weeks old," said Mr. Higgins.

"Oh, dear," said Ruth. Katie pressed her lips together. The situation did not sound good. Mr. Higgins looked back toward the house, where his wife and children watched from behind the sliding glass door.

"Okay," he sighed. "My wife is pretty distraught. She's not going to let this go. If you can't reach them, we have to do something else." He looked at the house again then, with a sigh, he turned back to Katie. "Can you step outside?"

He pulled open the other side of the double door and stepped up on the riding mower. The three of them pulled out the smaller mower, snowblower, and kid's bikes, creating an open space on the floor. Mr. Higgins knelt on the floor, cats-paw pry bar in hand. Carefully he wedged under the corner, working along the short side, popping nails up and loosening the four by eight-foot sheet of particle board. When he had one-half free, Katie stopped him.

"Can you hold it up a little so I can have a look?" she asked.

Mr. Higgins pulled on a pair of heavy work gloves. Kneeling on the short side, he pulled upwards until the board creaked at the halfway point. Katie ducked underneath, flashlight in hand. Ruth watched more and more of Katie disappear until even her feet were in the hole. Suddenly, her right hand reappeared, clutching a mewling ball of fur. Ruth grabbed for the kitten and the hand pulled back, only to return immediately with another kitten. When Katie's hand came back with a third kitten, Ruth, with one in each hand already, started putting them in her jacket pockets. Holding the fifth kitten, Katie crawled out of the opening. In the light of the forty-watt bulb, Mr. Higgins' face shone bright red with the strain of holding up the board.

Katie laid on the floor, blowing in and out through her mouth, eyes closed. Ruth took the last kitten. Before she could say a word, Katie held up her hand.

"Claustrophobic," she gasped. "Give me a minute."

By the time Mr. Higgins had finished tacking the floorboards back down, Katie had gotten back up on her feet. He declined her offer of help to replace the items they had removed, but asked her if she'd show the kittens to the children. Inside the house, Mrs. Higgins provided a box lined with a towel, and while her three youngsters oohed and aahed, she offered to let Katie wash up.

"How will they eat?" one child asked.

"Don't worry," said Ruth. "I'll take good care of them."

On the way home, Katie pointed out five young kittens were going to be a lot of work. Ruth reminded her that Sasha, the money cat, and a consummate mother, would do everything except feed the babies.

"I'll do the rest," she said. "We do what we have to do." But Katie could hear the worry in her voice. Two of the kittens were really tiny.

* * *

To conserve heat in the big house, Katie decided to keep the door to the cat room closed. Cardboard boxes lined with pieces of blankets or towels encircled the living room, while the laundry room held several litter boxes. The daily cleaning of the litter, mixed fifty-fifty with sand, remained Ruth's job, which she handled without a word. Katie shook her head. The kittens would need to be fed every two or three hours. How long before Ruth felt exhausted?

"Maybe," suggested Katie, dismayed that the cat-to-people ratio kept rising, "we should see if the vet will help out with these kittens."

"Stop at Beauregard's, so we can get some condensed milk," directed Ruth, ignoring Katie's suggestion.

In the general store, Katie picked up three cans of milk and two of Ruth's favorite candy bars.

"You're going to need these," she said, passing the chocolate over the box of kittens to Ruth.

As Katie turned the key in the ignition, a soft sigh wafted through the darkness from the other side of the bench seat. Ruth peeled open the first candy bar.

Chapter Twenty-Three

The first night with the new babies proved rough on all the humans. Even though Ruth sent both Katie and Rick to bed, where they tossed and turned, she stayed on the couch with the box in reach. Other than Sasha, the other cats were of two minds about the new arrivals. Some were nosy and wanted to get in the box to look, a move that put Sasha on the defensive. Others stayed away and when the people went upstairs, they followed. Katie grudgingly left the door to her bedroom cracked open to lessen the stress on Ruth. Soon her bed filled with circling felines.

She got up early, as she normally would have to go to work. Then watched as Rick packed his solitary lunch.

"Don't worry," said Rick, "Stan is going to call the attorney general's office and complain that he's shorthanded."

"I don't think that's going to do any good," said Katie, rubbing her back.

"You never know," said Rick. "There's always a chance those guys were out of line." He stopped in front of her. "What's wrong with your back."

"Too many cats," she groaned. "They held me down like twenty-pound weights."

"Hey," he said. "I knew letting them in would be bad. Good thing I followed my instincts."

With a laugh, he left. After helping Ruth get the babies fed and set for a while, Katie drove over to Charlotte. The town library had lately proved to be her best source of information. This visit netted her a three-year-old telephone book and a library card.

"You're in here often enough, Ms. Took," said the librarian. "You should be a member."

"Ah, thank you," said Katie. *Great, another way for big brother to track me.*

She barely got seated at the reading table when she found exactly what she needed, a physical address for Scott Ash. She also learned that Geoffrey and Phyllis Ash lived on Hoover Road, but did not find any listing for Robby, Robert, or Bob Daudlin.

"So, what?" she muttered. "The real son moved out, but the adopted son didn't?"

Katie copied down the new information she'd found and drove over to the vet's. Doctor Veronica gave her some supplementary vitamins for the kittens and some advice.

"If it gets to be too much," said Doctor Veronica, "bring them over. We'll do what we can."

Katie knew from the way the doctor spoke Ruth would be the kittens' best bet. She left there, headed toward Taft's Five Corners and Essex Junction.

The listing for Scott's address was on Lime Kiln Road in Essex Junction. Katie remembered Lime Kiln as a cutoff road used by locals to get from Williston on one end to the chapel on Saint Michael's college property on the other. Lime Kiln Road had always been a narrow dirt track and usually deserted, a good place for parking or drinking parties. Driving over, she found though still narrow, it had been paved and now boasted several apartment buildings sided with Texture 1-11, each complete with a rutted parking area. The phone book had offered a house number and street name, but no apartment listing.

"Time to knock on some doors," said Katie, climbing out of the pickup.

She had rapped on several doors across the first building before someone answered. A couple of barely awake co-eds told her the apartments were rented mostly to upper-class men from St. Michael's, an all-male college. The girls also said most of the renters living around them were foreigners.

"Yeah," said one girl, "They have money, so it isn't like they have to work to pay rent."

"Well, that explains it," grinned Katie. "I'm looking for a guy who lived here around Christmas the year before last. I can't remember his apartment number. But he wasn't foreign."

"Don't know," said the girl, "I'm new myself." But her friend, a couple years older, had been living in the complex for several years.

"Are you talking about the party guy?" she asked. "Didn't work, didn't go to college as far as I could tell. He always had some good junk to sell?"

"Sounds like my man." Katie's eyelids slid downward in a knowing look.

"He disappeared around Christmas," said the girl. "Yeah, I remember a lot of people were buzzing around looking for him."

"Cops?" asked Katie. She got hunched up like the idea worried her.

"Nah, guys from the college." The girl started to wander away from the door and the conversation. Katie put her foot out in the event her friend pushed the door shut.

"So, you saw him here, what? Just before Christmas?" she asked.

"Yeah, maybe the day before Christmas, I think. He had a big sale on everything you can imagine. Then poof, by New Year's, he'd disappeared."

"You actually saw him?" asked Katie, moving back as the door closed. No one answered as the door clicked shut.

Though she wanted to take the girls' word on when Scott had been here last, their giggly manner lead to a question regarding how stoned they were. *How much of that can I trust?* She wondered, walking back toward her truck.

A late-model Datsun pulled in. Katie flagged it down.

"Hey guys, can you help me out?" she asked, leaning in the driver's window. "I'm looking for this guy I knew who lived here. Tall, fair, a kind of life of the party guy, ya know?"

"Don't know," said the driver, but his passenger leaned forward, leering at the hick in her flannel shirt.

"Dude's been gone for a while," he said. "You're too late, lady."

"Crap," said Katie, keeping both hands on the driver's door. "When did you see him last?"

"Dude took off during the winter, like, phfft, over a year ago." the guy leaned closer. "What'cha looking for? Maybe we can help you out."

Both guys broke out in laughter. The Datsun jumped ahead and kept rolling. Katie flipped the guys off and went back to her own vehicle.

"Idiots," she said.

She had no reason to go to Saint Michael's. Without a warrant, she couldn't even find out if Scott had been enrolled, a theory she seriously doubted.

From Taft's Five Corners, she drove down the Parentville Road, turning onto Shelburne Road to take a shortcut back to Charlotte. Driving along, she cussed herself for not thinking of this other little gossip hub she'd discovered in August. Back then she had been in the bank on Main Street a few times while she trapped a rogue skunk who had taken up residence under the back staircase to the dismay of the employees. Those women knew everything going on. If they had a happy memory of her removing Old Stinky, there might be a slim chance one would help her out.

She lucked out. Boredom ran riot in the banking world.

"We aren't allowed to share information about customers," said the redhead.

"Unless," said the brunette, "it's like, personal information we would, you know, from our outside lives."

Katie moved over to her line. Even though she had the list of names she had copied from the yearbook in her pocket, she offered only one. With any luck, instead of arousing suspicion, she'd get a direction to follow.

"So, did you know Paul Childe?" she asked.

"Yeah," said the brunette, a lazy smile growing, along with the faintest blush that ran along the ridges of her cheekbones. "Do you mind telling me why you're looking for him? You don't have a kid or something, right?"

So Childe got around, thought Katie, but she said, "No, my brother is getting married. We wanted to throw him a surprise party, you know. Invite some of his old buddies."

"Cool," said the brunette. "Who's your brother?"

"Gary, ah, Moore," Katie gulped.

The brunette frowned. Moore wasn't a name she remembered from high school.

"They were on opposing school sports teams," Katie blurted out. "Friendly rivals. I'm sure I don't have to tell you how guys are, about their buds." Her eyes jerked to the older woman, the redhead, had a customer and not listening.

"Yeah, I totally get it," said the brunette. "Paul is attending the University of Vermont in Burlington. He lives there. I haven't seen him in forever. So, who else is coming to this party?"

Katie bit her lip. The brunette watched her with hungry eyes, and the redhead had finished with her customer.

"Why don't you give me your address, or number," smiled Katie. "I'll pass it on, see if I can get you an invite."

She left the bank, wadding up the scrap of paper before shoving it deep in her pocket. She had other names. One of those guys might still be in the area. Somebody who could give her some insight on why Scott would take off on a snow-machine headed toward an area where he had no business going, where even his family believed he hadn't been.

Over time, the downtown area of Charlotte had expanded to be much bigger than Parentville with its single Main Street. On the southern end, Charlotte's Main Street crossed US Route 7. That's where the Italian diner and the park were located. Katie drove down parking across from the diner.

"Think," she said, "before you open your mouth." Besides the diner, there were several businesses, two gas stations, one a repair shop and the other a mini-mart. The library, town hall, and fire station were back the way Katie had come. Any one of these might give up the location of one of Scott's friends.

"I'll start here," she said, "go up one side of the street and come down the other. Maybe, though," she paused in the middle of the street. "I'll avoid Ash's office." Diverting slightly, she headed towards the fire station.

Chapter Twenty-Four

The volunteers at the fire department gave great directions and Katie didn't have any problem finding Daniel Sly's house. If she hadn't been positive, she'd parked in front of the right place, the plethora of firefighter bumper stickers on his pickup attested to his voluntary commitment.

Daniel invited her in when she explained she did investigative work for the insurance company listed on Scott Ash's driver's license. In a more urban area, she would have been questioned more closely. Her clothing would have been a hint she wasn't what she professed, or she would have needed a briefcase, not the single spiral notebook she carried.

"I just came in for lunch," said Daniel. "I have to go back to work. Do you mind if I finish up?"

They hadn't been sitting for more than a few minutes when Daniel's wife, Marcie, came in, a toddler in her arms.

"You're here about Scott?" frowned Marcie. "We weren't in the same class."

"I understand," said Katie, feeling her mouth drying up. "I've talked to several of his classmates, but to be honest, all I'm hearing is about his sterling character. Everybody's statement is almost word for word the same."

Marcie snorted.

Hoping to get the woman to expound, Katie continued. "I understand that you two were good friends with Scott's brother Robby. I thought you might share your views." She clicked open her pen.

"Yes, we were in the same grade as Robby," said Daniel. He wore heavy mud-covered boots, which he laced up in preparation for leaving. The same gray mud caked his jeans all the way to the knees.

He reached for his jacket, allowing his wife, who sat on the very edge of her chair, to take over the conversation. Katie pinned him as being a hard-working laborer, soft-spoken, and more prone to letting someone else have center stage.

"Why are you checking into Scott?" asked Marcie.

"We're trying to establish his mental health at the time of his disappearance," said Katie. "It's standard procedure, what with the new issues being raised."

"Mental health?" Marcie snorted again. "His mental health showed everybody he could be a toad."

"Marcie," warned Daniel. Marcie continued as though her husband hadn't spoken.

"Maybe the first thing you should know," said Marcie, "is they weren't brothers."

"I know Robby is adopted," said Katie.

"No, wrong," said Marcie. "And it wasn't because Scott and Mrs. Ash didn't want it to happen. Wanting Robby to be his brother is the nicest thing I can say about Scott."

Katie waited.

Marcie set the little girl on the floor where her brother stacked blocks and zoomed plastic cars.

"Robby is a great guy. I'm sure you talked to him," said Marcie.

Katie nodded at the pause.

"Dan and Robby hung out all the time, were in the same clubs all through high school." Marcie beamed at Dan. "Robby is kind, generous to a fault, even that little lisp of his is cute."

"Hey," laughed Daniel, giving Marcie a shove.

"We've only spoken on the phone," said Katie. "I didn't notice a lisp."

"Yeah, it's the ess at the end of a word thing," said Marcie. "Anyway, Scott grew up to be the opposite. For him everything came back to me, me, me, I, I, I. He had to have the biggest, the best, the coolest. Robby is a straight-A student. Scott would have flunked out if Robby hadn't helped him. All Scott thought about were things like kick the ball, drive fast, or bang the girl. Didn't even matter which girl."

"Except you," whispered Dan, and kissed the top of her head.

"Yeah, lucky for me I'm way too plain Jane," laughed Marcie. "That and I didn't like him at all."

"And you kept telling him so," said Dan.

"How did Robby take that?" Katie asked.

"He didn't care. They were brothers, and Robby loved him. We were friends, and he loved me. Robby stood as the best man at our wedding. Right up until his brother died, we spoke with him at least once a week." Both Dan and Marcie saddened. Neither seemed to realize the conversation had diverted from being primarily about Scott.

"Scott's death changed that?" asked Katie.

"We haven't heard from him since," said Dan.

"We sent cards, letters, and every time we call, the answering machine picks up," said Marcie. "We finally got a letter back stamped by the post office saying moved left no address." She looked uncomfortable. "I drove over to the house to talk to Mrs. Ash. She got all teary, didn't seem to understand either, but wanted to help. Then Mr. Ash showed up. He told me Robby had gone on his own way, and he, Mr. Ash, would rather I not come back again."

"Like they're estranged?" Katie asked.

Dan nodded.

"It's so bogus," said Marcie. "They were so alike, Robby and Scott. As long as they didn't open their mouths, most people wouldn't know one from the other. But we knew, we always knew. Robby is part of our family. Scott's nothing but garbage."

Marcie leaned back in the chair, closer to where Dan stood. Her eyes drifted toward her children.

"Robby had a girlfriend," said Dan. "Daphne something. Her family came from out around the great lakes. Maybe Robby went out there, transferred colleges. We're hoping he's just too busy, and that one day he'll remember to call."

"Do you think he dropped out of college?" asked Katie.

Both of the Slys' laughed.

"No," said Dan. "Robby loves learning. He wants to be a doctor. He's still in college somewhere."

"Maybe Mr. Ash cut off the money," said Katie.

Dan frowned. "That wouldn't make any difference."

Before Katie could ask why not, Marcie said, "That big house the Ash's live in? That's Robby's house. His parents owned it. All that money they spend, that's his too. Geoffrey Ash had nothing until Robby's parents died. Now he runs the whole she-bang. Robby knows it, and never once begrudged them. That's how big his heart is."

Chapter Twenty-Five

By the time Katie left Dan and Marcie, the sky had grown overcast. The smell of rain tickled her nose, tingling her senses. Instead of taking a right onto the Parentville/Charlotte Road, she drove back to the village library. Her stop here lasted only a few minutes. Katie left her car in the library lot and walked across the street to the municipal building.

"Hi, Katie." Mrs. Deyak rose from behind her desk, smiling a genuine welcome. "What brings you to our fair town on this miserable day?"

"To be honest," Katie smiled in return, "I didn't know I would end up here. I came doing some research, and the librarian told me to talk to you."

"More research on your grandmother's property?" asked Mrs. Deyak. She had been instrumental in Katie's education on the Roser property Gram had inherited, and which Katie had known nothing about.

"No," said Katie. "This is more like historical information on landmarks. The high school and such."

"Wonderful," said Mrs. Deyak, "You probably want to look at the archive records." She motioned Katie to follow her out of the office and toward a door at the end of the room. "Is this related to the fundraiser the vet is doing?"

"Sure…ah…yes," Katie agreed, stomach tight.

The door led to a staircase to the basement. Mrs. Deyak opened one door, throwing several light switches on, illuminating a huge cavern filled with rows of wooden and metal shelves. Each shelf held thick oxblood binders or rolled maps. An oak table with chairs and dusty desk lamps waited for researchers near the door. On the wall hung a six-foot by eight-foot map of Charlotte. Lines crisscrossed the map in a grid pattern. Only the slats of wood nailed into the concrete kept the stained edges of the fragile paper from curling.

Katie stopped in the doorway.

Mrs. Deyak laughed. "Are you feeling overwhelmed?"

"Absolutely." Katie nodded.

"Use the map to find the section you want," said Mrs. Deyak. "The corresponding grid numbers are on the end of each row of shelves. After that you're pretty much on your own." She shook her head. "None of us has had time to work at sorting out down here in years. Older information will be closer to this end or at the bottom of the stacks."

Mrs. Deyak left, leaving the door open, for which Katie thanked her lucky stars. Main roads on the map were labeled with their names, while smaller ones were just a squiggle. The printing company had clearly marked the Pear Mountain region in a slightly different shade of green. Large blocks were marked out and labeled as FOREST, but one slightly smaller block said WELDON.

"That's got to be an estate or farm," said Katie.

Searching other areas, she found similar blocks outlined in magic marker and also labeled according to ownership, such as BROWN FARM or CHAMPLAIN TRUCKING. Taking a chance, she went to the rack identified as containing the grid block for the Weldon property. Her efforts were rewarded with a written record in one of the binders about the original owners. By flipping through the dusty, brittle pages, Katie found subsequent records regarding transfers of ownership. Marcie had been correct; the current owner did not list Ash. The last reference Katie found identified Everett Daudlin as owner. Beside the binders were stacks of scrolls. The first few were brittle maps showing a smallish house, barns, and a duck pond.

"Hm," said Katie, "there should be something newer. A survey or a county map."

She opened several for other pieces of property before finding one dated fifteen years earlier. A penciled in notation said the survey and corresponding Mylar seal were at the request of Everett Daudlin.

"So," said Katie, "Mylar means a permanent record. This guy got serious. He wanted to know exactly what he owned and made sure no one could argue with him."

This map showed the large estate house already in place, which meant she had missed maps. Leaving that one on the table, Katie went back and searched further. Her efforts turned up the building plans provided by the Weldon family when they replaced the small house with the much grander manor.

"Guy must have come into money," Katie muttered.

A different map turned out to actually be a blueprint provided by E. Daudlin on upgrades being done on the manor house. The upgrades included converting the stable building to a multi-vehicle garage.

"Cool," said Katie.

Sitting at the table, she sketched the information from the maps into her notebook, including any pertinent information she found. Upstairs, she found Mrs. Deyak tied up with another resident.

"Can I leave her a message?" Katie asked the woman at the center desk.

Katie left a short note of thanks. *I shut off all the lights and closed the door. Thank you.* She wrote.

As she turned away, a thought crossed her mind. Turning back to the elderly woman manning the clerk's desk, Katie asked.

"I found a lot of information acknowledging the Weldon family or trust," she said. "Can you tell me who they were?"

"Oh, my goodness," gushed the woman. "The Weldons were an enormous presence here. He owned all the tin mines. Whole families worked there. At one time they owned most of the village."

"Huh," said Katie. As she walked out, she thought, *I could use a tin mine.*

Chapter Twenty-Six

Katie didn't get home until late in the afternoon and found Ruth napping on the living room couch. The older woman lay on her side with one hand dangling inside the cardboard box which held Sasha and the kittens. Even though the babies with their short, pointed tails and oversized heads were sound asleep, the adopting mom kept busy bathing her charges.

Smiling, Katie tip-toed into the kitchen. She found a small pot of chicken noodle soup on the warming shelf and a bowl and crackers already on the table. Katie crept around the room, getting her lunch, hoping she wouldn't wake Ruth. The cats followed her every move, mewling for attention or a bite to eat.

"Sh," she said, "sh." Relief came when she finished and stepped outside. To save time, Katie hadn't donned her coat and gloves before leaving. In the house's shadow, with the wind whipping past, she felt the icy blast blow through, chilling her to the bone. Katie looked skyward in another hour it would be dark.

"Well, I guess I know what I'm doing," she said, turning back for her coat.

The hens had been left shut in the hen house, but their bucket of feed was kept stored in the kitchen. Katie got enough cracked corn in the metal pie pan so it would rattle when shook. Almost immediately, the geese appeared. When she had placed the chicken wire fence in the coop, Katie had boxed the hens in on the door side and left the smaller chicken door as access to the penned area. Opening the door, she could only hope a hen wouldn't jump the fence and wander out before she could lure the geese in.

Backing towards the hen house and rattling the pan, Katie kept a nervous eye on the geese. They followed with their necks extended and their wings slightly spread. Katie didn't trust them at all.

"Chick, chick, chick," Katie coaxed, rattling the pan. "Come on, I'll feed you."

She backed up to the hen house and then threw corn in through the small door. The hen noise rose. To Katie's surprise, the male goose rushed in to ward off the poachers. The female goose stopped halfway through the door. Close enough for Katie. Using the pan as a shovel, she shoved the wayward female inside and slammed the door shut. Though her original plan had been to go inside and feed and water both the hens and the geese, the hubbub coming through the walls changed her mind.

"I'll come back in a little while after everybody calms down," she promised.

In the barn, Bonnie lay hidden beneath a pile of straw.

"It's too cold in here for you, fat girl," said Katie, opening the stall door. "Let's go for a walk."

Bonnie followed her to the corner of the lawn closest to the Dean's farm and stopped. She had been trained to know the lilac bushes were as far as she should go. Katie offered a carrot, but the pig wouldn't budge. So, Katie went back up to the house and returned with a casserole dish half-filled with leftover tuna noodle surprise.

She circled the pig, dropping a spoonful of noodles right in front of Bonnie's snoot. Bonnie gobbled it up. Katie circled the pig again. This time stopping further along in the middle of the road. Bonnie hesitated. Katie wiggled the dish. Bonnie moved closer. They began a slow walk down to the Dean's driveway, but Bonnie only got a bite when she stubbornly balked to go further. Behind her, Katie heard someone call out pig, pig, pig. Bonnie paid no attention.

Raymond Dean appeared at Katie's side. She had taken a minute after trapping the geese to call Raymond and tell him she wanted to bring the pig down.

"I'm almost out of tuna," said Katie. "We're not going to make it."

Laughing, Raymond said, "Watch this."

He had a metal milking pail in his hand. Steam rose from within, and Katie could smell the luscious velvet scent of warm milk.

"Hey, baby girl," said Raymond, slowly approaching Bonnie. "Want some? That's a good girl." He let her get a good sniff, then turned and walked away at a steady pace.

Intrigued by the whiff of the milk, Bonnie gave a soft grunting chuckle and followed the bucket up the drive, into the barn, and then into the waiting sty. While she slurped happily, Katie left, knowing the pig would nap when finished.

Ruth worked at filling the cook stove, when Katie came back in from mucking out the stall.

"I wish I'd had a camera when you and Bonnie were going down the road," she laughed. "It would have made a good greeting card. Look at LG."

Seated on the windowsill, the black and gray cat gazed off in the direction Katie and Bonnie had gone. Stepping closer, Katie could hear the soft prrttt call LG used for Bonnie.

"Poor baby," she said, giving a pat and getting a swipe in response. Laughing, Katie followed Ruth into the kitchen. Together they fixed supper, and barely finished when Katie turned to Rick.

"Didn't some old guy, Galileo, I think, say that if you drop two things from the same height at the same time, both would fall at the same rate of speed?" Katie flipped through the pages in her notebook.

"Ah. Okay," said Rick, a frown on his face.

"My point is," said Katie, "if Scott and the snow-machine fell, once again, at the same time, how did Scott end up mostly under the machine? The report Marlie left said the snow-machine covered fifty-seven percent of the remains. That's a lot, and Lewis and those people found the machine lying on its side, not upside-down"

Rick looked incredulous. "I hate to say it, Katie, but I think you're talking about something irrelevant."

"No, if I had accidentally driven off the edge of the cliff, I wouldn't have let go of the handlebars. I'd be gripping those suckers for dear life and still be wrapped around it at touchdown," Katie edged closer. "Then consider the huge weight discrepancy between the two. The machine had thrust, not the man. All that stuff. How could both land in the exact spot and the lighter of the two, underneath?"

"Well," Rick rubbed his jaw, "Maybe, unlike you, Scott pushed himself away from the machine while it fell."

"Then," Katie pointed out, "he would have landed in the water, not on that narrow shale ledge."

"You aren't going to let this go, are you?" he said.

"Let what go?" asked Ruth, carrying the big gray tom from the living room towards the cat restroom.

"I'm telling you," said Katie. "I don't care what the pathologist said. Scott Ash did not die in an accident. It had to be murder."

"*Murder!*" squeaked Ruth, letting go of the cat. Old Tom hit the floor, running back in the direction he'd just come from. Ruth lowered herself into the nearest chair.

Rick looked westward.

"And," said Katie, "that pompous A-hole is going to get away with it."

"Murder," Ruth whispered again, pulling her cardigan tighter around her shoulders.

"But," said Rick.

"How?" Katie demanded, slapping her palm down on the table.

A shudder ran through Rick's frame as enlightenment struck.

"I'll tell you how," he said, yanking his coat off the rack. "Someone shoved Scott over the edge of the cliff. Then, the murderer pushed the machine over on top of him."

"Who?" gasped Ruth, but the other two were ignoring her.

"I don't know if old man Ash killed his own son intentionally," said Katie, "but I'm not going to let him get away with it. Get your coat, Ruth. You're going down to visit Grace for a while."

* * *

Katie and Rick rode in Rick's truck, getting lost, then finding their way again.

Eventually, they drove up Hoover Road onto Pear Mountain. Above them, standing proud in a large, cleared area, they could see the Ash house lit up against the dark forest and the darker mountain. Its positioning offered a view over the valley from above, and to a lesser degree, a view of the structure from below. Rick pulled onto a maintenance road, parking deep in a new-growth pine forest. He cut the engine.

"Holy cow, look at the size of that house." Rick eased the door of the truck closed.

"Yeah." Katie pointed to the six-foot steel mesh fence. "Electric?" she asked.

"Way out here?" asked Rick.

Katie whipped the screwdriver she'd picked up off the truck floor at the fence. When a ball of sparks flew out from the point of impact, both Katie and Rick threw themselves to the ground.

"For crying out loud," yelped Rick. "How about a head's up?"

When the screwdriver lit up the fence, large searchlights along the fence top flashed on for a length of fifty feet in either direction. Out of the corner of her eye, Katie saw a big rectangular box swivel.

"Stay down, Rick," she said. "There's a camera."

She levered up just enough to verify they had parked the pickup hidden from view in the scrub. They waited for the lights to go off. Several minutes later, the red light on the camera disappeared, indicting it had also been deactivated. Then the searchlights clicked off.

"Look at the size of that camera lens," said Rick, "that's an incredibly expensive set-up."

"Why would anybody around here need all that?" Kate asked, getting to her feet. "Keep an eye on the camera."

"What? Wait! What are you doing?" Rick hissed.

Katie stood up, and in short darts approached the fence. Nothing happened. She walked along, keeping close to the brush line for several yards, then walked back. Neither the lights nor the camera came on.

"So," said Rick, also standing, "the lights and the camera are all connected to the fence, not motion activated."

"I'd say so," Katie agreed. "A deer hits it, everything comes up. A sparrow, maybe not. But I don't think the whole fence is electrified. There are strands of shiny wire running horizontally woven in the fence. I think that's where the electricity actually is."

"I'll take your word for it." Rick frowned. "I'm not interested in getting close enough to get fried."

Leaving the truck, they walked back to the road, then up towards the house until they encountered a drainage ditch coming from under the fence. There wasn't enough clearance to crawl safely under so they kept going, eventually breaking out of the brushes onto a wide swath of mowed verge hemming the driveway. The estate's entrance gates were about four car lengths off the dirt road. The same chain-link fence crossed the drive, interrupted only by a gate of the same material mounted on sliding access wheels.

"Did you notice barbed wire before, Katie?" asked Rick, looking upwards. "Because this section of fence has got some mean-looking hardware on top."

Peering through the steel mesh, Katie could just make out the original stone entrance columns with the wrought-iron gates. A fleur-de-lis wreath encircled a solidly blocked W.

She pointed out the second set of gates and the wreath. "Probably left over from the original owners."

"Those gates look pretty old," Rick agreed. "I'm willing to bet replacing them with a capitol A for arrogant would have cost plenty." He flashed his light back and forth along the fence.

Katie sunk to the ground in the middle of the gravel driveway. She could see the lights from the house, hear music playing, but she might as well be looking at the moon. Rick moved between the gatepost and the tree cover.

"You know," he said. "I don't think the original gate included any fence."

"Don't get too close," Katie warned. "If you touch that electric fence, you'll end up with permanent curly hair."

"I'd have to get hair first," laughed Rick.

Katie's eyes followed the drive as far as she could see in the pale moonlight. "The road curves off away from the house," she said.

"Makes it look further away, more majestic, before it swings back. It's an architectural thing." Rick's voice sounded muffled.

Twisting to better hear him, Katie realized he had disappeared. "Where are you?" she called.

"Right here." Rick popped out of a copse of leafless birches. "As near as I can tell, the fence is pretty new."

"How's that?" Katie got to her feet, stopping short when an audible click sounded. At the top of the drive, they could hear people laughing and talking. The voices were almost clear enough to understand. Rick clicked off the flashlight.

"They're leaving." She rushed for the birches. "Somebody is coming out. Hear that? The buzzing stopped. The fence is shut off."

"Don't take a chance touching it," Rick warned.

"Phfft, don't worry," snorted Katie. "I'm not interested in a frizzy 'do."

The voices continued, then mixed with the sound of car engines starting. Through the brush, lights appeared. Katie tracked their progress as the cars followed the serpentine sweep of the drive, moving slowly but steadily toward the gates.

"Like I said," whispered Rick, "It looks like they cut all the trees and brush out in the last few months for the fence."

"I checked the land records, trying to get any information I could," hissed Katie. "I didn't see a building permit."

"Yeah, like Ash would bother." Rick's voice rose.

"Sh," whispered Katie. "How many cars? Three?"

Rick stood taller, craning his neck while moving side to side. "Three," he agreed. "Get ready."

They squatted behind the birches, waiting. The first car passed without pausing. The second. As the third car pulled even with where they hid, Katie and Rick darted out from the edge of the birches closest to the fence. Hunched over, his hand pushing her from the back, they circled close to the edge of the chain-link gate, and once past the iron gates; they threw themselves down onto the lawn. Katie lay on the damp grass, eyes on the taillights. Only the briefest flash indicated the driver touched his brakes. There was no interruption of their forward motion. And then, slowly, the steel mesh gate rolled to meet its partner on the far side. They touched with a faint clink. The twin top and bottom U-shaped hinges dropped into place, and with the same audible click, the buzzing resumed.

Katie and Rick were locked on the inside.

Chapter Twenty-Seven

Katie swallowed convulsively. They were in a good and bad place. She had wanted to get to the house, but she hadn't planned on being trapped on the grounds overnight. She could hear Rick breathing and saw his dark silhouette as he sat up.

"Ah, Katie," whispered Rick, looking back at the locked gates. "Why are we here again? And do you have a plan for getting out?"

Katie rolled over, eyeing the tall metal mesh with its crown of barbed wire.

"Well," she gulped, "I wanted to see if anything suspicious might be happening around here. To be truthful, I didn't expect to get locked in."

"Now what?" Rick asked.

Katie licked her lips. "As long as we're here, we'll scout around. Then we'll leave."

"But, we're not going in the house, right?" asked Rick.

He walked back toward the gate, looking for a control box that would open the locks. The beam of his flashlight showed nothing.

"Right," said Katie, *and I don't know how we're going to get out*, she thought.

"Okay, then," she said, pushing up and brushing off her shirt. "Let's see what they're serving for leftovers."

The house sat above them on a rise. Everything they could make out in the moonlight appeared designed to impress. The long sweeping drive cleared back twenty feet on either side, had been edged with smooth, perfectly mowed lawn. It would have been quicker for them to cut through the woods, but who knew what they'd fall into in the dark.

"If I remember correctly, the estate is three hundred and fifty acres," said

Katie. "That's a lot of fencing."

"Well, when you've got money and powerful connections, you can always work a deal," said Rick. "Or if he didn't want to lay out the big bucks, just the area surrounding the house is fenced in."

"That's true," said Katie. "Ash has owned this place for ten years, anyway. If he put up the fence recently, he might have only done it for privacy, not safety."

"Well," said Rick, "which one changed to make him go the expense?"

They had reached the top of the rise. Ahead of them, the bright lights on the side of the house went off. The music also stopped. The drive split, circling around a garden area enclosed by a low stone wall. In the center, a dark spire rose. Katie thought it might be a fountain, shut down for the winter. Rick hesitated. But Katie cut across the compass garden, staying on the flagstone path, and headed straight for the front door. Rick caught up with her just before she stepped through the open space in the stone wall across from the entrance steps.

"Wait," he whispered. "There might be surveillance cameras."

"Is this when they let out the drooling, barking dogs?" she whispered back.

"Dogs?" he gulped.

Before she could respond, Rick grabbed her by the arm, darting across the drive to the right. They circled the house, coming to a narrow driveway filled with two black vans. Rick squatted behind the first van, studying the area.

"According to the blueprints," said Katie, "this would be the service drive."

"So, if Mr. and Mrs. Ash were having a soiree," Rick said. "These are probably the caterers." He leaned back, trying to read the van's logo in the dark.

Katie agreed. "Come on," she said.

Rick turned to see her disappearing around the back edge of the second van.

"Crap," he swore, following her up a bricked path toward an area where large multi-pane windows unencumbered by drapery glowed with light. He stayed low, finally catching up while she knelt near the door, peeking through the bottom of the window.

"It's the kitchen," she looked at him wide-eyed. "It's *huge*, like a restaurant."

Rick took a peek, "And full of people."

Katie tried the door handle. It twisted smoothly, and the door drifted open a few inches. "What do you think?" she whispered. "Should we try it? To get in there?" Her words were met by silence. "Rick? Rick?" Katie turned. Once again, he had disappeared. She swiveled back toward the small opening between the door and the casement. A hand landed on her shoulder. Katie yelped, falling forward on her knees and barely catching the door frame before she tumbled inside.

"This way," Rick whispered.

She reached out to smack him, but he had snuck away, squeezing between the house and the shrubbery. Katie followed, ducking as they crawled beneath another set of long windows. They came out behind a wall of potted evergreens on the end of a gracious veranda. A single man stood on a stepladder removing ambiance lights from the cross wires. Rick pointed toward the open glass doors, tilting his head in an obvious invitation to follow him. Slowly, quietly, they crept along the glassed wall to the door. Once inside, they squatted on the raised rim of a sunken lounge. The four-foot-wide, edge led to two wide downward steps. Awed, Katie looked around wide-eyed at the opulence until a voice in the hall caught her attention. Ash. And from the sound, right outside the door.

Rick dove one way, Katie the other. She ended up curled in a ball behind a Queen Anne chair. Rick lay hidden by a low eight-foot-long, sofa. The voice got closer. Then a woman spoke.

"No, go ahead," said Ash. "You might as well go to bed. I'll wait for the clean-up."

This time, Katie heard the woman more clearly. Or as clear as the slurring voice got. From where she hid, Katie could see a section of staircase and the lower edge of a deep blue, sequined gown drifting upwards. She took a breath, then scuttled across a few open feet to a loveseat. Letting out a sigh, Katie considered herself safe until Ash entered the lounge, walking up to the bar. He faced the wall of shelves pouring liquor, the rich, amber color of maple syrup into a snifter. If he turned even slightly, he'd see her. She had nowhere to go.

Ash took a long drink. Katie crushed herself smaller. He swiveled. Smaller still. But then, whistling to himself, he left the lounge, pausing only long enough to remove and leave his dinner jacket on the arm of the loveseat. The falling sleeve grazed the top of her head.

I'm going to puke, Katie thought. A chill ran down her spine. Bracing her hand against the floor, she prepared to stand, but the scuffing of a shoe on stone stopped her.

The caterer came through the glass door, closing and locking it. He tested the lock to make sure it held, and then with the ladder and strings of lights over his arm, left the room, closing the hall door behind him. Katie counted to ten. Then rushed to where Rick should have been lying and found an empty space. She swung around, mentally swearing at the old man and searching frantically before spotting a pair of pocket doors between the bookshelves on the wall behind the sofa. One panel had been pushed open about two feet. Beyond the door, she found a dining room, stripped of its raiment and in darkness.

"Rick?" Katie called out in a hoarse whisper.

No answer. She crossed the darkened room to the sliver of light that showed another entrance. This door, like the pocket door, stood slightly ajar. Katie slid out into the well-lit hall. After a single fleeting gaze upward, she moved towards the back of the house, crouched and ready to bolt either way at a moment's notice. If she had gone to the front, she would have passed by the doors leading back into the lounge. Across from her, a smaller door opened under the staircase. Inside, she found a closet with only a few umbrellas hanging from the hooks. She kept moving, and the hall narrowed. She could hear voices. Light drifted from a room in the interior of the house. It appeared to be an office. A single lamp burned, but no one sat at the desk. Finally, she stopped outside the kitchen. Just within, one man spoke to another. The second man sounded like Ash. They were discussing the dinner party. Katie listened for the clatter of the caterers, but heard only the two men.

"Go ahead," said Ash. "The caterers have got just about everything loaded. I need to lock up. We can sit down and discuss the rest of this mess after they go."

Katie heard footsteps, perhaps one set coming towards her. Katie ran back to the office and hid in the darkness, hoping Ash would retire for the night. Back the way she'd originally come, a door opened and shut. A bolt struck home. She stayed still for what felt like hours. When she crawled out of her hiding place, the single desk lamp still burned. Ash hadn't come in, nor had she heard him come back from the kitchen. Standing in the hall with her feet sinking into the lush carpet, she thought, *He could be walking up right behind me, and I'd never know.* She turned, stumbling backwards. A man advanced towards her, moving fast. Katie opened her mouth to scream, but Rick tackled her, smothering her cries and almost knocking her to the floor.

"Where have you been?" he hissed.

"Where did you go?" she whispered.

Instead of answering, he pulled her toward the front of the house. They were standing on the opposite side of the heavy front doors from the lounge. Sliding a framed picture silently to the side, Rick peered at the markings on the electric box, threw two switches, and eased the front door open.

"Run," he hissed, "run like those big slobbering dogs are chasing you."

Ignoring the driveway, they ran through the woods. Katie could barely hear Rick's panting breath over the horrible pounding of her heart trying to break free of her chest. They reached the gates. Ahead of them the metal gate trembled, the wheels squeaked as the gate started its slow progress back across the drive where it would again lock in place.

Rick grabbed Katie just as she reached for his jacket. Together they exploded through the narrow space, landing spread eagle on the gravel.

"Ow," said Katie. "Ow. Ow. Ow."

"I think I broke both my knees, and maybe my hands," Rick groaned.

They had all they could do to crawl out of the open.

"How did you...?" she asked.

"When I came back downstairs from following the lush, I spent a few minutes studying the box in case we had to break out," he said.

"How did you know you'd find the control panel there?" asked Katie.

"I didn't. Ash showed me when he let the caterers out," said Rick. Then his wheezing gave way to a deep cough.

Katie got to her feet, palms burning from their impact on the gravel. Looking back, the house was dark, with the exception of a single light burned bright on the upper floor.

Chapter Twenty-Eight

Rick's cough continued even after they got home, where Ruth waited anxiously.

"I've been sitting here waiting," she said, wringing her hands. "You have been gone for hours."

"Well, not exactly hours," said Katie. "Here Rick, have a glass of water." She watched him with concern. The coughing had started quickly and persisted for quite a time, leaving Rick unable to talk, and Katie worried about his driving ability.

Ruth left the room, returning a few minutes later with an asthma inhaler in hand. Rick took a draw from the puffer, holding the medication in his lungs for the count of five.

"Where did you get near Rhododendron bushes?" she asked.

Rick shrugged, slowly releasing his breath.

"They must have been around the patio," said Katie.

"No," said Ruth, "he'd have to fall into them. That's the way his allergy works. He can get fairly close, but for an attack like this he has to handle them."

"Then it had to have been in the woods," Katie said.

"Rhododendrons are expensive and don't just grow anywhere, like the woods," Ruth scoffed.

"I'm okay," said Rick, "you two can settle down." Ruth patted him on the back as she moved past, but he jerked away. "I said I'm fine, stop fussing."

"Alright," said Katie, "explain what you meant about the lush and the circuit box."

Rick spoke slowly, each breath, a little less wheezy. "Laying on the floor behind the couch, I could see the door behind me open a crack, but out in the hall, I could hear Ash talking. I belly crawled through the dining room to the door leading into the hall. Am I losing you?"

Katie shook her head. Ruth nodded.

"Ash went into the living room, but his wife went up the stairs. I took a chance and followed her. She was kind of stumbling along. I didn't figure she'd notice me. There are several bedrooms up there. She went into the big one at the end of the hall and shut and *locked* the door."

"Locked?" asked Katie.

"Yeah," Rick nodded. "Locked."

"Why?" asked Ruth.

"Who else besides Ash would be in the house?" asked Katie.

"No one I saw," said Rick. "Anyway, I crept around upstairs, and Ash comes back into the hall just as I hear the vans pull away. Before I could move, I saw him slide the picture out of the way and fiddle with the switches. It's all marked, security system, main gate, back gate. Like I said before, that's a heck of a lot of security. And it's rigged so that a light shines on a small panel beside the front door if the gate is open. When I got back downstairs, I went across the hall from the dining room. There's another parlor and rooms, for I don't know what. I didn't dare turn on any lights, so I went back to the hall."

Katie sat back. The timeline Rick gave her didn't jibe with what she had experienced. Which meant she had missed something while hiding in the small office or hadn't been there as long as she thought. She told Rick what she had seen. Ruth looked like she would faint any second.

"I never heard Ash go back up the hallway after the caterers left, and I didn't hear the vans leave," she said.

"Thick carpets," Rick pointed out, "and if you were in an interior room with no windows, you could have missed the outside noises."

"True," she said. "Did Ash go up the stairs after he opened the gate for the caterers?"

"No," said Rick, "he went back the way he'd come. I guess that would be toward the kitchen. I stayed on the floor upstairs watching and wondering where to hide if he came up."

"Oh, my," gasped Ruth.

"So," said Katie, "the caterers left. Ash locks everything up. He walked past where I hid twice. Why did he go back to the rear of the house? And who's the man I heard him talking to?"

"Maybe the other kid, Robby," said Rick.

"No," said Katie, "Daniel and Marcie Sly said Robby hasn't been here in months. There's some kind of bad blood. I need to find out why."

"How are you going to do that?" asked Ruth.

"I guess I'll have to drive over and talk to him," said Katie. Picking up the telephone receiver, she dialed the operator. "Hello," she said, "I need directory assistance for Syracuse, New York."

Chapter Twenty-Nine

Rainy days were coming more often. Quick fall showers with lasting pattering episodes that chilled to the bone were becoming the norm, but this morning the word storm or deluge or even sleet would have been a better fit. Katie parked at the Charlotte ferry landing, waiting for the first thirty-minute run over to Essex, New York. The sun had barely risen and showed a wet world ahead. Beyond the thumping windshield wipers, the lake surface rose as a churning mass of dark waves warning of a freezing fall to depths no set of human lungs could endure. There seemed to be no singular direction, and most of the tall waves were crested with white foam. Katie's heart sank even as her stomach rose. It wouldn't be long before the only ferry to be crossing over for the winter would be the ice breaker out of Burlington. Never a conveyance Katie would have chosen.

Only six vehicles crept aboard. Drivers were told to stay in their transport because of the rough water and wind. Katie clutched the steering wheel, trying to squeeze her eyes shut. She didn't want to see her end coming. Her determination, a losing battle, ending with the first wave breaking over the bow. No matter how hard she tried not to, she couldn't stop looking. Watching the far shore creep closer seemed to be the only small victory on the entire crossing.

Finally, on the Essex, New York side, Katie found a picnic pavilion just off the ferry docks. A wooden roof covered four redwood, stained tables. She sat on the innermost bench, gulping cold air. Her hands encircled her head, elbows on the scarred wood riddled with the initials left by travelers over the years. Other than the occasional squawk of an indignant seagull, no one bothered her.

"Fools," she whispered, watching as other travelers loaded onto the ferry.

The weather once on shore did not improve, the four-hour journey to the college took almost five. She barely made her appointment with the provost.

"I thought the weather might be a hold-up," the man, Gene Lyons, said. He looked exactly as expected: five feet six inches tall, pot-bellied, pinstriped gray suit, and quite bald. "I took the liberty of making notes for you."

His examination of the letter of introduction she offered consisted of a casual glance. The Provost's indifference to the missive which had taken Katie an hour to create irked her. She stomped down the feeling that the pompous little man couldn't be bothered checking credentials and accepted her letter back.

"Thank you for seeing me," she smiled. "My employer, Attorney Wilkins, is keen to get everything in order."

"Yes, you mentioned a failing client. Too bad. Just too bad," Mr. Lyons shook his head as though the sorrow were his own.

"Mr. Daudlin?" Katie prompted, reminding the Provost of her errand.

"Yes. Of course. This is Mr. Daudlin's third year with us. As you probably know, he no longer resides on campus. I've included a listing of his course schedule, related sports, and club affiliations."

Katie scanned the pages, hoping to find a home address. There was none. Nor did she find a fraternity listed. The last page showing the current year's schedule seemed mostly blank.

"There doesn't seem to be a lot of information available," she frowned.

"No," Lyons' tone was disapproving. "When Mr. Daudlin first came here, we had high hopes. He exhibited enthusiasm, drive, and I personally found him to be a happy, well-adjusted young man. Then the next year, around mid-term, something happened. He dropped out of every extra-curricular he had signed up for. His grades began slipping. I didn't see him around campus as often."

Katie raised her head from the pages. "That would have been after Christmas break?" she asked.

"Yes, or shortly thereafter," said Lyons. "He's an orphan, but has an uncle listed as next of kin. Our office notified him that Mr. Daudlin could be failing out. I remember his arrival, very tall, sharp, obviously used to giving orders and being listened to."

"Mr. Ash?" asked Katie.

"Why yes." Lyons brightened for a moment, then paled. "Oh, the failing client?"

Katie merely lowered her eyes.

"Mr. Daudlin's uncle took the boy on a two-week sabbatical," said Lyons. "When they came back, the boy had greatly improved. Caught up with his classes, and even though he didn't step up at a point level as we expected, he did move to the next year in the top third. This year he's much improved. It looks like he will graduate with high honors." Lyons smiled, his eyes disappearing as his cheeks rose.

Among Mr. Lyons' notes, Katie found a short list of two names. These were the only other young men Lyons remembered as being friends of Daudlin. Each name followed by the address of the same frat house. That would be Katie's next stop.

She only found one boy at home in the frat house. He had twenty minutes, he explained, to talk with her. They sat in the lounge, which would have been the original parlor in the old Victorian-style house. The boy slouched in his seat, picking zits and acting as though he were the King of Cool.

"Yeah," he said, "Robby and I are friends. Who're you again? A lawyer?"

"No," sighed Katie, "I work for a lawyer. We've been asked to establish Mr. Daudlin's history here at the college."

"Is his rich uncle checking up on him again?" grinned the boy.

"No, this is from the other side of his family." Katie got right to the point. "I've spoken with other members of academia. They seem to be spot on until around a year ago. As one of his friends, I thought you might have some insight into how he is currently getting on." She held her pen poised over the notebook on her knee.

"Is there like a finder's fee or something on this?" asked the boy.

"Hm," she gave a sly grin. "There could be."

The boy's attitude went from wanna-be jock to information spewing junkie. He straightened up in his seat.

"Yeah, well Robby is way cool, you know?" His hands crept to his face. "Good looking, always has plenty of jingle in his pocket, and he knows all the babes."

Yeah, thought Katie. *So, there's the connection between you two.*

"But he wasn't the type of guy to be stuck up. He always has something going on, some sports practice or club meeting, and like, no matter what people said, he could still be my friend. We were roomies. Then he went home for Christmas. To Vermont, I believe. When he came back, he acted all bogus." The boy looked out the window, possibly considering his friend. Katie waited.

"He didn't want to do anything or hang out with me anymore," said the boy, turning back to Katie. "He, I don't know. He acted uptight, not friendly anymore. And then his moods were all over the place. One minute a smile, the next he screamed till I thought he would have the big one. We got into this really major argument. One day he started screaming about something bad happening back where his family lived. He said, me and Max should grow up. He stopped going to class, started smoking weed, in the room and drinking heavy. To be honest, he freaked me out. When he started getting stoned all the time, I buggered out of there and moved in with a couple of other guys I knew. I'm here on a scholarship. I can't take a chance the dean is gonna take him down, and me too."

"Then what happened?" asked Katie.

"Someone must have told his family," the boy shrugged. "The uncle showed up. Guy's a piece of work. Robby flipped out. They were screaming all over the dorm. I think the cops even showed up." The boy's stress had ramped up, the face picking a serious manifestation of his state of mind. Katie gritted her teeth.

"The next morning, Robby disappeared. He didn't come back to class for a couple of weeks. And when he did, he didn't live in the dorm anymore. He had a pad somewhere else. It's no big deal. A lot of guys do. But Robby used to talk about the college experience." The boy laughed. "I always thought he sounded kind of hokey about the whole thing."

"Where?" asked Katie, clearing her throat. "Where is his apartment?"

"Don't know. He never invited me. But it's clear he's all done with everybody here, for more reasons than one."

"What does that mean?" asked Katie.

"So now, he's gotten all bitching and nasty, only the assholes want to be around him. Then someone found out he'd been in dry out and spread the word." The boy had a sly, knowing grin that made Katie's skin crawl. "Even the stoners who had been coming around before he left, don't show up anymore. Plus, the uncle put the kibosh on that shit."

"And?" said Katie.

The boy stood up, stretching and scratching his crotch before he walked to the door. Just before exiting, he turned back. "Robby didn't pass to the next year on his own. That rich uncle? He pays us to get him through. We don't tutor him; we just flat out do the work."

It took Katie a moment to come up with her next question. By that time, the boy had already walked down the front steps. She rushed outside, grabbing him by the arm.

"Where is the dry-out?" she demanded.

"Whitney House in Glen Falls," he grinned, reaching out a hand to touch her face.

Katie jumped backwards like from a hot grease fire.

Flipping her off, the boy sauntered away.

* * *

She walked back to her car in the rain, hood up on her slicker and both hands shoved in the pockets. The wind blew wet and raw, smelling like incoming snow. Glen Falls lay to the east and south. If she went that way, she could drive around the southern tip of Lake Champlain to get home. She had a map in the car.

"I'm this close," she said. "I'll take the detour."

Across the street, a coffee house offered a hot drink and maybe something a little sweet. Done with the pastry and on her second cup of coffee, Katie asked the waitress if she could look at the phone book. Under the d's, she found an R. Daudlin and wrote down the address. The waitress directed her to a street five blocks away.

There weren't any cars parked in the alley next to the building, or in front. On the porch were four flip-top mailboxes. A bit of paper taped on number two said DAUDLIN.

That's what I'm afraid I'm going to find, thought Katie. *Number two.*

She entered the hall and found the apartment door on her left. With no idea what she would say, she knocked on the door. No one came. She knocked again. While she waited, the clatter of a girl coming down the stairs caused her to turn. The girl wore heavy shoes which looked like the bottom of a buccaneer boot and had a heavy platform heel, and no socks.

"If you're looking for Bob," the girl said. "He's probably in class."

"Thanks," said Katie, eyes flicking back to the door. "Are you sure?" she asked, looking back, but the informant, who had never stopped walking, had gone.

The rain didn't let up for Katie's entire journey south to Glen Falls. Her map got her into town, but once within the city limits, nothing was mapped out. At her second stop for directions, a clerk pointed the way to the Whitney House. She parked on the street across from a tall iron gate complete with a notice: locked at 7 P.M. and unlocked at 8 A.M. A thick red line crossed the walk. The building had the ambiance of a Saturday Late, Late Horror Show.

I don't want to go in there, Katie's insides cried as her feet followed the water darkened concrete walk.

Katie produced the fake letter of introduction she had carefully prepared for Mr. Winkler to the administrator's secretary. The woman came back in a few moments.

"You'll need a warrant," she said when she returned.

Outside, a young man had appeared, perched on the wide granite step.

"Didn't talk to you, did they?" he chirped.

He was wearing scrubs. Katie hoped he might be an intern, not a resident. While she silently tried to figure it out, he watched her without moving.

"Who you looking for?" he asked. "Got any smokes?"

"No," she said.

He shrugged and turned away.

"I've got a five-dollar bill, though," she offered. "That would buy smokes."

His eyebrow raised. She pulled the bill out of her jean pocket but didn't offer it. Red-rimmed eyes stared hungrily at the money.

"Robert Daudlin," she said.

"Wait here." The man sprinted around the corner.

Katie moved slowly toward the main gate. If someone from the admin office witnessed their exchange, she might need to make a quick getaway. The man came back to the exact spot where they had been standing. His head snapped back and forth until he spotted her. He stopped at the red line. Katie moved back to him.

"Daudlin hasn't been here for a long time. Before I came. Word is, he did a quick detox, then got hauled away, most likely by his family. Lots of folks don't want their kin here."

"And?"

"That's all I got, other than my buddy said Daudlin could be the worst kind of conceited ass."

Katie handed over the money. Seated in the car, she made notes before checking the map. She could drive further southeast to Whitehall and cross into Vermont. It wouldn't be a much longer ride than driving all the way back to where she'd come over the water. The idea of wet roads didn't terrify her half as much as the ferry crossing had. The ride from Whitehall, New York, to Parentville, Vermont would take an hour and a half on a good day.

"It'll be dark by the time I get home," she said to herself, turning the ignition key. "That's okay, at least I'll still have fingernails when I get out of the car."

* * *

The long day had exhausted her, but she had plenty of time to consider what to do next. Four times she pulled over to the side of the road to write a note, or add a question. At the end of three of her scribbles she penciled in the initials T. A. Though her plan had been to call after a good night's sleep, minutes after walking through the door, she dialed long-distance.

"Ms. Adams? Tessa? This is Katie Took." An answering machine had taken the call. Katie wasn't sure what information she could leave safely. "I went to Syracuse today. Perhaps we should more closely compare notes." With any luck, Tessa would understand and call back.

Chapter Thirty

Katie made it to her chair in the living room before the telephone rang. Hoping to hear Tessa, she found Stan telling her the attorney general's office said she could go back to work.

"I know it's late to call," he said. "But you might want the pay."

"Are you sure, it's okay?" she asked.

"Absolutely," said Stan. "They seemed a little surprised when I asked about it. Like maybe, they didn't know Detective Riffle ordered you not to come to work. The clerk said Riffle would call you, but I'm letting you know because that jerk detective probably won't call until four-fifty tomorrow afternoon."

Katie had to agree with her boss. Letting out a sigh of relief, she turned to Ruth with the news she would be returning to work the next morning. Before she could say a word, the phone rang again.

"Is it too late to talk?" Tessa Adams asked.

Katie asked Ruth to leave the room while she took the call. Ruth gave her a frowning look.

"She's older," Katie explained to Tessa. "I'm worried she'll get all agitated, and she might accidentally talk to someone else. There have been several people at the door lately looking for information." She almost bit her tongue in an effort not to say reporters.

"I totally understand," said Tessa. "You said you had information to share?"

Katie told Tessa what she had learned while in New York.

"I ran out of time," said Katie, "and I didn't think of the questions I should have asked until hours later."

"Well, I think," said Tessa, "I might do a little research around here. How

160

about if I give you a call back in a day or so?"

"The evening would be best," said Katie, before ending the call.

She returned to the living room to find Ruth wrapped in her flannel bathrobe, seated on the couch feeding two kittens. Rick sat right beside her; a fuzzy tiger barely visible in his hand. The kitten had a firm grip on Rick's finger with its tiny claws, while Rick nervously watched its every move.

"If you relax, Rick," said Ruth, "the kitten will too." Sasha stood in the box, front legs on the edge, watching the man.

"I don't think Sasha trusts you, Rick," laughed Katie, peeking into the box. The remaining two kittens crawled around mewling. Obviously, concerned about their dinner. One of them only half the size of its sibling.

In response to Katie's observation, the mama cat reached out a tentative paw, letting Rick know she'd take the kitten back any time. Carefully, he laid the precious bundle down under the female.

"Whew," he said, dropping back into his seat. While Katie laughed, he wiped his brow. "Did you notice we're down two cats?"

"What?" said Katie, swinging around trying to count. LG sat in the chair, giving Katie a sour look. "Why are you so grouchy?" Katie asked her hairy buddy. In response, LG snapped at the extended fingers.

"They're all a little nervy right now," said Ruth. She placed her two kittens back with Sasha, who immediately began a vigorous washing of all. Ruth sat back, a new kitten in her hands. "Every time someone disappears or actually just leaves, they get all edgy."

"Who left?" asked Katie, relieved Ruth had not used the word passed.

"Barbara from the nursing home came around," said Ruth, her displeasure at being ordered out of the kitchen still evident in her frown. "She wanted a couple of older cats for the residents, and Doctor Veronica sent her here. Why are you so touchy?"

"I'm sorry," said Katie, "I had a long day. Why don't we have a cup of tea and I'll tell you about it?"

"I'm for that," said Rick, jumping up.

"So, who went with Barbara?" Katie asked, filling Ruth's cup. The older woman coaxed the tiny kitten to suckle on the bottle.

"The bird sisters, Dove and Pigeon," grinned Ruth.

"Perfect," said Katie. "The identical twins. There won't be any fighting over them, because you can't tell them apart."

"I called Doctor Veronica to say thank you," Ruth called out, her voice following Katie into the kitchen. "I also told her we would have five kittens ready to go the week before Christmas."

Doctor Veronica, the vet in Charlotte, helped with the spaying and neutering for the feral cats, giving Katie a special rate. Ruth sounded pleased, but Rick, leaning on the counter, frowned into his cup. Katie took it to mean at least one kitten might be in danger. She'd wait until Ruth wasn't right there and take a good look at the litter. If there was an issue, it would probably be the tiny one.

"Let me tell you what I found out in New York," she said.

Ruth twitched around in her seat while Katie spoke. Watching Ruth, Katie tempered what she said, sure the older woman's apprehensive about the remains found on the ridge caused her unease. And then, Katie's involvement also created tension. But Rick wanted to know it all. While Katie spoke, Ruth moved around, still carrying the last kitten. Again, Katie thought about how tiny it looked.

I hope she hasn't already named it.

"Wow," Rick said. "I think you uncovered a lot. Are you sure you can trust this reporter person?"

"Yeah, I think so," said Katie. "Actually, I really hope so because I am not riding that ferry again this winter."

* * *

The next morning, Katie left for work wearing one of her new shirts and carrying an old one in the event she got sent back to working in the feed shed.

"Glad to get back?" asked Cindy, taking the cash drawers out of the safe.

"Yeah," Katie smiled. "Looks like everything here is pretty cool."

"You don't know the half of it," said Cindy. "I, for one, am glad to see you back. I don't think, a single one of those guys can make change correctly. The cash drawers were screwed up every night. And, if someone they knew walked up, it doesn't matter how many people waited, they had to jaw until they were done."

"I've seen that before," nodded Katie. "They talk about women gossiping, but it's a joke."

She walked out of the office with the cash drawer in her hands, ready for the sideways glances and snide innuendos sure to come her way. Instead, she found hustle, bustle, and friendly smiles.

"Heads up, people," Stan called out. "Doors opening."

Katie rushed to her designated spot, dropped the metal tray in the cash drawer slot, and turned to the first person in line.

"Good morning," she smiled enthusiastically. "What can I do for you?"

The snow shovel business had dropped off until the next storm, but the bird food and straw business were still roaring along. In the mid-morning, she looked up to see Mrs. Higgins with her arms full of bird feeders and a suet tray.

"Holy cow," laughed Katie.

"Yeah," said Mrs. Higgins. "When the kids get home from school, we're going to set up a bird yard. We couldn't do this in the city. They're pretty excited."

Katie helped her drag everything up onto the counter, including the thirty-pound bag of winter bird seed.

"Is this everything?" Katie asked.

"No," said Mrs. Higgins. "I'd like to find out about the kittens." Before Katie could say a word, the woman went on. "We'd like to get one if we can. I mean, if the kittens are...you know?"

"Alive?" asked Katie. "And doing well. Ready to leave by Christmas. Why don't you go up and pick out the one you want before Ruth starts calling people on her waiting list? Just call and tell her you're coming. Take the kids. Ruth will be thrilled to see you." She scribbled her phone number on Mrs. Higgins' receipt and got one of the guys to help the woman lug everything out to her station wagon.

The adoption offer forgotten as soon as the next smiling customer stepped up. Katie had a great morning.

On her lunch break, a man in a suit found her squatting out back in the sun enjoying her leftover fried ham sandwich.

"I'm with the *Burlington Free Press*," he said.

"You need to talk to someone over at the sheriff's office," said Katie. "The attorney general has sealed my lips." It sounded like a viable excuse to her.

"Phfft," said the man. "Are you kidding? They're so wound up over there right now, you could get shot walking in and asking a question."

At Katie's quizzical look, the man added, "I guess one of the deputies, quit cold. Just stopped coming in. The sheriff is really pissed."

"Which deputy?" asked Katie, rising slowly to her feet.

"I don't know," the man said. "The one I wanted to talk to. The one that found all those bodies."

Marlie. Katie watched the man walk away, his trench coat flapping around his knees as he rounded the corner.

Rushing over to the police station wouldn't do her any good. She'd have to go to Marlie's apartment in Charlotte.

"Rick," Katie called out as she passed the feed warehouse loading dock. "I have to make a stop on my way home. You guys just eat, I'll be late."

Rick popped out of the doorway. "Have you got a trap, your snare stick?" he asked, thinking she'd gotten an animal call.

"Yeah, I'm good." *I just don't know about Marlie.*

The rest of the afternoon seemed eons long. Then on the ride over the Parentville-Charlotte Road to the farmhouse converted to small apartments, she found traffic backed up and doing a fast twenty-five miles an hour in a forty-mile an-hour zone. Katie didn't worry about hitting a deer, but she did want to jump out and beat the pulp out of the moron who couldn't pull over and let the long stream of cars pass.

"Calm down," she muttered, arguing with herself. "It's probably a farm tractor going as fast as it can."

Her guess proved correct when, a half a mile later, the tractor turned off into a barnyard.

CHAPTER THIRTY

* * *

Katie knocked on the door, called Marlie's name, knocked again, and finally pounded, screaming at the top of her lungs.

The door on the apartment below yanked open.

"For crying out loud," shouted the woman standing in the light coming from inside her apartment, a toddler in her arms. "She's gone. Moved out bag and baggage." The door slammed shut.

Resisting the urge to kick the door in and check for herself, Katie descended the wooden steps to knock on the other woman's door.

"What?" demanded the woman when the door yanked open.

"I'm sorry," Katie said, humbly. "I'm worried about my friend. Can you tell me anything? When she left?"

The woman let out a long sigh. "A few nights ago, sometime after nine, a guy shows up. Then I could hear them arguing. I'm already in bed, so I didn't see anything. He left, roared out of here in what must have been a big car. When I got home the next day, she had already gone. That's all I know."

"Thank you," said Katie, turning away. The door closed without a harsh bang.

Katie drove up the Charlotte main street until she found a building whose sign declared. *G. H. Ash, Investments.* A light shone in the back office and a Crown Vic parked in the alley. Katie didn't stop.

Arriving home, she found the farmhouse still lit up. Ruth sat in Katie's chair knitting. A cat in her lap, another in the yarn, and a third resting on the chair back. Rick lay stretched out on the sofa, snoring.

"Sh," said Ruth. "I left a plate for you on the warming shelf of the stove. I fed the hens and the geese."

After retrieving the plate, Katie sat with her back to the wood stove. But the warmth did nothing to thaw her heart. LG loped in, her purring caress rewarded with a generous portion of Katie's supper. Biting her lips, Katie dialed Marlie's number. A recorded operator voice told her the number was no longer in service.

Katie didn't climb out of the bath until she shivered in cold water. Ruth and

Rick had already retired. She paced alone except for the cat that shadowed her. Upstairs, her room was cold, with little frills of icy lace forming on the inside of the windows. Pushing the pads of her fingers through to the pane created ovals of clear glass. Saddened at the loss of the Jack Frost art, and by the feel of her own flesh compacting to preserve her body heat, Katie rolled up in her blankets. Though she didn't think sleep an option, her eyes closed, and her numbed brain allowed the outside to fade away.

Chapter Thirty-One

"LG?" screamed Katie. She ran through the woods in the dark. Overhead, naked tree branches danced like witches weaving terrifying spells. "LG, where are you?" Rain froze around her. She wore only her Bahama Mama t-shirt and underpants. "BONNIE," she screamed. "RUTH." She pushed through the brush, panting for breath. Suddenly she felt herself falling, far out in the air and for a long distance. She sucked in trying but unable to force air down into her lungs.

A heavy pounding interrupted the scene, calling her attention elsewhere. The fist beating against wood as loud as the voice yelling her name.

Katie struggled to a sitting position, wound inside the quilt. The doorknob twisted and Rick, dressed in striped pajamas, burst in.

"Katie," he called out, groping for the light switch. "Katie! Are you alright?"

"I, ah, think I had a nightmare." She gripped the covers with icy fingers, trying to control the shaking.

Rick stood beside the bed, looking down. The light from the overhead light cast his face in a shadow but she could still see all the deep furrows.

"I'm good," she said, gathering the covers closer as the chattering of her teeth abated. "Go back to bed."

"You're shivering," he said.

"It's cold in here, go to bed." Only then did Katie become aware Ruth had also come into her room. "I'm sorry to have wakened you," Katie said. Ruth felt the younger woman's forehead, tugged the blankets back into place, and with a small smile, pushed Rick out of the room.

No stranger to nightmares, Katie lay back, eyes wide while she waited for the dregs to evaporate. Once the frightening picture was gone from her mind, she'd be able to sleep again. A tiny worry bored into her chest. She had never before called out, never thrashed, yet tonight she had done both. Why?

* * *

Where Katie had been thrilled to go to work the day before, the new dawn brought apprehension. This differed from her inner turmoil about the farms' financial woes. She could not seem to shake the hard lump buried within her rib cage. It made her feel emotionally strung out, flighty and frail.

"Marlie," she whispered as she drove into town, "where are you?"

As soon as she had a few moments, Katie called the sheriff's office. To her surprise, Sheriff Lewis answered the phone.

"Good morning," said Katie, "I'm looking for Deputy Foster. She told me she'd get me some information I needed about permits on renting out land on the farm." She waited, lips pressed together, hoping he'd offer a tiny scrap of information.

"Sorry, Katie," Lewis said. "You don't want us; you need to talk to the zoning officer." The line immediately went dead.

Katie went back to work no wiser than she had been ten minutes before and spent the rest of the day wrapped in the aching of her heart. She spent her mid-morning coffee break sitting with Rick. She told him about both the reporter stopping in at the feed store and then what she had learned at Marlie's apartment.

"She never told you she planned on leaving?" he asked in surprise. "She didn't tell the sheriff? I thought she liked being a deputy. Taking off like that's going to stop her from getting another job anywhere."

"I know," said Katie, replacing the cap on her thermos.

Rick watched her walk away. Katie didn't have many real friends in Parentville. Thus far, Marlie had been the only one. At noon, he drove over to the town hall. Neither Janice nor Brad could tell Rick why Marlie had left so hurriedly.

* * *

At the supper table, Rick told Katie. "Brad said, he thought something more than finding a few bones on the ridge scared her."

"How come you're taking tomorrow off?" asked Katie. She didn't want to reveal to Rick how badly she felt and changed the subject to one less likely to crush her heart.

"I missed my regular day off when we were shorthanded at the store," he said. "Tomorrow, I'm going to light the furnace. I want to be here while it's burning at first to make sure there aren't any problems."

Ruth watched Katie while Rick explained what could possibly go wrong with the furnace. Katie didn't respond, like she hadn't really listened. Ruth frowned when Katie turned away. Both Ruth and Rick had expected Katie to raise the issue about Rick selling his trailer and using his money to pay expenses at the farm, but Katie had not said a word. Rick watched Katie too, sitting head down over a plate of chicken and mashed potatoes she barely touched.

What now? He wondered.

Finally, Katie realized her two housemates were too quiet. "What?" she asked, looking from one to the other. No one answered. "Okay, so yes, I am a little upset about Marlie leaving. Maybe more than a little. I thought we were friendly enough, so she'd have at least said goodbye." Katie pushed away from the table. "Let's face it. Finding body parts out in the woods, and no word from her, and no one knowing where she is all makes the worst part of my imagination work overtime. Somehow, I believe Geoffrey Ash has a hand in all of this." She stopped, unsure how much to reveal. "He didn't like Marlie, and he was clear about it. Maybe he doesn't like anyone. He's angry. Lashing out at whoever is standing in front of him. Every time he went in the sheriff's office, she was right there. He probably dumped on her and now she's gone."

Katie left the table, moving back through the living room. Other than the cat beds, they had little in the way of furniture. Her footsteps made a slight echo and the big room felt empty, like the space in the center of her chest.

She considered the meager furnishings, seeing it as another failure. The sofa, chair, and lamp table were old and there when she had returned from Illinois. The recliner, television, and its stand had come out of Rick's trailer. Another donation she couldn't pay back. By the door was a small maple table currently stacked with the newspaper and that day's mail. She flipped through the mail morosely, looking for more past-due notices. There were two envelopes for Rick, each envelope with a long yellow sticker covering the original address. The stickers had the farm's address typed in place.

"What's this?" Katie wondered aloud.

Ruth looked over her shoulder. "Oh, those are for forwarding his mail. You know, when you move, you tell the post office, and they send your mail on to you."

"Huh, I didn't know," said Katie.

"Haven't you ever put in a change of address, Katie?" asked Ruth. "Like when you moved back from Illinois?"

"No," said Katie. "I never thought about it because I don't believe I ever received mail I wanted, anyway."

Ruth laughed, and with a pat on Katie's head, went back to her knitting. Katie sat for a while, studying the envelopes. Finally, sure was Ruth focused on the television, Katie wrote a short note to Marlie asking her to call, or at least let Katie know not to worry. Addressing the missive to Marlie's old address, Katie slipped out the kitchen door to the mailbox, lifting the flag with a prayer the postmistress would send the letter on.

Katie still leaned on the mailbox when Rick stepped out the kitchen door, calling her name. She came in through the front.

"Ha," he said, "I thought you were checking those stinking geese."

"They don't stink," declared Ruth, carefully heating kitten formula, "they're just noisy. And they have names. Squeak and Squawk."

Katie rolled her eyes, knowing once Ruth named the geese, she planned on keeping them.

"Phone," Rick said to Katie over Ruth's head. Then he shushed his lady friend ahead of him out of the room in the same manner they moved the geese across the yard.

CHAPTER THIRTY-ONE

"Hello," said Katie.

"Well, it's nice to hear some laughter in your voice," said Tessa.

"Hi, Tessa," said Katie, gripping the phone harder.

"I'm calling to give you a quick update," said Tessa. "Is this a good time?" Before Katie could answer, the reporter started talking. "I got nowhere with the dry-out clinic. They want a warrant, and I couldn't find anyone close by who had any information. As a matter of fact, the locals were pretty protective and ready to run me off on a rail. So, I went back to the frat house and found one of Robby's old buds. Guy's name is Dork. No, that's not right, James Riley."

Katie laughed. "Could it have been Zitty?"

"No, I must have missed that one," said Tessa. "Anyway, this guy told me Robby didn't chase girls as much as they chased him. He remembered one particularly aggressive female who showed up in the early fall. Jimmy says the whole episode got to where she stalked Robby, and a heated discourse ensued."

"Is this guy studying to be a lawyer?" asked Katie.

"Maybe," said Tessa. "Anyway, campus security got involved. There were a couple of screaming fits on the lawn. Robbie's car got vandalized. The problem escalated, and the girl of Robby's choice stopped seeing him. Jimmy couldn't remember her name, but said she had brown hair and came from someplace with cowboys."

"Do they have cowboys in Michigan?" asked Katie. "So, we don't know if the girl of choice might have been Daphne?"

"No," Tessa replied. "But I'm working on both names. The description of the second girl is close to what Daphne looked like. From there, I went to the apartment. I found out Robby drives an older Chevy Vega and likes a good time. While I was rooting around, one of the young ladies I spoke to identified Robby's favorite bar. Lo-and-behold, I found the man himself supporting a bar stool. I think he had a little hinky side business going on. But I can't prove it. I did sit beside him for a short time, casual conversation, but I don't think I'm his type. The guy is crude."

"So, you actually talked to him?" asked Katie, awed at the other woman's bloodhound abilities.

"Yuppers."

"You're sure it's the same guy? Fair, good looking, money to blow, and the lisp."

"Hm," said Tessa. "Now you've got me wondering. I didn't notice a lisp. Maybe this isn't the same guy."

"Maybe he can suppress it," said Katie.

"This guy had been there a while, totally loaded, Katie. You should have heard his mouth. I don't know that he had the wherewithall to be able to suppress anything."

Tessa promised to check further before hanging up.

Damn, Katie thought, replacing the telephone receiver. *I should have asked her how I can track down Marlie.*

It turned out Rick had an idea on that front.

"You know," he said, "the post office and probably the Sheriff will not give you any information about Marlie. However, she took off in the middle of the week, and I'm willing to bet she has a paycheck coming to her. Maybe the town clerk has a forwarding address for her check?"

* * *

"Hi Janice." Katie barely caught the town clerk before the window closed for lunch the next day. "Real quick, Marlie Foster, the deputy? Yeah, the day we found the remains up above my house, she left her jacket on my porch. I'd like to mail it out to her, you know, because it's a nice one. Do you have an address for her?"

"Well," said Janice, moving towards a locked file cabinet. "I have her home address on her file. I don't do her payroll. It comes to us from the county. I just pass the checks out. She left me a different address to use for that."

The clerk unlocked the file cabinet and pulled out a slim binder. After copying down the address, she locked the cabinet before returning to Katie, whose knees jittered in anticipation. Marlie's check would go to a post office box in Williamsberg, Vermont, a town Katie had never heard of. She studied the note before raising her head to ask if Janice were sure of the information. The window, however, had closed.

Back at the feed store, Katie went looking for Cindy.

"You handle all the business here," Katie said. "If you're sending a bill to someone in Charlotte, and they've moved, how long will it take for the people to get your letter?"

"Four or five days," said Cindy. "It might come back a little quicker if the postal service can't forward it."

At Katie's look, Cindy said, "If somebody gives us a bad check, or doesn't pay a bill, I send out a notice. If the bum moved without a forward mail order, the post office stamps it saying they can't forward it and sends it back, so I'll know."

"The bum," whispered Katie, walking away. *But who is the actual bum that made Marlie take off?*

She stopped at Beauregard's General Store for more canned milk. Being after work, locals swamped the village store, making her arrive at home later than she expected.

"There you are." Ruth rushed up to Katie. The older woman's face flush with excitement. "Your friend called."

"Marlie?" Katie's heart jumped.

"No, the newspaper one," said Ruth. "She said to tell you, the fraternity housekeeper said Robbie left on Christmas break the Monday before Thanksgiving. She said you could do the math." Ruth paused. When Katie didn't respond, Ruth said. "You also got mail. And I think you're going to be very happy!"

Ruth danced in place, holding an envelope in each hand. Katie snatched the first one away. The construction company that had contracted to remove gravel from the farm pit during the summer sent a request for additional winter sand they would be removing. Bookkeeping had enclosed payment.

"Holy cow," beamed Katie. "Check it out! L & F is going to take sand out too. This is an advance for half of what they're expecting to take out for the next three months." Grabbing Ruth's hands, she spun them both around.

"What's going on?" asked Rick, coming through the kitchen door from outside with an armful of wood.

The open door offered an escape route for cats frazzled by Katie's antics. Rick dodged to avoid stepping on felines, and Ruth whipped past him, trying to catch the escapees. As she went, she thrust the second envelope in Katie's hand. This one had the town's stamp as a return address. This envelope also included a check, as well as a notice from the Parentville Historical Society informing Katie that she had been awarded $475 of grant money to be used for repairs on the one-room schoolhouse at the end of their road.

"Like I said before," said Katie, "holy cow! We can fix the roof on the school, and I can pay you back for the cordwood."

"That's great, Katie," said Rick, picking up the letter from the contractor. "What's for supper?"

Undeterred, Katie stuck out her tongue at her stuffy friend and happily put together a one-pot meal for their supper. While they ate, Rick remarked that the grant money wouldn't be enough for a roof, but it would do for fixing the windows.

"If we do it ourselves, we might be able to get all the broken panes replaced and have a little money left for paint," he added. Then he took the tin off the fridge where Katie stored the household bills and put it on the table beside the letter from L & F Construction. "These before me."

"You're ruining my good time," Katie sighed.

"Did you happen to notice at all since you've been home, how warm it is in here?" Rick asked, changing the subject, and sat down with a fresh cup of coffee.

Katie stopped midway between the stove and the table, allowing the interior of the house to surround her.

"It is," she said, in awe. Leaving the pot on the table, she went back to the living room where the rug normally covering the four-by-four-foot steel heating grate had been moved. Cats, wise enough not to step on the hot metal, surrounded the edge. Stepping onto the grate, Katie felt the rush of hot air run up her body. Above her, she saw the grates leading to the second floor already open.

"Oh, this," she smiled, "is going to be wonderful."

When warm to the point of over-heated and smelling the melting soles of her work boots, she stepped off the grate. Immediately a shiver ran up her calves, a reminder not all problems get solved on the first try. *No more of that,* she thought, more chilled now than before. She watched Sasha herd the kittens away from the edge. Ruth also kept a close eye on the babies.

"Supper is getting cold," Rick called out.

While Katie had luxuriated over the heat grate, Rick had put their meal on the table.

"Do you know," Katie asked, "where Williamsberg, Vermont, is?"

"Hm," said Rick. Rising, he went outside, returning shortly with a folded road map in hand. With it spread on the table, he traced routes with his finger. "You can't get there from here," he finally said.

"How then?" asked Katie, pushing her plate aside.

"Well, Route 7 to White River Junction, then west to Brattleboro, then north, looks like the quickest way," said Rick. "Then you're stuck traveling over a mess of side roads and switchbacks."

"Couple of hours," said Katie.

"Closer to three and a half," Rick answered.

After he put his plate in the sink and went down the cellar steps to stoke the furnace, Katie folded the map. Williamsberg seemed a long way off. Why would Marlie have gone that far? Behind her, the whir of a portable mixer revved up.

"What are you making, Ruth?" Katie asked.

"Brownies for the fundraiser meeting for the cat clinic," Ruth answered.

"You should mix brownies by hand, Ruth," said Katie, pulling the plug out of the wall socket.

Doctor Veronica invited Katie to participate in the fundraiser, but Katie explained she didn't have enough time. Ruth had stepped forward, willing to take her place. Grace Dean, also a member, would provide a ride for Ruth.

"I'm kind of nervous," said Ruth, spooning batter into a baking pan. "Mrs. Ash sits on the board. She's one of the co-chairmen."

"What?" said Katie. Mouth open, she moved closer.

"Yes." Ruth continued spooning, brownie mix, oblivious to the look passing between Katie and Rick. "Lately she's been sort of, I don't know, odd. Like at the Historical Society meeting we went to."

"I didn't see her there," said Katie.

"But she should have been." Ruth carefully closed the oven door. "Mr. Ash isn't the head of the board, she is."

When Ruth turned around, both Rick and Katie stood directly behind her. Rick to check on the brownies, Katie to hear what Ruth had to say.

"What is wrong with you two?" Ruth asked. "Mrs. Ash is a big philanthropist. She's involved in a lot of committees and boards. Let's face it, you heard how Mr. Ash talked to people. He's not a very sympathetic person if you're trying to raise money, right?"

"Absolutely," agreed Katie.

Chapter Thirty-Two

"Telephone, Katie," said Stan. Her boss took her place at the cash register.

"I'm sorry." Katie sighed. *In my whole life, I never received so many phone calls.*

Stan nodded, his mouth a straight line. Aware this must be something different from an animal control call, which Stan tolerated. Katie hurried into the office.

"This is Katie," she said.

"Hey Katie," said Tessa. "Your friend gave me this number. I didn't realize it would be your job. I can call back this evening."

"No, go ahead," said Katie, chewing on her lip.

"I wanted to let you know I went back to Robby's apartment. I passed the chatty girl from upstairs leaving. She told me Robby left yesterday morning with a suitcase."

"Did she know where he went?" asked Katie.

"No, I asked," said Tessa. "And I asked if it could be a permanent move. She said she didn't think so, he leaves on a regular basis for a few days at a time. Keep your eye open. Maybe he's going to visit his aunt and uncle."

* * *

Katie pulled into her driveway after dark. Rick right behind her.

"We need to go back to Ash's house," said Katie, rushing into the house to grab her barn jacket and stuff a flashlight in the pocket.

"What about supper?" Ruth asked.

"Later," said Katie, tersely.

"We'll take my truck," said Rick. "It's better if we run into snow or mud."

"Oh, dear," cussed Ruth, jumping from foot to foot, pulling on her boots. Both Katie and Rick looked at her.

"Where do you think you're going?" Rick asked.

"If you think for one moment," snapped Ruth, eyes blazing, "I'm going to trust you two not to break into somebody's house, you're out of your minds." She pushed past him. Outside, she climbed into the truck to sit in the middle of the bench seat with her black, vinyl purse held securely in her lap.

"I don't think taking her is a good idea," said Katie.

Rick didn't answer.

They rode in silence along the Parentville/Charlotte Road for a mile or so before Rick reached under the dash and flipped the switch on the CB radio attached there. Pressing the com button on the mike, he said,

"Niner, Niner, this is Ripsaw looking for eyes on Hoover Road or up on Pear Mountain."

"Hey Ripsaw, this is Coppenhagen, I'm in the vicinity, come back."

"'Evening buddy," said Rick aka Ripsaw, "I'm looking for an older light blue Chevy Vega with New York plates. Seen anything resembling?"

"You sure it's got New York tags?" asked Coppenhagen.

Rick looked across at Katie. She nodded in affirmative.

"That's a ten-four," said Rick.

"Bugger blew past me faster than I thought one of those little crap heaps could go," said Coppenhagen.

Ruth snatched the mike away from Rick. "You should watch your mouth," she said into the mike.

"Wha...? Who is this?" said an obviously surprised Coppenhagen, "Is that you, Bird Lady?"

"It is for a fact," gushed Ruth. "We're riding with," she looked at Katie, "Little Miss Piggy."

Katie could only gape.

"You up for a cup of coffee?" asked Coppenhagen. "You and me?"

Rick glowered out the windshield.

"Sorry, good buddy," chirped Ruth. "We're out on business. Maybe next time."

Rick made a move at getting the mike back, but Ruth leaned over Katie, pushing her back in the seat and he couldn't reach.

"Well, your ve-hicle, went by ten minutes ago, headed south on Route 7 with a black Crown Vic in hot pursuit."

"A bear?" Rick shouted toward the mike.

"Nope, a privately owned," said Coppenhagen, signing off.

Rick slid up to a stop sign, barely slowing down before he took a left-hand turn onto Route 7.

"Rick," sputtered Ruth, "you're going to get us killed or arrested."

"CRS," said Katie.

Ruth spun to look at her.

"California rolling stop," Katie explained. When they leveled out, she asked, "What kind of name is Little Miss Piggy?"

Rick laughed.

They sky-rocketed down Route 7, checking back in on the CB for another sighting. Nothing showed up. Finally, Rick rolled to a stop on the side of the road near a T intersection.

"They could have gone anywhere," said Rick.

"And if Robby headed out of town, why would Ash follow him?" Katie asked.

"Follow or chase?" Rick asked, turning the truck around.

They pulled into a little hot dog diner south of the Charlotte village.

"Maybe," said Ruth, squirting an ample amount of mustard on her wiener, "they were going to the airport."

"It's the other way," said Rick.

"Not Boston," said Ruth.

Katie groaned. On the counter in front of her, stood a tiered glass-covered cake plate. The silver stem held the plate high, offering a stack of fig bars, fudge, and brownies.

"Ruth," said Katie, "did you see Mrs. Ash at the meeting this afternoon?"

Ruth nodded, mouth filled with the last bite of hot dog and roll.

"Did she seem to be in a good mood? You know, not confused?"

"She seemed just fine," said Ruth, concentrating on her French fries. "Her friend Jala came with her." After taking a bite, she said, "Jala is going to be sitting in for Mrs. Ash for a little while so we can, you know, keep on schedule."

Katie nodded. She hadn't felt the six-woman committee would be able to collect enough funds for their plan to capture, then neuter, or spay ten feral cats in both Parentville and Charlotte. The women, however, had proved to be quite dedicated. Now that Halloween was over, they would attend Christmas craft fairs in pairs. There, they would collect donations, sell cookies and brownies, and raffle tickets. Grace donated goat cheese, Ruth knitted mittens as fast as she could, but Mrs. Ash had stepped up persuading local businesses to donate goods to their cause.

"So, you won't be going with Mrs. Ash?" Katie asked.

"No, the first weekend, I'll be going with Grace." Ruth licked mustard off her fingers. "Why?"

"I think we should make sure Mrs. Ash gets you all the information you ladies need to make sure this venture works," said Katie.

"What are you talking about?" Ruth asked.

On Ruth's other side, Rick smiled.

* * *

"Okay," Katie said, "stop right here."

They were creeping up Hoover Road with the headlights off. Rick pulled up before the gates to the Ash estate. Much to Katie and Rick's surprise, the heavy gates had been left rolled back, leaving the drive open.

"Huh," said Rick, sitting back and sucking on his teeth.

Jumping out and firmly shutting the door behind herself, Katie told him, "I'll walk from here. Find a place to park where nobody pulling in will see you."

"Wait, Katie," Ruth called, but the young woman had already walked away.

Once inside the double sets of gates, Katie cut across the lower lawn, headed toward the woods, the quickest route to the house. The thin snow cover crunched beneath her boots.

"Hold the phone," she said. "If they have cameras, someone might see me coming from the woods and shoot first. Yeah, or I could get lost in the dark and fall into the duck pond."

Back-tracking to the gravel drive, she looked back the way she had come. The truck had disappeared from sight. Other than the skitter of fallen leaves across the gravel and the wind in the trees, she couldn't hear anything. Songbirds had moved south to a warmer clime. Only the crows were left, but Katie thought they, too, must be banned from the property. Rounding the last curve, she could see a cottontail sitting on alert ahead. Two more steps in its direction, and the small bundle of brown hip-hopped away. The bunny's disappearance alerted foraging deer Katie hadn't yet seen. Their heads came up, eyes alert, watching from afar, large ears flickering and mouths busily chewing up Ash's lawn. There were no vehicles in the circling drive in front of the house, and the stable converted to a garage far out of sight. She had to assume Ash hadn't beaten them back to the house. The doorbell echoed within the house. From her spot on the uppermost step, the echoing bell had a deserted, haunted sound of a death toll.

"Can I help you?" The woman who opened the door wore a dove gray uniform with a crisp half apron.

"My name is Katelyn Took," Katie said. "I came to see Mrs. Ash regarding the cat clinic fundraiser."

The woman looked beyond Katie at the empty driveway.

"I left my car at the gate," Katie smiled. "I hope that's alright. I've been driving for hours and needed to walk off a few of the kinks from sitting so long."

"One moment," said the woman. "I'll check with Mrs. Ash." The door closed.

Katie had been left standing on the doorstep for so long, she decided to have a seat on the granite edge. Just as she moved away from the door, the woman returned with Mrs. Ash flowing along behind, wrapped in a floor-length chiffon robe with deep sleeves and a dark violet print. The garment billowed and ballooned around her as she moved. The lavender leisure outfit beneath clearly visible, rendering the robe more fashion than warmth.

"Hello! Hello!" beamed Mrs. Ash, brushing the woman aside. "Move Jala, let our guest in out of the cold." Mrs. Ash, tall and svelte, appeared every inch a woman born to a more sophisticated society than one found in a small farming community. Her eyes were bright, smile wide, and it took Katie only a moment to realize the look in her eyes screamed lonely. Or bored. Or both.

Mrs. Ash reached out and took Katie by the arm, drawing her inside.

"Tea," she said. "We'll have tea. Jala?"

"Yes, ma'am." Jala gently closed the door, blocking Katie's escape.

"Would you rather sit in the living room, or the lounge?" asked Mrs. Ash. Then immediately answered her own question. "Oh, the lounge, it's so much more comfortable there. And the fire's lit so it will be warmer. Let's, shall we?" She flowed away, tugging Katie along.

"Mrs. Ash," Katie protested. "I'm not really dressed to be wandering around in your house. I, ah, just came from work to pick up the meeting notes. You know, for the cat clinic fundraiser?"

"Yes, Jala told me," Mrs. Ash continued to beam, "but let's have tea first." Then she faltered. "Is that okay?"

Katie looked Mrs. Ash straight in the face. She could see the confusion, the hurt, and the aching loneliness.

"It's been a long day," Katie sighed. "I'd love tea."

"Fabulous," Mrs. Ash smiled again. "JALA?"

"Here, Mrs. Ash." Jala came around the corner lugging a large tray. "Right here. You sit, okay?"

"Isn't she fabulous," said Mrs. Ash. "She's absolutely my brick and mortar."

Jala laid out the tea items, a blush tinting her face, as well as a tiny, prideful smile. She poured for Katie, then Mrs. Ash. After placing a plate of small shortcake cookies between them, she left.

"I thought," said Mrs. Ash, "your aunt took your place on the committee,

CHAPTER THIRTY-TWO

Ms. Took?"

"Katie, please," said Katie. "Yes, Ruth is my good right hand on this project. Unfortunately, tonight she's tied up with a new litter of kittens we just picked up, so I'm doing the running. Did she tell you about the kittens?"

"No, are they adorable?" Mrs. Ash clasped her hands in joy. "And they're all okay, and mama?"

"Orphans," said Katie, sadly. "Ruth is so good at taking care of them. All five."

"Five," gasped Mrs. Ash, dropping her cookie. Jumping up, she ran across the room to a secretariat against the wall, returning with several file folders which she laid on the coffee table.

"Thank you, Mrs. Ash," said Katie, searching for a polite way to ask Mr. Ash's whereabouts.

"Phyllis," she smiled. "I organized the notes and all the other bits according to subject." She spread out the folders, opening each one to show Katie the information inside and how best to read it. Everything looked concise and clear. Having expected Mrs. Ash to be a rambling drunk, Katie gaped, stunned at the layout.

"Holy catfish, Mrs. Ash," she said. "This is an incredible amount of work."

"Nonsense," said Mrs. Ash, sitting back, admiring the spread silently.

"This is a beautiful house," said Katie. "You must love living here. And the grounds are beyond gorgeous. You're living in a piece of paradise."

Mrs. Ash gave a small laugh. The metallic undertone raised Katie's curiosity.

"I bet you can walk for hours out here watching the deer, oh, maybe foxes?" Katie remarked.

"I never go outside," said Mrs. Ash. "I mean, other than to the garage or patio. It's a lovely house, but not what I would have selected." Mrs. Ash faded.

Katie, who had been looking around the room, turned back to her hostess. The dead silence raised the hair on Katie's arms. Both Mrs. Ash's smile and the lights in her eyes were gone. A blank stare had replaced them.

"Mrs. Ash?" said Katie.

"I'm sorry, dear," Mrs. Ash said, shuddering delicately before reshuffling the files. "It's just, well, I'm a little sorry to see my part in this getting ready to finish up. It's kept me busy." She paused. "This has been a difficult time for me."

"I know," said Katie, softly.

Mrs. Ash exhaled before busily stacking the files. "Well, whoever gets these now will be all set," she said. "I believe they won't have a problem continuing on from here."

Katie didn't touch the files. Instead, she leaned back, sipping tea and looking around the room, then nodding back toward the files.

"You know," she said, "you're very good at this."

Mrs. Ash smiled.

"Have you considered staying involved in the project? You know, seeing it to the end? I work. Doctor Veronica is so busy at the animal hospital, and my aunt doesn't drive, so we are continually looking for a ride."

Pinching her lips together, Mrs. Ash looked away.

"And," Katie whispered confidentially, "I bet you know all the right people to hit up for a contribution."

Mrs. Ash had a low chuckling laugh. "You know, I do." Then she sobered. "However, Geoffrey is not pleased with what I'm doing. He made it very clear I shouldn't be involved."

Raising her eyebrows, Katie asked, "He doesn't like cats? He thinks letting the feral cats breed indiscriminately is a good thing. Maybe he doesn't understand after the spay or neuter, we're going to release them to live out their lives in their natural environment."

Mrs. Ash sat upright on the low divan; the hem of the chiffon robe twisted in her fingers. Looking everywhere except at Katie, she said. "Geoffrey doesn't care for cats, or pets in general. I've had some beautiful Cavalier Kin Charles Spaniels," she pointed to small pictures on the table. "He, Geoffrey, believes that if I'm out and about, someone is going to accost me because of all this ugliness regarding Scott." The last sounded like a faint moan.

Katie slid an inch closer, placing her cup and saucier on the coffee table. "Why," she asked, "would he believe that?" She knew this pushed the ticket.

Mrs. Ash's manicured fingers rubbed at her forehead. She seemed to cave in upon herself. Katie opened her mouth to ask if Mrs. Ash needed assistance, when the older woman said, "I didn't do well when Scott disappeared. Geoffrey called the police, the sheriff. I'm afraid I got distraught. Geoffrey gave me some medicine to help me relax, and I gather I must have helped myself to more because two days passed before I came back to my senses."

"Two days?" Katie gasped.

"Yes, I woke up and Jala waited, taking care of me." Mrs. Ash reached out, almost touching Katie. "She's so good. If she left, I'd be beside myself. But that's not the worst of it. One other time, I drove to the sheriff's office looking for Geoffrey. The only people there were the deputies. I lost control and lashed out at the sheriff's people." She gave a dry laugh. "I'm not even sure how I got home."

"Now, it's all rising up again. Perhaps, as Geoffrey says, it's better I stay here. Away from people. I had to drop out of some other committees, too. When this is all straightened out, when things get better, I'll go away. Maybe Europe, somewhere the voices can't find me."

"Voices?" asked Katie through dry lips.

"I hear him talking, Scott, he's angry, so angry." The color had drained from Mrs. Ash's face. Her voice rose, and her eyes darted around the room.

Suddenly, Jala stood beside her.

"You come with me," she said to Mrs. Ash. "We will have a bite of supper, a nice bath, and you'll feel better." She helped her employer to her feet and, without a word to Katie, they left the lounge and climbed the stairway to the second floor.

Katie left as well. This time she walked straight into the woods and, in doing so, through a hedge of Rhododendrons. Pushing the heavy branches apart, she stumbled into a small grotto lit by cold white starlight. A Buddha lorded over an array of toys, stick figures in children's clothing, and faded photographs tacked onto the trees.

"Whoa," she cried, stopping so short she almost toppled over. "Ca-ree-py."

Beyond the wall of trees, circling and moving up toward the house, the sound of a car engine snapped her attention from the grotto. Like a deer, she sped among the oaks, away from danger, mindless of her path as long as she escaped.

Arriving at the road, Katie had no idea how to find Rick. Just as she decided to head down the hill towards the place they'd parked the truck before, a voice hailed her from above.

"KATIE!" Rick and Ruth stepped out of the brush. He waved Katie in his direction. "Ash just pulled in. Did he see you?"

"No," gasped Katie, running for the truck. "Go. Just go."

Chapter Thirty-Three

Sunday morning, Katie opened the door to find Jala in street clothes getting out of a white SAAB. Before Katie could say a word, the geese Rick had released before he and Ruth went to church, rushed out from under the porch. Nonplussed, Jala spread her arms wide and rushed toward the geese, making a loud, harsh noise. The female turned immediately and ran away. The male held his place only long enough to make sure his mate got away. Then he, too, ran. Katie could hear them cackling and hissing from beneath her feet.

"Good move," said Katie.

Jala shrugged but kept walking. Instead of her uniform, she had on beige trousers, a cream-colored silk blouse with an ascot bow, under a high frilled edge collar, and a wool jacket of burnt orange. The colors hi-lighted her olive skin and green eyes. Katie considered Mrs. Ash's companion to be a fine-looking woman.

"What can I do for you?" Apprehension chilled Katie's skin.

"If you have a few minutes, I would like to speak with you about Mrs. Ash," said Jala.

Katie stepped aside, allowing Jala to precede her through the door.

"You're not allergic to cats, are you?" Katie asked. Every window held a feline sunbathing.

"You said you didn't wish to come into Mrs. Ash's home," said Jala, "but you, too, live in a big house."

"It has a history," said Katie. "Originally it was built to be a hotel for the stagecoach company and riders."

"I brought you the files Mrs. Ash wanted you to have. I found them still in the lounge after you left," said Jala. She sat in the single chair before pulling the files out of her large leather handbag. "I wanted her to come with me, but she refused. It took me a long while to find where you live. Many people here would not give me directions."

The evasive testament of people whose small-town concern to protect their neighbors warmed Katie.

"I hate to say it, but you don't look like you're from around here. Even though you don't have an accent," said Katie, "your speech is different."

Jala nodded, "I am not from here, though I have lived in Vermont for almost twenty-five years."

Watching the cats snoozing, she seemed to forget her mission.

"Would you like coffee? Tea?" Katie offered.

"No, as I said, I wish to talk to you about Mrs. Ash. And maybe her son."

Once again, her attention turned to the cats. LG came in from the kitchen, pausing for a quick wash and to scrutinize the unknown person. Silent conversation traveled between the animals; others turned their attention to Jala.

"Have you worked for the Ashes long?" Katie asked, ignoring the cats.

"When I first came here, I worked for Mrs. Daudlin. After she passed away and when the Ashe's came, I stayed. Mrs. Ash needed help with the two boys. It became my job. Over time, I came to be more of a help, to Mrs. Ash." Jala sighed. Turning to face Katie, she said. "Mrs. Ash is not like her sister. Mrs. Daudlin had always been strong, happy. Mrs. Ash is timid, her feelings are easily hurt. Both her husband and son recognized this. Mr. Ash uses it to his benefit. Scott adored his mother, as she loved him. If she asked, he did. Both the boys were like that. It is one of the reasons I don't understand why Robby won't return."

"I have heard," continued Jala, "rumors Mrs. Ash is, um, alcoholic or maybe addicted to pills. It's not so. I know. I am the only person there. No one else is allowed unless Mr. Ash is home. He never lets outsiders near his wife. I used to live in the house. There are rooms on the second level back of the house for live-in staff. However, even though I no longer live on the property, I am there early every day. But I need to be gone by 6:00 P.M. unless he's absent."

"Why?" asked Katie. She thought about the lights on the back of the house she had seen the first time she and Rick had been there.

Jala shrugged again. "Mr. Ash is not my concern. His wife is. I tell you this, the day Scott disappeared, Mrs. Ash took it badly, beyond distraught. Her husband gave her medicine to calm her down. Those were his words, just to calm her. Within minutes, she passed out. I thought she might be allergic, having a bad reaction. I don't know. I thought she might die and stayed with her for two days. I wouldn't leave. The only time I went out of the room was to get food."

LG advanced toward Jala, who held out her fingers.

"She bites," warned Katie.

"One time I came back into Mrs. Ash's bedroom and her husband stood over her. He has his own room and hasn't been in hers for years. He had something in his hand. When he realized I'd come back, he got all red in the face and rushed out. I think he gave her more medicine. I can't prove it. But she had been waking up, trying to talk, and moving around a little. After he left, she had sunk back into that heavy sleep. I did not leave again. Eventually, she woke."

LG stepped close enough to sniff Jala's fingers. Suddenly the cat snapped ahead, lunging toward the extended hand. But Jala moved quicker. She grabbed LG by the scruff and held the cat just off the floor. Katie didn't have time to react before Jala released LG, who ran away. From six feet away, the cat watched the strange woman while calmly washing her front paws.

"I am so sorry," said Katie, getting to her feet to shush the cat away.

"It's okay," Jala smiled. "Now she knows I won't play her game. We had many animals where I grew up. Your cat is not the first one wanting to be the boss." She looked pointedly at Katie. "I know people who are the same. Only by letting them know you are not afraid, are you safe from them tormenting you."

Katie felt captured by Jala's eyes. She nodded slightly, unable to break the contact.

"So," Jala continued, "Mr. Ash has forbidden his wife to leave the house. He did that after she went to the police station looking for information about Scott."

Katie blinked rapidly, clearing away the intense feeling Jala's stare had left.

"Yeah, I heard Mrs. Ash showed up at the sheriff's office," said Katie. She swallowed, wiping the corners of her mouth with her fingers.

"I believe her husband goaded her into that reaction. A while ago, he began giving her vitamins to help make her strong," said Jala. "I think this is again a medicine misrepresented. Her thinking seems to be more confused. She found a note saying Mr. Ash had left to visit the sheriff. The note said he wanted to talk to the authorities and plead for their help. But he didn't think he would be strong enough alone to convince them to help. The note asked for her to back him up."

"Do you think he left it on purpose?" asked Katie. "How could he have known she would go there?"

"I don't know," said Jala, "Sometimes I stand outside her room even when she is alone, and always when he is there. I worry about what happens when I leave."

"That's why you showed up so quickly the day I visited," said Katie.

Jala inclined her head. "Before? When she went to the sheriff's office? I heard her husband say they should go together, a united front. I think he believed she would act on the memory of that conversation with a small amount of prompting."

"Hence the note?"

"Exactly," Jala agreed.

"What kind of vitamins is he giving her? We had an issue with Ruth because of a mistake with her medicine," said Katie.

"I don't know," said Jala. "He doesn't give them to me or put them with her other medicines. I'm concerned he is telling me they are one thing, when they are actually something much different. And perhaps, something Mrs. Ash should not be having."

While Katie considered her words, Kole stretched and jumped down from the furthest window sill. Kole, a deep, brushed black cat, with ocher eyes, and a thick-boned body, stretched longer than most of the other cats. He had double paws in front and the hunched shoulder walk of a predatory animal. He advanced toward Jala, then sat. His long pink tongue making a surprising splash as it flickered out to wash his face. He had never been a threat, but after LG's behavior, Katie watched him closely.

Sticking out his nose, he sniffed, advanced a step, and sniffed again. Satisfied with the knowledge he had acquired; he went back to the windowsill. Jala didn't pay him any attention and gathered her bag to leave. Katie held out her hand. She had other questions. Jala sat back down.

"Mrs. Ash said she heard voices," said Katie. "Is it a possible side effect from the vitamins?"

Jala looked toward the windowsill where Kole lay in the sun. "In the last few weeks, maybe two months, she has started walking around within the house after I leave." She looked directly at Katie. "A few times I have found her in the morning somewhere other than in her room. These are the nights she speaks of the voices. I worry she will walk outside, lost and unfound."

Katie shuddered at the implication of Jala's words.

"You, said you used to live in the house? On the back, like the second story?"

"Yes," said Jala.

"How do you get up there?"

"Just beyond the kitchen and laundry doors at the end of the hall is a door leading to the staircase," explained Jala.

"Who lives up there now?" asked Katie.

Jala blinked. "No one," she said. "Since I've moved out, Mr. Ash keeps the door locked so Mrs. Ash can't get up there and get lost."

Katie sat back on the sofa. "Ah-huh," she said. "And I bet you don't have keys?"

Jala looked at Katie suspiciously. Taking the other woman's silence as an affirmative answer, Katie considered her memory. Her eyes roved around the room, returning to Jala.

"One last question," said Katie. "Does Mrs. Ash have any peculiar religious beliefs? You know, that might make her create some kind of off-beat temple?"

She felt foolish asking, but the grotto still bugged her.

"No," said Jala, "we attend the United Methodist church in Shelburne."

"And she never walks outside, even maybe in the copse between the house and the road?" asked Katie.

"Where the summer house used to be?" asked Jala. "No. Even when the boys burned it down, playing with matches, she wouldn't go with Mr. Ash to survey the damage."

* * *

Ruth, returning from the Dean farm, joined Katie at the door as Jala drove away. "Did you offer her tea?" she asked.

"Of course, I did," said Katie. After the SAAB pulled out onto the dirt road, she followed Ruth into the kitchen, where the older woman spread the open files on the table and the counter.

"Ruth, before I left, Gram didn't have this small table. There used to be a wide board farmer's table here. Maybe six feet long, old, and none of the chairs matched. Did you guys burn that too?"

"Don't be foolish, Katie." Ruth barely looked up from the file in her hand. "It's upstairs in the back bedroom with all the rest of the things Irma took out of the house."

"The room with no doorknob?" Katie's jaw fell.

Ruth looked up at the surprise in Katie's voice. "Haven't you looked in there?" she asked.

"I have never in my life been in there," said Katie. "To be honest, it's become invisible to me."

Ruth took a screwdriver out of the junk drawer and said, "Well, let's go check it out."

Inserting the screwdriver into the hole left by the missing knob, Ruth gave a twist and the door creaked opened. Katie stood in the hall with her bottom jaw almost on her chest. The room, as large as her grandmother's bedroom, had furniture, wooden boxes, and way in the back, the top curve of a spinning wheel crammed up to the rafters.

"Ruth," she croaked, "when I spent all that time going through the junk Gram left, why didn't you mention this?"

Ruth pouted. "You said you wanted all of Irma's papers. That's what we dug out. You lived here longer than I have. How could I know it would be a surprise?" Turning with a huff, Ruth stomped down the stairs.

"Ruth," Katie called out as a tail disappeared behind a tall dresser, "there's a cat in there."

"Leave the doors open. It'll come out at supper," Ruth called back.

From where she stood, Katie could see items she recognized, including the old kitchen table leaning against the wall. Its location and her desire to move it created another problem. Taking one more look, she considered the possibility asking about the table had been a mistake.

Chapter Thirty-Four

Katie, Ruth, and Rick shared Sunday dinner with two of Rick's friends, Philip and George, who had been on the roof cleaning the chimney. After eating, Katie went down to visit Bonnie. The pig woofed excitedly to see Katie but wiggled all over when given the leftover biscuits. Katie stopped to check on how boxing in a tractor work area in the barn progressed. The men also had a pot-bellied wood stove Rick found at the dump. While Katie watched, they discussed the best place for the stove.

"If we can get it set up to heat this smaller area, it will be warm enough to work on the tractor," Rick explained. "If we put it on the back side of the barn, smoke won't blow toward the house."

Katie nodded and left. She was antsy, unable to sit still, and unsure why. She went by the chicken coop. All the fowl had been released for the few warm hours in the middle of the day. Circling the place where the geese pecked at the frozen ground, Katie climbed the steps and entered the house through the front door. The telephone rang. Ruth appeared to be elsewhere. Katie ran across the living room, skidding to a stop as she came around the corner and found Ruth standing directly in front of the wall-mounted unit, staring.

"Ruth," exclaimed Katie, exasperated at the older woman's behavior.

Ruth continued to stare, making no effort to reach out as the shrilling began anew. Katie yanked the receiver off the hook inches from Ruth's face.

"Hello?" said Katie.

"Is this Katie?" The voice, masculine and muffled.

"Yes, this is Katie."

Ruth's eyes opened in surprise.

"I only have a minute." The voice had a juvenile, whiny timbre. "I need to talk to you. Soon. There's something you need to know about the dead lady."

"Who is this?" Katie demanded.

"Can you meet me at the old high school in Charlotte at seven tonight?" asked the voice. "I can get there. I, oh, oh, I gotta go."

The phone went dead.

"Hello?" said Katie.

No one answered. She returned the receiver to the chrome hanger before turning to Ruth.

"Who talked to you?" asked Ruth. "Every time I've answered this afternoon, no one spoke."

"Huh." Katie looked at the phone again.

"Did they tell you what they want?" Ruth asked again.

"Hm? Oh, it's just a bill collector reminding me to get my payment in on time," said Katie. A shiver of unease ran up her torso and down to her fingertips.

"Really?" Ruth looked even more surprised.

Before Ruth could ask anything further, Katie walked away, considering what the caller had said.

Why would a kid call me? She considered, then paused for a step. *No, not a kid, had to be a teenager.*

She stood in the middle of the room. Finally, she gave herself a mental shake. The idea of driving over to Charlotte because of an anonymous phone call was ludicrous.

* * *

At 6:45 P.M., she slowly approached the bottom of the entrance staircase outside the high school. A blustering wind skittered leaves across degrading asphalt through the dark. The building had been abandoned long enough to have taken on the derelict and shabby countenance of an old and broken hobo. The last street light on the short Main Street line shone several hundred feet outside the edge of the driveway. Only a feeble glow lit the space closest to the road.

"Idiot," muttered Katie, cursing herself for having driven over on this fool's errand, and not having told Rick where she intended to go.

There was a rustling sound behind her, different from the whisper of the wind. She swung around and immediately, a flashlight held inches away from her face snapped on, blinding her. Katie's arm flew up attempting to block the light. She still could not make out who stood in front of her.

"Katie?"

A definite adult male, not some high school youth, she thought. Goose flesh popped out along the outer ridge of Katie's cheeks. Before she could step back, a fist swung out, catching her flush in the mouth. She stumbled backwards, almost falling. Just as she got her feet under her, the fist struck again, this time deep in her gut, knocking the air out of her. Katie folded over, dropping to her knees. The next hit made solid contact high on her cheekbone. This time she fell over, slamming against the truck's running board. She coughed, trying to draw in a breath.

"This is your only warning," hissed the voice warm against her ear.

The rustling repeated before fading away. Then all she could hear was the wind soughing through dry leaves. Katie willed herself to move, but her body refused. Somewhere a dog barked. A sob broke free. The noise of her own making terrified her. With a heave, she got to her feet heavily dependent on the truck. Once in the cab, she locked the doors before collapsing across the seat. Her heart jumped out of control and her breathing caught as she sobbed. Tears leaked down the side of her face, creating a puddle on the vinyl seat beneath her cheek.

* * *

"Katie," Rick called out as the door swung open. "You forgot to shut the headlights off."

He looked up to see her hanging onto the doorjamb, blood from her split cheek, a dark stain on her chin, and the neck of her thermal shirt. Surging to his feet, he crossed the space in long strides. Startled by his actions, Ruth looked up unable to see Katie until Rick stood by the young woman's side, wrapping his arms around her.

"KATIE!" Ruth screamed.

Katie's knees gave. Only Rick's arms stopped her from collapsing. He half dragged; half carried her to the sofa.

"Get some warm water, a cloth," Rick ordered Ruth.

She darted away, shooing cats as she went. Back and forth to the kitchen and bathroom getting a basin, more cloths, ice, and finally a first aid kit.

While Ruth ran for what he asked for, Rick questioned Katie.

"Were you in an accident?" he asked. "Are you hurt somewhere else?"

Katie shook her head, trying to push him away. When he finally understood she wanted him to stop, she told him what had happened.

"You went alone?" he asked, his tone sharp and unbelieving. "In the dark, not knowing who waited out there? Are you foolish?"

"No," she groaned, one hand holding a cloth filled with ice to her lip, another to her eye. "I'm an idiot."

"I'm calling the sheriff," he said.

"No," said Katie. "He won't be able to do anything other than arrest the night and the wind. I didn't see anybody or a car. There wasn't anyone around, so no witness. And– " she added, miserably, "what is Lewis going to do to me when he finds out I've got my big nose stuck in his business again?"

"Oh, Katie." Ruth stood near Katie's feet, wringing her hands.

Katie fought to sit up. Her guts reminded her they had taken a hit too. Nausea rose.

"I think I'm going to be sick," she whispered.

Ruth pushed the basin closer.

"Lay down," said Rick. "Just stretch out and try to relax, okay?"

He adjusted the cloth on her forehead before shooing Ruth away. Ruth went only as far as the recliner, sitting and pulling an Afghan over her lap. Almost immediately the mewling kittens were crawling up the knitted wool. Rick brought a chair from the kitchen. Positioning it next to Katie, he sat silently.

Katie wanted to tell them to go away and leave her alone, but that, like the wish to be lying in her own bed, proved beyond her abilities.

"I'm so stupid," she muttered, just before she fell asleep.

Rick shook her knee. "Wake up," he said.

"Need to sleep," she slurred.

"No," he demanded louder. "Wake up. You can't sleep. If you have a concussion, you could die."

Ruth pulled the Afghan and kittens closer with icy fingers. Tears fell silently down her face.

For two hours, Rick kept Katie awake. When her voice cleared and the nausea had passed, he finally allowed her to doze off. Across the room, Ruth snored lightly, the Afghan covered with kittens and cats. LG alone lay with Katie. Rick brought blankets from upstairs, covering the women and leaving one for himself on the low chair. Only then did he realize the headlights on the truck still glowed dimly in the dark.

"Well," he said, locking the door on his way back inside, "that's not going to start in the morning." With the furnace stoked and only the kitchen light offering illumination, the old man settled in the low chair, hopeful for a few hours of rest.

Chapter Thirty-Five

True to Rick's prediction, the next morning the truck wouldn't start, barely offering a small croaking growl. Katie and Rick rode to work together in his truck. Both were sleepy-eyed and a little cross. Rick, because Katie had taken such a risk without saying anything to him. And Katie, because no one would miss the black eye and swollen lip she now sported.

Just before Katie went to lunch, a woman's voice spoke beside her.

"What happened to you?" Surprise evident in Janice's voice.

"Foraging raccoon and black ice." Katie had taken to using this same story to any who asked, and all that gawked. She tried to smile, but the painful tug on her lip stopped her cold.

"Yeah, well, you might want to consider a different line of work," said Janice. At Katie's nod, she continued. "I came over to tell you if you haven't mailed Marlie's jacket, I've got a different address for her."

"What?" Katie frowned.

"Yeah, apparently the Williamsberg address is her grandmother's. Marlie is working in Rutland at the glove factory, or maybe some store. I can't remember what her grandmother said when she called this morning." Janice passed Katie a slip of paper while eyeing the bruising. "There's a lot of ice out there," she said, nodding toward the parking lot, "eat soup. It won't hurt as much."

Eyes on the slip of paper in her hand, Katie barely managed to wave goodbye. Rick walked by, headed for Stan's office with the tally reports for the weekend.

"Check this out, Rick," called Katie. She showed him the note with its physical address.

"Great," said Rick. "Is there a telephone number?"

"No," Crestfallen, Katie looked at the note again, then brightened. "But this time I have an address, maybe I can get one."

Slipping into Stan's office when her boss stepped out, she dialed 555-1212 for directory assistance.

"City and State," the operator said.

"Rutland, Vermont," said Katie. "Marlie Foster at 14C Hatchet Street."

"I have a new listing for M. Foster at 14C Hatchet Street," said the operator, "Please hold for your listing."

Katie grabbed a pencil off Stan's desk. The operator had barely finished when Katie broke the connection, the telephone number scribbled across the scrap of paper. She dialed 1, then stopped. Not only should she have been on the floor waiting on customers, but this wasn't her telephone and she'd be calling long distance. Returning to the cash register area, she hustled customers along, smiling but no longer interested in chit-chat. She wanted the day to be over, to be home and able to make the call that might, just might, ease her pain.

"Hello, Ms. Took," said Colleen Johnston. "Have you taken up boxing?" The Montpelier Sentinel reporter, Katie had previously thrown off her front porch, had returned and stood in front of her register. The reed-thin woman looked exactly as Katie remembered her, all teeth.

This time Katie bared hers, a smile that would have frightened small children.

"This register is closed," said Katie, turning the lock key and walking away.

She only went as far as the rack filled with new barn coats. She could see Johnston but stayed out of sight herself. The line behind Johnston began grumbling, and the woman, holding her head high, stalked out the front door. Katie rushed back to her place.

"What's that all about?" Arthur Fortin asked.

"Sorry," Katie whispered, "bit of nasty indigestion."

They both had a giggle as Katie rang him up.

"Did you know who the woman you were talking to is, Katie?" asked the next customer, Charlene Garland, the diminutive Historical Society treasurer.

"Vaguely," said Katie, "she's been giving me grief about the mess on Eagle Drop Ridge."

"Hm," frowned Charlene.

Katie snapped open a paper bag for Charlene's purchases.

"Why?" she asked.

"She came into the Historical Society Museum," said Charlene. "Asking questions, touching stuff, and being all snooty and nasty."

"Really?" Katie paused.

"Yeah, but she's not as bad as the guy from a couple of days before." Charlene added a can of bee balm to her purchases.

"What guy?" asked Katie, trying to sound as though the news was of no importance.

"Somebody Riffle," said Charlene, "wearing a suit, looking for maps on boundary lines. I sent him to the zoning office." Hefting her bag, she said goodbye and moved away.

Katie totally forgot the questions she had regarding the disbursement of the grant money. Her eyes roved over the people in the store. The crowd had thinned, and she could see most of the remaining people. She didn't see Johnston, or Riffle, or the man who shadowed him. She also didn't see any way of ending the investigation on the two sets of remains. Throughout the afternoon, Katie worked with one eye on the entrance, ready to run if Riffle or Johnston entered.

The day's mail lay on the small table when Katie returned home. The letter she had mailed to Marlie at the Williamsberg address on top with a yellow sticker stamped RETURN TO SENDER/NO FORWARDING ORDER ON FILE. Katie's hopes fell, then soared anew. It didn't matter that Marlie hadn't gotten the letter. Now Katie had an address and a telephone number. Uncaring what the other correspondence might be, she placed it all on top of the refrigerator.

Later, while Ruth cleaned up from supper, Katie started making telephone calls. Her first call to Corinne Cox. Katie wanted to know if the forensics team had discovered anything new.

"There isn't much," Corinne admitted. "You heard the female victim suffered a broken neck, right?"

"No, I hadn't. Wouldn't that have been evident at the site?" asked Katie.

"Animal perdation," said Corinne. "It took us a while to rebuild bones that were broken apart, and reassemble the skeletal structure. The information went out to the police working the case."

"The sheriff or the state police?" Katie asked.

"I don't know," said Corinne, "that's not my part of the job."

Katie didn't feel slighted, she wasn't on the list of people who needed to know. Next, she called Tessa, who reported not having seen hide nor hair of Robby.

"But," Tessa said. "Get this, the apartment is empty."

"What?" Katie's jaw dropped.

"Yup, just found out this afternoon," Tessa explained. "The chatty girl didn't know, but the super told me a moving company came in with a signed release dated the day before Robby left the last time. Their instructions were to show up yesterday, pack and remove everything to be held in cold storage until further notice."

"How can that be?" Katie asked.

"I went down to Grover Movers," said Tessa, "and told them the schmuck owed me money. All the guys there would tell me is Robby Daudlin came in, filled out the paperwork, paid two months' storage fees, and left. I specifically asked if they knew who they were talking to. The guy in charge told me Robby provided identification."

"Now what?" Katie asked.

"Well, you're not going to find him using the telephone," said Tessa, "because the number he provided the movers has been shut off, probably from the apartment. Your only hope is for him to show up there."

"Okay," said Katie, "one more question. You said you knew the girl's mother."

"Yes," said Tessa.

"Do you know if either she or the police had information they didn't pass on to the public?"

"What kind of information?" asked Tessa, interest in her voice.

Katie paused for a moment before saying, "Something that wouldn't degrade over time outside, like jewelry."

"Katie," said Tessa, slowly, "what are you asking me?"

"I can't tell you," said Katie.

"Sandra Carter said she could positively identify only one thing missing from her daughter's belongings," said Tessa. "A silver charm bracelet Daphne had gotten at her high school graduation. She said Daphne never took it off, which meant Daphne had to be wearing it."

Katie waited.

"It had several graduation reminder charms attached," said Tessa. Both women were silent but thinking about the same thing. "Katie, do you know where the bracelet is?"

"I can't answer that Tessa," said Katie. "I can't put you in a position where you have to make a choice that might prevent further investigation."

"I trust you," said Tessa. "And hope you will eventually be more forthcoming. But I have to say, I don't like it at all."

Katie leaned her head against the telephone receiver hanging in its silver cradle. The pain emanating from her eye and lip spread to her head. She looked up to find Ruth, dressed in her coat, watching her.

"What?" Katie asked.

"I got the kittens all fed and Rick is going to watch them while we're at the knitting club meeting," said Ruth. "We're going to be late."

Chapter Thirty-Six

On the ride into town, Ruth explained Rick had told her to go back to the knitting club and collect the gossip going around about the bone folks and Geoffrey Ash.

"I told him what he wants me to do is rude," huffed Ruth. "I'll knit; you can gossip."

"I'm not staying!" said Katie. "I don't even knit."

From across the seat, Katie could see Ruth watching her in the glow of the dash lights.

"Well, that's just a nice kettle of fish, isn't it?" snapped Ruth.

Rarely did Ruth come across as out of sorts. Right now, Katie didn't want to deal with her, but they were already moving up Main Street and almost to the library. Once in the parking lot, with Ruth staring out the window on her side of the truck, Katie spoke.

"Look, Ruth," she said softly. "I know you don't like this, and truly, I am sorry. But it's a little late now for me to back up. Rick isn't asking you to spy on your friends, or even to ask questions. It would be better if you didn't. You shouldn't be connected to what I'm trying to figure out. All we need to know is if somebody else is talking, what they're saying. You know, like all those War World Two spy novels you read? You can be the lovely village maiden serving beer and biscuits and hearing the invading soldiers running off at the mouth when they get drunk."

Ruth giggled. "Maiden?"

Katie grinned back. "Would you rather be the floozy?"

"Heavens, no," said Ruth, opening the truck door.

Because the town, did not offer a diner to wait in, Katie decided to step inside and peruse the bookshelves. After Ruth got settled with her friends, Katie stopped in front of a tall vintage teacher's desk. A display of booklets relevant to Parentville was spread on the desktop. Katie fingered one and jumped when Charlene, who doubled also as the librarian, spoke from the other side of the desk.

"We have snacks," said Charlene. "You can help yourself."

"Thanks." Katie smiled. "I just saw these pamphlets. They're pretty cool."

"You've never seen these before?" asked Charlene. "The historical society asked older residents years ago to help document the original village because things were changing so fast."

She reached past Katie, selecting one pamphlet.

"A lot of the older residents came forward with tidbits we used to create village memories. Some of them knew a lot about specific things. You know, the town hall, the old high school, the creamery, all kinds of stuff."

"This one," said Charlene, "is one of the two your grandmother wrote."

"My grandmother wrote a book?" Katie's jaw dropped.

"It's not really a book," Charlene smiled. "And yes, she wrote two. They were your grandfather's memories and words, but Irma set them down. This one is about the schoolhouse, the other one is about the history of the stagecoach house."

Charlene fished through the pile until she found the second pamphlet. While the librarian returned to the knitters, Katie sat at the reading table. As had happened too many times for her comfort, her chest tightened and her breathing felt harsh.

The glossy cover identified the town, the structure written about, and gave credit to the memories of Fred Moore as recorded by Irma Roser Moore. Katie sucked in her lower lip and opened the pamphlet.

An hour later, the knitters meeting had finished, and Katie had read through both pamphlets twice.

"Are you ready?" Ruth asked.

Sadly, Katie replaced the pamphlets back on the tall desk.

"Yes," she said.

"Hold on a second, Katie," called Charlene, disappearing into the stacks. The small woman returned a few minutes later.

"Here these are for you," she smiled.

Katie looked at the desk where a notice asked for a donation for copies. She reached into her pocket.

"No," said Charlene. "Those are yours. They were supposed to go to Irma."

Cocking her head, Katie considered the other woman. Ruth had wandered off to the side, saying goodbye to her friends.

"I think," said Katie, "you might be misrepresenting this."

"Nope," said Charlene, pulling on her coat and shooing everyone toward the door. "But if you lose them or mess 'em up, you have to pay for a second copy."

Katie drove home with the pamphlets on the seat beside her, mind elsewhere as Ruth chattered on.

* * *

Well past 8:00 P.M. with Ruth and Rick settled in front of the television while Mork and Mindy ran amok. Katie dialed the phone, crushing the small piece of paper in her hand while many miles away, a different phone rang. Eight times, nine, ten, no answer. Katie hung up. Leaning against the wall, she considered her next move.

"Rick," she called out, "how long would it take to drive to Rutland?"

Chapter Thirty-Seven

When her repeated calls had gone unanswered, Katie settled at the kitchen table, pretending to read the paper. The telephone rang, startling her. Frowning, she reached out to snatch the receiver from its cradle.

I don't know, she thought, *if the telephone is a friend or a foe.*

"Am I calling too late?" Marcie Sly asked. "Dan is out on a fire call, and I just got the kids down."

"No," said Katie, "this is good. What's up?"

"After you left the other day," said Marcie, "I started thinking about what you were asking. You know, about Scott and Robby? And well, around here, among our friends, there's been some gossip. This one says this, someone else says something different. But if you put it all together, it doesn't make any sense."

"And?" Katie cut in.

"Well," Marcie didn't sound offended or ruffled, "the last time we all saw Robby, he came over a few days after Thanksgiving. He stayed at the house on Pear Mountain where the Ash's live. Remember we told you it's actually his family's home? Anyway, we saw him several times over a few days. He called, so excited he lit up the entire world. His girlfriend had decided to come for a visit. He wanted us all to meet her."

"Wait!" Katie cut Marcie off again. "Do you remember exactly when the girlfriend arrived?"

"As near as I can recall, she had a few days off around Christmas and showed up then," said Marcie. "But that's not all. Scott lives less than an hour away from here in Essex. His mother wanted him to come home and stay over the holidays, which he did."

"One afternoon a bunch of those guys went out on the snow-machines. We don't own a sled, so Dan used one of the Ash's. Dan told me at one point they went up the mountain onto Eagle Drop Ridge. He said they stayed on the old road, but they were close to where you guys found those old bones. Which is a disgusting thought. Anyway, Dan said Scott and Robby got along fine together. Two weeks later, after the girlfriend arrived, they went for another ride. I guess Robby said she showed up exhausted from working long hours before the holiday. Anyway, she didn't go with them. Dan said the guys weren't right, there seemed to be some awkward tension between Scott and Robby. They had been out for a while when Scott made an off-color remark about the girlfriend. Robby got mad and left the group."

"Then what happened?" Katie clutched the telephone receiver so hard her fingers ached.

"That's all we know," said Marcie. "I'm sorry, I thought I'd make sure you knew the truth in case you're hearing all the other gossip."

"Did the police ever talk to Dan, or maybe one of the other guys?"

"I don't think so," said Marcie, "not Dan anyway. Oh, and when Ash called early in the morning looking for Scott, he said to tell him to come back home. The entire conversation was weird. He didn't ask if Scott had been here the night before or spent the night. I don't know why Ash would have called here looking for Scott, anyway. To be honest, we weren't his great friends."

Sounds like Ash made calls in case the police checked, thought Katie. *Like maybe he wanted people to say he was all concerned and calling around in case they found Scott stoned and holed up somewhere. Bet daddy didn't want folks to know his boy was pushing.* Katie's thoughts swung to everything she'd heard so far about Scott being a party boy. In the distance, she vaguely heard Marcie speaking.

"What?" Katie asked. "Say that again."

"I said, Dan's back, I have to go," said Marcie. A door closed behind her.

"One more thing," said Katie. "Why did Dan ride with Scott instead of

Robby?"

"On the same sled?" Marcie laughed. "Don't be silly. Ash has three sleds, one for each of them. Bye."

"But," said Katie to herself as she walked upstairs after Marcie's call, "Marlie said they only found one sled at Ash's house when she and the sheriff arrived. I wish I could ask her, if she was sure. I mean, maybe it was buried under the snow, or in the garage, right?"

* * *

Even with the addition of the wood furnace blowing heat through the living room and the open floor vents to the second floor, her bedroom stayed chilly. Katie snuggled under the covers, waiting for her multi-layered cotton cocoon to get warm. LG nosed around looking for a place she, too, could get among the covers.

"So, we know," the young woman told the cat, "one snow-machine is parked in the yard, and the second one on top of Scott's body in the bog. If Dan had been riding a third machine, where is it?" LG had made it under the quilt and stretched her long body out beside Katie's, her warmth already spreading. "I know they have to be registered. How am I going to find out about another machine without Marlie to help?"

LG reached out, poking a sharp claw into Katie's side, a subtle hint to stop wiggling around and go to sleep.

Chapter Thirty-Eight

Katie walked into the sheriff's office early the next morning. An unknown man wearing a sheriff's department uniform and heavy glasses sat at Marlie's desk. Fortunately, Brad worked at the second desk there.

"Hi Brad," said Katie, tearing her eyes away from the bespectacled deputy. "Is Sheriff Lewis around?"

"He's over in the town hall," said Brad. "Want me to call him?"

"Sure," said Katie. "I'll wait in his office."

Though Brad hadn't indicated she should step inside the sheriff's private domain, as soon as he went through the connecting door, she did. The new deputy watched her go, never saying a word. Katie didn't turn around, but knew the man kept an eye on her until Lewis returned.

Sheriff Lewis and Katie had experienced a rough patch when she'd first returned to town, and it hadn't smoothed out yet. They circled each other like two wary adversaries. If there were any other choice of a place to go for help, Katie would have gone there first. Taking the initiative, Katie closed the office door. She began speaking even as Lewis opened his mouth.

"I'm sure you've had a conversation with Detective Riffle," she said.

From what she had experienced of Riffle's attitude; Katie expected Lewis' interaction with the detective had also gone badly. She had taken a chance and received her reward when Lewis's face tightened up.

"And even though this is your jurisdiction, and you're probably higher on the command chain, he told you to back down." She waited, still watching the sheriff closely.

Lewis' eyelid's lowered to half-mast. A muscle twitched in his jaw.

"Well," she continued, "in case you didn't hear, he pretty much did the same thing to me. It doesn't matter I own the property, or I stumbled on the remains, or anything else I can think of. Riffle ordered me off." She spread her hands, palm side up, in front of her. "He even got me thrown off the job for a while. I can't afford to not be working, and you know it."

"So, what is it you want, Katelyn?" Lewis asked.

"People are talking. A lot," she said. "Right now, there is all kinds of gossip swirling around. People stop me on the street or call my house. Some are scared there might be some roving sicko. Others are just sticking their noses in."

Lewis cocked a hip, his impatience showing.

"Okay, this is the deal," said Katie. "I want to know how many snow-machines, or snow-sleds, Ash has registered. Either to him, or Scott, or Robby. Maybe even Mrs. Ash."

"Why is that?" Lewis took a half-step closer.

"Because you found one at the house, and one in the bog, and according to Scott's friends, he had another one he loaned out to his buddies." Katie didn't move. "I want to know where it is because I believe somehow that machine is going to give up a lot of information."

"How do you know what we found at the house?" Lewis asked.

Katie blinked.

"The ah, Fish and Game guy stopped by. Wanted to know if I'd rehab wild animals." She tried not to blush. "I can't do it. I'm not trained and qualified. But we were talking about the mess on the ridge. Like I said, everybody wants to know."

Lewis turned away. Katie's eyes rolled back, and her shoulders sagged. As soon as Lewis moved again, she straightened up.

"And you're sure about this third snow-machine?" asked Lewis. "How's that?"

"A couple of Scott's buddies were talking about how they all used to go out together," Katie explained. "Not all of them have sleds, but Scott had an extra one they used. I think one of them might have called it a super horse.

I have no idea what it means." She bit her lip. If Lewis didn't buy her story, she would be up to her neck in trouble.

"Which guy?" Lewis asked.

"You know, I never knew any of these guys," Katie swallowed. "I don't know one from the other. They were all hanging around at the feed store, yapping about it. I missed most of the conversation because, ta-da, Stan, made me get back to work. But what I heard made me curious. I just want to know if a third sled exists." Lewis opened his mouth, but Katie already had her hand on the doorknob. "I have to get to work." She reached out, twisting the knob to open the door. "If you find out, and it's okay with Riffle, can you let me know?"

She hustled out of the sheriff's office, knowing Lewis wouldn't breathe a word to Riffle. She also hoped the ruse would slide Lewis a little closer to her side.

Katie's chance paid off when Lewis walked into the feed store an hour later. Nodding to her, he stood to the side until there were no customers in front of the register.

"You were right," said Lewis. "There were three. The one that's missing is registered to Robby Daudlin." Lewis hooked his thumbs in his gun belt. "Now tell me about these friends."

Katie ticked off some first names, keeping Daniel's way down the list. When Lewis pressured her for the surnames, she told him she had barely been interested enough to remember the first names.

"Okay," Lewis said. "If you remember, or better yet, the next time they come in and you see them, call me."

Katie nodded in agreement and Lewis left.

"What's up?" Stan had stepped up silently behind her. "You and Lewis aren't usually so cordial."

Katie jumped slightly at Stan's sudden appearance. "He's mad at Detective Riffle. I think Lewis believes Riffle is trespassing on his turf, and he's running his own independent investigation."

"Well, don't get too cozy," said Stan, "because he might get a call that's going to put you back on the top of the crap heap."

CHAPTER THIRTY-EIGHT

"How's that?" Katie looked at Stan.

"Geoffrey Ash called. He's been trying to talk to you since day one and you keep blowing him off. He wanted to warn me you might be more guilty than you're letting on." Stan looked around the store. "He also said you showed up in Charlotte and were disrespectful and rude."

Katie gaped. "That's not what happened."

Cindy walked up.

Stan shrugged. "Can I offer you a piece of advice? Make an appointment to talk to Ash. Not out in public, but not at his home either. Make sure there's a third person to mediate the meeting. It'll keep him from spreading rumors or getting out of control. When I have an issue with a particularly touchy employee, that's how I handle it, by taking them to neutral ground with someone there as anger management."

"I think it's an awesome idea," said Cindy. "Call Ash," she told Katie, "tell him to meet you here at five. The two of you and Stan can use his office."

Katie and Stan watched open-mouthed as Cindy walked away. Stan groaned.

"Go ahead," he said. "She's probably right on the money."

At noon while she was on her lunch break, Katie called Ash's office in Charlotte. Ash himself answered the phone and accepted Katie's invitation.

Just before the feed store doors locked for the evening, Ash arrived. Stan showed him into the office before taking a seat behind his desk. Ash's eyebrows rose, but Katie had considered he might question Stan's involvement and prepared for an argument.

"I'm sorry," she said innocently, "didn't I mention Stan would join us? Yeah, I'm having a rough time and he's like a father to me."

Ash looked from one to the other. Stan studied his fingernails.

Whatever Ash's original plan had been, he merely spoke of his need to know what transpired on the ridge. Katie walked him through the morning she and, as she referred to Marlie, a deputy had been on top.

"The next morning," Katie explained, "the forensic people were there. I took them up top to where the remains were. Once we got there, Sheriff Lewis wouldn't let me near enough to hear or see anything. I was on the other side of the clearing when one of them found the second site."

"Then you took them there?" asked Ash.

"No sir," said Katie. "Lewis wouldn't even let me into the bog. I didn't see anything."

Katie didn't mention she had made subsequent visits. She noticed when she said she hadn't actually been on the site, Ash's face brightened slightly before the mask of grief returned.

What is he trying to find out? And why is he glad I can't help him? She wondered.

"Perhaps," she offered, "you should talk to Lewis. He might have more insight than I do."

Ash went rigid. "That inconsiderate idiot? He wouldn't know a brick if it hit him in the face."

"I beg your pardon," said Stan.

Ash held his hand up. Rising, he collected his coat. At the door, he hesitated.

"Don't take my words personally," Ash said rather gruffly. "I've asked. He knows nothing either."

After seeing Ash out, Stan came back to get his own coat.

"I'm willing to bet, Katie," Stan said. "Ash wants to know what the detectives are snooping around about. He probably figures there's a piece of information someone isn't sharing. I'd almost say that tidbit is scaring Ash."

And well, it should be, thought Katie as she followed Stan out.

Chapter Thirty-Nine

As soon as she walked in the front door after work, Katie told Rick she planned on driving to Rutland.

"Okay, the fastest way to travel after dark is to go over to Charlotte Village, and pick up Route 7. That'll dump you in Rutland in about an hour and forty-five minutes," said Rick. He dropped the armful of wood in the wood box, then took a step toward the door. "Maybe I should go with you."

"No. If you want to help," Katie grabbed a thick envelope off the top of the fridge. "This came in the mail yesterday. I bet it's the contract agreement from the climbing school. Read it and see if you can figure it out." Coat in hand, she went out the door.

By the time she got to Charlotte, her belly started growling, reminding Katie about supper. At the hot dog diner south of the village, she got a cup of coffee and a garlicky wiener to go. In Rutland, she stopped for another coffee and directions. She found Hackett Street three blocks off Main. Sixteen Hackett, the second building up from the corner. Right out front, she saw Marlie's car parked on the street.

Katie sat in the Subaru chewing her lips while studying the windows. Most were lit, several had shades. The paint on the older building, gray with white trim, looked neat. Children's toys sprinkled the hard-packed dirt yard, in the middle of which she could see a large pile of maple leaves.

"Which one?" she mused, focusing again on the windows, one hand on the inside handle of the driver's door, the other clutching the collar of her jacket together. "Where are you, Marlie?"

With hesitant steps, Katie climbed the stairs to the narrow porch filled with bicycles, a stroller, and an old fashion hanging swing. Inside, she found sixteen C on the second floor. Once in the building, Katie smelled multiple suppers cooking. Somewhere a television newscaster talked, and a child squealed with joy.

Katie knocked. Footsteps came towards the wooden panel. Then, before Katie could prepare, Marlie gazed back at her. On the other woman's face, Katie saw a quick succession of emotions; surprise, joy, followed immediately by anger.

"What are you doing here?" Marlie demanded. The words and frown were meant to convey she wasn't happy to see Katie there. But shining happiness pushed all that away.

"I wanted to make sure you were all right," said Katie, not waiting to be invited, but stepping into the light.

Marlie gasped, "What happened to your face?"

"Black ice and a raccoon." Katie tried to grin, but her mouth still hurt.

She disappointed herself when the lie jumped so readily forward. But she soothed the pain by telling herself the truth would add to Marlie's fear. They sat in the living room and shared two tacos and a bag of chips. Marlie had a pitcher of orange Kool-Aid.

"It's cheap," she blushed.

Katie nodded. There were questions she wanted to ask, none of them having to do with Parentville, or the sheriff's office, but Marlie started talking, so Katie listened.

"I had to leave," said Marlie. She sat back; the plastic cup of Kool-Aid held between both palms. "Ash came to my house."

"I know," said Katie. At Marlie's look, she added. "I went there. The woman downstairs told me a man came, and an argument followed. I knew Ash had to be involved."

Marlie's lips pinched together. "He needed someone to crush. I made an easy target. He knew things. He said he'd destroy me and the integrity of the sheriff's office. I couldn't tell anybody. I just got out." She gave a little laugh. "Now, I'm selling gas and chocolate bars ten hours a day." Her eyes filled. "I hate it. But I'll never be able to go back."

"Never say never," said Katie. "That ass is going to go down. Then maybe things will straighten out."

She didn't mention the new deputy with thick glasses. Katie told Marlie what she had learned about the remains on the ridge, and how she had to ask Lewis for help. When she stopped for breath, two hours had passed since her arrival. It was time to go.

"I'm sorry," Katie said, getting to her feet. "I didn't mean to take up your evening, all I wanted was to make sure you were okay."

Marlie caught her hand. "Don't apologize. Please. I only want you, to not be angry with me."

Katie gave a watery smile. A chaste kiss on Marlie's forehead, and a squeeze of her fingers over Marlie's.

"I could never be angry." She pulled on her coat. "Call me, okay? Or better yet, can you come over on Saturday? Sunday? Or I can come here." Katie felt sixteen and floundering.

"I work weekends," said Marlie. "Let me see what I can do."

Driving back to the farm, Katie clutched the vague promise to herself. It wasn't much. In Charlotte, she passed the bottom of Hoover Road. The overwhelming urge to drive up there and beat the crap out of Ash caused her to depress the gas pedal. The road curved toward Parentville, and Katie barely made the turn regaining control on the other side of the road. Not far ahead, headlights shone. Pulling back into her lane, she slowed down. Opening the window, filling her lungs with cold air, she promised herself to push harder. Three lives had been irreversibly changed, the two on the farm and Marlie. Somebody needed to answer for that.

Ruth and Rick were still waiting when she pulled into the drive. They were sitting on the sofa together, and from the bleary look on Ruth's face, she might have dozed off. Katie told them about finding Marlie as Ruth put the kittens into their overnight crate with Sasha.

"Did she tell you why she left?" asked Ruth, her back to Katie.

"No," said Katie. "There's another thing."

Ruth didn't seem to notice Katie's remark and wandered into the kitchen to check the stove.

"Lewis came into the store today," Katie told Rick. "He told me the missing snow-machine is registered to Robby. Why, if Scott died lying on the bottom of the ledge, did he have someone else's snow-machine on top of him? There's more," she continued. "You had to have seen Ash's car in the parking lot when you left for the day, right?"

Rick nodded. "You said you were going to talk to him with Stan right there." Rick's face took on an ugly red color. "What did the bastard say?"

"It's more what he didn't say," said Katie. "Like not a word about the bruises on my face. I watched him. He didn't even so much as try to sneak a peek." Though the bruises were changing from violet to yellow and a dusky purple, they were still clearly evident.

"And I bet every other person you've come in contact with has, haven't they?"

Katie nodded. Motioning Rick to stay put, she went into the kitchen, returning with a flashlight, which she passed to him.

"I want you to hold this in your left hand," she said. "I'm going to shut off the light. When I tell you to, I want you to shine the flashlight directly into my eyes, try to blind me."

"Okay," said Rick, with a skeptical look.

The overhead light went off. Rick could hear her footsteps until she stopped in front of him.

"Now," said Katie, opening her eyes wide.

The flashlight came on. Katie raised her right arm defensively, then said. "Shut it off. Raise the light a couple of inches and get ready."

They repeated the exercise two more times. Ruth stood in the kitchen doorway, a question waiting to be asked. When the position of the light felt right, Katie told Rick not to lower his arm.

"Now," said Katie, flinching at the thought, "swing towards my eye with your right fist."

Rick, who stood only five-feet-nine-inches, less than two inches taller than Katie, swung, but the position of Katie's upheld arm made the movement awkward. She stepped away to turn the overhead light back on.

"For you to be comfortable holding the light high enough and getting a solid punch in," said Katie, "you'd have to be at least six feet tall. Do you agree?"

"Yes," said Rick.

"What does this prove?" asked Ruth, touching Katie's arm.

"It proves nothing," said Katie, "other than whoever beat me up had to be taller than Rick."

Ruth looked from one to the other, trying to decipher who they were talking about.

Katie's eyes met Rick's. Both pairs darkened. He exhaled slowly.

Chapter Forty

The next morning found Katie outside the Taft's Corner drug store. Her day off and she waited impatiently with a list of errands to do on the way home, including stopping at the post office. After she and Rick read the contract agreement from High Ridge Climbing School, they decided to have Gram's lawyer look it over. By the time she walked into the post office and handed the big envelope to the Postmaster, her palms were sweaty. She wiped them on her jeans. She hoped to hear back soon, and that the news would be good. Back at the farm, errands finished, she hid the photographs and negatives in the barn, exiting the back doorway to walk through the ragged orchard to the family plot.

"Hey, Gram, Poppa," she said, walking through the wooden gate. Metal bars running between granite uprights sunk deep in the soil encircled the plot. A falling apple tree had bent one of the metal bars, but the granite posts stood unyielding. Katie sat in the bent spot; feet caught on the bottom rail.

"So," she began, "I just wanted to tell you in person we got money to work a little on the schoolhouse. I found the old kitchen table and I'm sorry Gram, but I'm going to haul it back downstairs." As usual with these visits, her heart swelled, and tears clogged her throat. "I miss you, we're having a bunch for Thanksgiving, and I don't know who's going to carve."

Overhead clouds skid across the sky, fluffy white ones, shape shifting in the wind. The sun cast bright, brittle light across the plot and the lower meadow. Katie blew one last kiss before walking back to the house.

"What did she say?" Ruth asked as Katie hung her coat on the peg.

"That we should dig that table out," said Katie.

Getting the taller than the doorway table onto its side and out into the hall required moving a lot of other stuff out first. Four chairs went downstairs to the kitchen. A maple coffee table ended up in the living room. Other furniture and boxes lined the upper hallway, where they would be out of the way while the women fought to get the table free. Belatedly, they realized the cats should have been shut downstairs. It took time, but eventually, the trestle table leaned against the wall in the second-floor hallway.

"How did you old ladies get this in there?" panted Katie.

Ruth sat on the top step, wiping her brow. "Who said we did it alone?"

Katie groaned. "Well, it's going to stay here until we get more help."

She looked back through the open doorway. Several cats were crawling among the stacks. Familiar items vied for Katie's attention, with others unrecognized.

"You could hide anything in there," she said. "Right in plain sight."

"Yup, poof, gone like magic," said Ruth.

After tea with Ruth, Katie announced she had to go into town.

"I'm going to the dump," she said. "Got anything for Chet?"

* * *

"Hi Chet," Katie called across the piles of refuse. "Ruth sent you a plate of lunch. Where do you want it?"

While the old man peeled back the tinfoil and hungrily eyed the sandwiches and brownies stacked underneath, Katie looked around.

"Is there any rhyme or reason here?" she asked.

"Course there is," said Chet. "No salt, right? I'm not supposed to have salt."

Katie's eyebrows rose.

"Okay, so wrecked equipment; lawnmowers or snow-machines are where?" she asked.

Chet pointed the way. Katie left him to eat and followed a zigzag path to the mountain of corroded metal. Among the cracked hoods and twisted handlebars, skis stuck out like porcupine quills.

"What were you expecting to find," Katie said aloud, "nice, neat rows of machines all tagged with the name of the person who dropped them off?"

Nearby were piles of steel or fiberglass parts or cushions. Katie walked back to where she had left Chet. He had taken the food inside the Silver Bullet. Katie knocked and at his invite entered.

"Ooh, nice in here," she said. *Well, warm anyway.* "You probably don't keep track of who brings in what, do you?"

"Nope."

"Can anyone dump here?"

"You mean from other towns?" Chet asked around a mouthful of chicken salad.

Katie nodded.

"Nope."

"So, each town has its own dump?"

"Yup."

"And they all look like this?" Her hope faltered.

"Nope."

"Really?" Katie smiled.

"Yup." Chet smacked his lips, handing the empty plate back to Katie. "Most aren't as nice and organized as this one. I keep right at it, ya know?"

The last flickering light of expectation she would be able to find the missing snow-machine vanished.

Katie stopped at the Baldwin's Feed and Hardware. She pulled around back to pick up her six fifty-pound bags of kitty litter and found Rick working while Philip and another man sat nearby.

"Are you guys just having a gab session?" she asked, helping Rick load the back of her pickup.

"We're planning our hunt tomorrow," said Philip.

"Hunt?" said Katie, straightening up to look at Rick, who visually shot daggers at Philip.

"You just gotta talk," Rick said to his friend.

"Let me guess," said Katie, rocking back on her heels, "you aren't going to bother with the deer on the farm, right?"

"Nope," said the third man, "we're going to Pear Mountain. It's in

Charlotte."

Both Rick and Philip were throwing dark looks.

"There's a fence," said Katie.

"I have it from a reliable source," said Rick, "that if you drive further up Hoover Road, there's a fire lane that leads into the woods past the end of the fence."

"What are you expecting to find?" Katie slammed the tailgate shut.

"Seems Weldon dug a mess of test holes on his property looking for tin," said Rick. "People have been dumping all kinds of stuff in there for years trying to fill them up."

"Yup," said Philip. "Then there's them that take old cars out and leave 'em. A small one, like a, I don't know, Vega might never get seen again."

"Well," smiled Katie, "it's a good thing all the snakes and bears have gone to bed."

Chapter Forty-One

Katie decided while she worked the next day, being in the warm store felt nice, but the more physical labor in the feed building kept her brain busier. By mid-afternoon every time the door opened, letting more than one person in at a time, she checked the newcomers hoping to see Rick and his comrades. At four, she went out to set up a live trap for a foraging raccoon living under a family's deck. When she finished, she promised to come back and pick the trap and passenger up as soon as the homeowner called.

"I don't want it to freeze," said the woman.

"Just call me," said Katie, "don't touch it."

Rick sat at the trestle table, reading the paper when she walked into the farmhouse.

"Holy cow," she grinned. "How did you get this downstairs?"

"The guys helped," said Rick. "I told them if they did, they could have turkey here."

"Nice," she said. He seemed tense. "Did you, ah, get a deer?"

"Nope, the whole place is posted," he said.

"So, you didn't really see anything?" Her stomach fell.

By now, Katie realized Rick didn't want Ruth to know what he had been doing. When she didn't ask a more direct question, a small amount of tension drained out of Rick's shoulders. Sitting back, he looked up at the younger woman.

"I didn't say that," drawled Rick. "We left our rifles in the truck and had a nice walk."

"Which is why, folks," said Ruth, dropping a plate in front of Rick, "we don't have venison."

They ate in silence for several minutes before Rick said. "We found some big test holes. Deep ones."

"Yeah?" said Katie.

"Filled with all kinds of stuff," said Rick. "Old furniture, household rubble, lots of old equipment."

At the reference to items that might prove salable, Rick had Ruth's attention.

"Anything worth picking up?" she asked.

"Nope." Rick looked directly at Katie. "Not a thing."

For the rest of the meal, Katie and Rick were silent. Ruth, however, had been scheming since the grant money check had arrived.

"If we replace just the window panes and paint," she said, "next summer we can open the barn sale down there. It's right on the main road. We'd get more customers. Rick cleared the sumac and saplings out with the bush hog..."

Katie's mind drifted away. Finding the third snow-machine had felt like the perfect idea. She didn't have a backup plan. Was this the end of her search?

* * *

Two evenings later, Katie received a couple of telephone calls. The first from Marlie asking if she could come over on Sunday.

"If I can trade shifts so I get done by eleven or so, I could drive over for a few hours. Would that be okay?" Marlie asked.

"That would be so cool," said Katie.

The second from Tessa. Daphne Carter's remains would be released the following week.

"Her parents are flying in to accompany the remains back to Michigan," said Tessa. "I can't tell you how badly I feel. I mean, it's good they don't have to wonder anymore. But Susan is my friend. I have a daughter who will attend college next year. I'm afraid to let her go."

Katie also felt badly. She'd been nosing around, found some questionable tidbits of information, but hadn't uncovered any answers.

"I think Monday," she said to LG, "I'm going to have a talk with Sheriff Lewis. It's probably time for him to be more involved in this."

Reaching out to stroke LG, Katie got caught by surprise when the cat turned, giving her a harder than usual nip. Because Katie didn't normally chase her after a bite, LG moved only a few feet away. But Katie, having watched Jala, swooped in, catching the cat behind the shoulders. With her hands around the cat, Katie held LG off the floor without squeezing or shaking her until LG quieted.

"No bites," said Katie firmly. "No bites."

Then she set the cat back on the floor. LG ran six feet away before turning to watch Katie.

"Do you think that's going to work?" Rick asked.

"I hope so," said Katie, rubbing the red nip mark. Now both her face and her hand were marked.

Chapter Forty-Two

Katie left the Dean farmhouse early Sunday morning, juggling a gallon of fresh milk, butter, and some of Grace's signature goat cheese. At the end of the driveway, she saw a flash of white and barely had time to recognize the Saab headed back into town to the high school craft fair. Jala would share space with Ruth at the fundraiser booth.

Rick worked at sanding down the top of the big kitchen table. He had decided a fresh layer of varnish would be better than an armful of splinters.

"Well, those two are going to have quite a day," he said, pausing for a cold drink.

"Yes," said Katie, closing the refrigerator door. She felt bad for Phyllis Ash, home alone for the day with Geoffrey. Suddenly Katie realized her thoughts. Ash *would* be home alone except for his wife. Her mouth popped open. *You're crazy,* she thought, snapping it shut.

"Okay, listen closely," she said to Rick, pulling her boots back on again, "I want you to make a phone call for me and I want you to be pathetic."

"What?" asked Rick, a frown pinched his eyebrows together.

"Call the Ash house," Katie directed. "Keep calling until he answers."

"What makes you think he's going to answer the phone?" Rick asked.

"He won't let Mrs. Ash answer the phone," Katie explained. "If it keeps ringing, she's going to get antsy about it, and Jala's not there." Katie yanked on her hat and stuffed a heavy pair of gloves into her jacket pocket. "She's afraid of the world. He did that to her. Now when he answers, I want you to sound like a harmless old man."

Rick's brows drew even closer together. "I'm not liking this already," he said.

"Tell him I'm on my way over there because Jala forgot something." Katie stood right in front of Rick. "Then ask him to give me a message."

"What message?" Rick's frown deepened. He didn't like this idea at all.

"Say, the forensic tech from Montpelier called. They're on their way over to pick up the rest of the metal machine parts they found on top of the ridge. Make sure he understands the part about on top." She paused. "Say something about some code number etched in it or something."

"That doesn't make sense," said Rick, stalling to keep Katie in the house. "Why wouldn't they have taken it with them before?"

"I don't know," she said. "Don't banter with him. Tell him and hang up. If I'm right, he's going to get scared and react."

"And you're going to?"

"Be waiting for him," she said.

"I don't think so, not alone," said Rick.

"I need to be there and hidden before he arrives," Katie explained. "Give him some time, then call Lewis. Don't let Lewis come into the woods until you're sure Ash is already there."

"Like I said, I don't like this," Rick repeated.

"Make the call."

As Katie dashed out the door, Rick dialed directory assistance.

"I need the telephone number for Geoffrey Ash in Charlotte, please."

Outside, the truck had already disappeared from sight.

* * *

Katie considered she should have found a hiding spot on the fire lane side of the fallen tree site, instead of the cliff side, when she heard voices.

She had expected Ash to be alone. He would come running up, be rooting around looking for pieces. She would step out of hiding with her .22, and then...she wasn't sure, but hoped for the best. Instead, two men were talking, and they had arrived much quicker than expected. In her plan, she had envisioned Ash coaxing his Crown Vic up the mountainside. Katie had no way of knowing he kept a heavy-duty pickup truck parked in the garage.

She watched them, Ash and Robby, kicking leaves aside, yanking at fallen branches. Ash had been livid when he found the fallen tree moved and a large section cut out.

"What the hell is this?" he raged. "Who's been up here?"

"Obviously the forensic idiots you've been carrying on about," said Robby. He seemed much less enthusiastic in searching than Ash, moving his feet, but keeping both hands jammed in his jacket pockets.

Ash swung around. "Get moving," he ordered. "We need to get out of here."

"Give it up, old man," said Robby. "You're over-reacting. There's nothing here."

"Yes," said Katie, standing up, rifle in hand. "Give it up."

Both men straightened. Robby didn't move, but Ash took a step further away from his nephew. Katie realized she had a problem.

"Nope," she said, "not that way." She motioned with the rifle. "Step over to Robby, or should I say, Scott?"

Scott's head jerked up. Ash didn't react. He didn't move as ordered but continued leaning on a long branch like he would a cane. Katie paid it no mind. A little worry niggled at her causing her to question her ability to cover both men. *I hope shooting is like riding a bike. It's been a long time since I did either.* Ash took another step away. When her eyes flicked to him, Scott took a step, except he moved towards the young woman. A drop of cold sweat chilled her back.

"I said," she ordered Ash, "move that way."

Again, the tip of her rifle jerked toward Scott. Katie's eyes were on Ash but jumped to Scott at his quick movement. Now Scott held a handgun taken from his jacket pocket. He looked much more relaxed in handling the firearm than Katie felt. She moved her right foot backward. Something blocked her, keeping her rooted. She couldn't move. Ash took another step, this one forward. Katie could barely take her eyes off the handgun. Ash took a long step, swinging the branch as he did. Though too far away to reach Katie, he caught the end of the rifle, pushing it away from Scott. Before

Katie could react, Ash jumped on her. She fell backwards, tripping on the downed tree which had stopped her movement before, but leaving her legs draped over the top.

"Get off me!" she screamed. The words barely echoed before Scott added his weight to Ash's.

Katie screamed again, bucking and fighting. Both men laughed at her.

"Who do you think is going to hear you, sweetheart?" gasped Ash. Holding Katie down took effort, leaving him winded.

"This is just great," said Scott. "What are you going to do with her?"

"Do you have any of that junk you're so fond of shooting up hiding in your pocket?" asked Ash, disgust in his voice.

Scott gave his father an offended look.

"Help me get her jacket off," his father ordered. "Then you can shoot her full of crap and we'll throw her off the edge of the cliff. When they find her and start checking, they'll think she over-dosed and jumped."

Scott yanked at the sleeve of Katie's jacket.

His father slapped him away. "Don't rip it. We want her to look like she did this to herself."

Katie screamed again. Scott held her down while his father worked on her clothing. Even though out of shape, he still had fifty pounds on her. Katie sobbed.

"No," she screamed, "NO."

Ash and Scott traded places. Ash sat on Katie, pinning her right arm down while Scott tied a tourniquet on the upper part of her left arm. Katie continued to sob as Scott prepped the hypo.

"Hold her still," Scott told his father. "It'll be a giveaway if the vein rips. Little prick," he laughed.

Just as Katie felt the sharp jab, Scott disappeared.

"Get off of her," Marlie ordered. "Don't make me shoot you dip-shit, because I can, and I will."

Rick and Marlie were facing down Geoffrey and Scott Ash. As soon as Katie had left, Rick made the two phone calls, not waiting as she had directed. Rushing out the door, he had stumbled on Marlie and dragged her with him up the ridge. The only pause had been while she unlocked the trunk of her car and retrieved her pistol.

Slowly, Ash rose. Katie pulled her legs, which had been caught over the log, toward her torso, and stumbled to her feet. The dislodged needle lay beside her. Three feet away, Ash held his hands up. On Katie's other side, Rick sat astride Scott, who lay on his belly with his arm twisted high on his back by the old man.

"We were trying to save her." Ash licked his lips. "She's a doper, she's ranting about some murder in the woods." His voice trailed off as his tongue ran over his lips again.

"Liar," said Katie, "LIAR!" Still shaking, she took a step toward Ash.

"Easy Katie," said Rick. "Back away, okay. Go over behind Marlie."

"Don't step between me and Ash," Marlie directed, taking charge. In her mind, it didn't matter about her size. She had sworn to stand for right and it did not matter she no longer held the job. Right then, Marlie didn't care how big a man Ash tried to be. It didn't hurt she had an experienced grip on her handgun.

Katie scooped Scott's gun up on a piece of bark. Then picked up the rifle, leveling it at Scott.

"Okay, Rick," she said, "you can let him up." Both women had the men in their sights and a finger on the trigger.

The thudding of running feet crashing through underbrush came up behind them. Marlie didn't take her eyes off Ash, but Katie spun around.

Lewis stopped beside Marlie. He had his revolver drawn and reached with his left hand, wrapping his fingers around the top and taking the gun out of her hand. "Stand down," he ordered.

Marlie let go, stepping back and raising her hands. Katie watched out of the corner of her eye. She would have argued with Lewis, instead, she followed Marlie's example, lying the rifle on the ground before Brad could take it. Rick also stepped away, circling around to the women. He knew to avoid going in the direction of the small pines and cliff edge.

The new deputy came running up, his glasses jumping slightly on his nose. A state trooper and the game warden who lived at the bottom of Kitteridge

Road, followed him.

Ash's superior attitude returned. He opened his mouth and dropped his arms. Lewis stopped him cold.

"We're going to hear it all," Lewis said, "before we decide who goes to jail. Ladies first."

"Go, Katie," Marlie whispered.

"You know the woman," Katie stopped to clear her throat, "found here is Daphne Carter. I know because I found the bracelet her mother said she always wore. It was buried in the ground under where the body laid, and I dug it out. I've been talking to a woman in Syracuse who has the inside on the story." Katie pulled the silver charm bracelet out of her pocket. "She told me Daphne came here from Syracuse to visit Robby."

"I loved her," said Scott.

"Drop it, Scott," Rick said, disgusted. "We all know you're not Robby."

"Right," said Katie. "It's nice you too looked so much alike. Nice for you anyway. The body at the bottom of the ledge everyone, including his father, identified as Scott, is Robby Daudlin. Dan Sly said you two had an argument the day before Daphne and Robby disappeared. I bet about Daphne. Am I right? You said or did something Robby didn't like. Did he throw you out of his house?"

Ash's head snapped up.

"*You* brought her up here, probably forced her against her will. You killed her," said Katie. She tried not to pant, but anger and sorrow were stronger than she. "Then you killed Robby to cover it up so he wouldn't raise a stink when she went missing, or maybe even turn you over to the cops. Your father helped you." Katie's throat hurt and her voice dropped. "Only your mother innocently also posed a problem. You couldn't go near her; she'd know you weren't Robby. But you were in the house, weren't you? You couldn't stay away. That's why she said she could hear you talking."

"She needs me. Us," Scott whined.

Katie laughed. Shaking her head at Scott, she pointed an accusing finger at Ash.

"Did your father tell you he's working to have her confined to the

Waterbury State Mental Hospital? He's been setting it up for a long time. I'll bet that weird voodoo grotto in the woods is part of his plan. Yeah, then he can live happily ever after on her money and Robby's." Katie drew a long breath.

Scott had gotten to his feet, rubbing his arm and looking crumpled and lost.

"No," he looked at his father. "You wouldn't do that? Would you? She's so fragile."

"She's weak and stupid," Ash spat out.

As Scott moved toward Ash, Brad jumped forward to grab his arms. The younger Ash wept.

"You bastard," he cried. "No matter what she does, you belittle her, treat her like nothing. Yeah, well, how about we get this all out? Okay? Okay, yeah," Scott turned to Lewis.

"Daphne showed up, so pretty, all about Robby. She had this kind of exciting feel about her." Scott stumbled, but the other two men held him up. "I tricked her. I could imitate Robby. I'd been practicing for years. We went for a ride and came up here. We were horsing around on the snow-machine and one of the front skis got caught and we went air born. She flew into that rotten tree. If it had been standing straight, not leaning, she'd have missed it. I knew she was dead. I had to walk out to get Robby and Dad because the snow-machine wouldn't run. Robby went nuts when we got back here. He said he'd throw us out. We were all done living on his nickel. He came at me, and Dad hit him with a branch."

"SHUT UP," Ash roared.

Scott shook his head. "It may have been my fault Daphne died, but I didn't plan for it to happen. Dad beat Robby to death. He must have hit him six or seven times. I couldn't believe it. I couldn't move. Afterwards, Dad made me help throw Robby's body over the ledge. The rotten tree Daphne hit leaned right over her body. We used rope and the two good sleds to pull it down. We threw my wrecked snow-machine on top of Robby. Dad said by the time somebody discovered it in fifteen or twenty years, they wouldn't be able to tell it was totaled before it went over. Later we got rid of Robby's sled." Tears streamed down Scott's face.

Ash pointed at Scott and said, "Insanity is hereditary. He's like his mother."

"Yeah," said Lewis, "sure he is."

He pulled handcuffs off his belt and handed them to Marlie. She walked towards Ash.

"Get away from me," he snarled. "You're not even a deputy."

Marlie reacted before anyone else. Scooping up the same stick Ash had used against Katie, Marlie smashed him in the face with it.

"That's right," she snarled. "I'm a private citizen." She moved to the fallen Ash, pulling one arm at a time around to his back.

"You have the right to remain silent," she said.

Everyone looked at Lewis.

"What?" he asked. "I didn't see anything."

Chapter Forty-Three

"Promise me, her mother will get this back," Katie said to Lewis as she handed him the charm bracelet in the farmhouse door yard.

"Yes," said Lewis, "I'll see to it."

Geoffrey and Scott had spent a long afternoon sitting in separate cruisers while the Sheriff and Trooper worked to sort Katie's story out. The warden had gratefully left after writing out his report.

"How did you get in the middle of this?" Lewis asked Marlie.

Having been coached by Katie, Marlie held up her parka. "I left this here the day we found the remains. I came back to get it."

"Is she going to get her job back?" Katie asked.

Lewis shrugged. "She walked off the job."

"Because of Ash," said Katie.

"Stop Katie," said Marlie. "It's okay." Explaining why Ash threatened to expose her to Lewis would destroy both women's lives.

"She can petition the state," Lewis said, getting into his cruiser.

The Saab pulled in to drop off Ruth.

"Is that Mr. Ash?" asked Jala.

"Crap," said Katie. Taking the woman aside, she explained Mrs. Ash, home alone, wouldn't know yet both her husband and son had been arrested that afternoon.

"They're guilty?" whispered Jala. "Both of them?"

"Perhaps," suggested Rick, "Mrs. Ash should find another place to stay for a little while. Where no one can bother her."

Katie nodded her agreement.

Jala left, intent on moving her employer before the media got wind of what had happened.

"Good luck," Katie whispered as the car disappeared around the bend.

* * *

Ruth opened the front door, beckoning them all in out of the cold.

"I think," said Rick, "we should all have a beer and then maybe a steak."

"We have hamburger." Katie laughed.

"Works for me," Rick said, putting one arm around Katie and the other around Marlie.

Chapter Forty-Four

Though Katie went to bed feeling as though the entire problem had been solved, and the episode done, it wasn't the case. Coleen Johnston showed up in Katie's door yard at first light.

"If I tell you one thing no one else knows, will you leave and never come back?" asked Katie.

"Yes," whispered Coleen, eyes growing larger.

"The identifying bracelet found because of the combined help of myself, and a member of a New York climbing club sealed the case on identifying the missing woman."

"That's it?" blinked Coleen.

"That's all I didn't tell the sheriff," Katie grinned.

She didn't bother to add she had shared that same information with Tessa, and it would appear that same morning in the Syracuse Daily News. True to her word, Johnston drove away.

Detective Riffle charged Geoffrey Ash with the First-Degree Murder of Robert Daudlin, impeding an investigation, fraud, identity thief, tampering with evidence, and mental anguish. He would eventually be sentenced and sent out of state to serve his time. Scott Ash, charged with manslaughter in the accidental death of Daphne Carter, resulting from careless and negligent actions, and also with identity theft and failure to report two crimes, one being Robby's murder, would be housed at Windsor Penitentiary. This was a request by his attorney so Scott would be close enough for Mrs. Ash, who filed for divorce, to visit her son.

Katie opened the door one crisp evening, pleased to find Jala standing on the porch.

"I've come for Kole," Jala said.

Though Katie knew nothing about it, Ruth had Kole crated and ready to go.

"She called the other day," Ruth explained as the Saab disappeared. "Mrs. Ash bought a condo in Shelburne. She and Jala live there now."

"Really?" asked Katie.

"Yes," Ruth sighed. "I certainly hope Kole can get along with a spaniel."

Thanksgiving Day Katie, Rick, Ruth, and Marlie shared their meal with three of Rick's friends. Instead of sitting on the living room floor, each had a seat, albeit miss-matched, at the newly refinished farmhouse table. Later, the last of the four bigger kittens went home with the Higgin's children. The small guy, Peanut, would stay with Ruth, who still carried him around in her apron pocket.

Later, while the men tinkered in the barn and Ruth napped, Marlie told Katie she had petitioned the state for her job back.

"What's going to happen when Sheriff Lewis finds out what Ash knew?" Katie asked.

"Supposedly this is a closed petition," said Marlie, "Lewis might never know."

"That would be nice," said Katie.

"Yes," said Marlie. She stood up and stretched. Reaching for her coat, she added. "You know, I could use a walk. Maybe," she smiled, "down lover's lane."

Acknowledgements

Getting here was way more complicated than I would have ever believed. Publishing is like raising a child. It takes a village. I'd like to assign all those that helped honorary titles and issue medals.

My partner, Glenn R Sennett, who took on washing dishes and doing laundry and didn't ask if I was through yet.

Tiffanee Rae Kendall, Izzabela Verrill, and Gracin Verrill, my sounding boards, and the 'what would happen if,' when I got stuck.

Verena Rose, Harriette Sackler, and Shawn Reilly Simmons from Level Best Books for their support, belief, and the education they have provided.

Margeret Hakey, Richard Goss, Joanne Clarey, and Anne Garland for Alpha, Beta, and repeat reading.

LaRee Bryant, copy editor. Who knew there were so many comma rules?

My rah-rah section, headed by Rose Ann Lombard and Charlene VanSleet.

Shawn Reilly Simmons for the awesome cover artwork.

My friends at Northwest Farmer's Market who listened to me rant and rave, sometimes in the pouring rain.

And a great big hug to the readers and complete strangers who shared my excitement as I went along.

About the Author

DonnaRae Menard began the journey to a writing career in the seventh grade with notes containing disparaging descriptions of other students. Being forced to stand and read those notes aloud, began her training for the one hundred-yard dash in track and field.

Time went on. There were diaries, journals, two tiny columns in small-town newspapers, and competition pieces for Toastmaster's International, not to mention the banana boxes under the bed filled with novels, finished and not.

In 2010, after a serious health scare, DonnaRae took on the biggest wish in her bucket list, to write and be published. A chance meeting with a small publisher at the Crimebake Writers Conference in 2019 was her springboard.

DonnaRae lives just outside of town in the type of place where people feel free to drop off cats, kittens, cages of gerbils or white rats, and even the occasional farm animal.

The door is always open, and the coffee is on.

SOCIAL MEDIA HANDLES:
  Facebook: DonnaRae Menard Author
  Twitter: @DonnaRae Menard
  Bookbub, and Goodreads

AUTHOR WEBSITE:
  DonnaRaeMenardbooks.com

Also by DonnaRae Menard

Murder in the Meadow, 2021, Level Best Books

Willa the Wisp, Amazon

In the Shadow of Pharaoh, Amazon